MY BIG GREEK HOLIDAY

LISA DARCY

BLOODHOUND
— BOOKS —

www.bloodhoundbooks.com

Print ISBN 978-1-914614-29-3

ALSO BY LISA DARCY

Lily's Little Flower Shop

To Mia, Josh and Noah, with love.

CHAPTER 1

I had it all planned. The *Mamma Mia* DVD playing on television (which I'd watched with Sophie and Tara ten times)... tzatziki, dolmades and olives for starters, then steaming calamari, moussaka and Greek salad for mains. Ouzo, wine. Nothing was left to chance. I'd even placed a bottle of Hawaiian Tropic on the dining table as a not-so-subtle reminder of our last holiday together. But the pièce de resistance? A photo of the three of us taken at a Polynesian theme night on said holiday! Ah, the memories.

'What gives with all the Greek stuff?' Tara waved her glass of wine.

'Guess?'

Sophie clapped. 'You're opening a Greek restaurant!'

'Not quite.' I sipped my wine, pausing for dramatic effect. 'I'm off to Santorini...'

'Way to rub it in!' Tara said.

'It would be if I was going alone, but I want you guys to come with me.'

They squealed.

'You're kidding,' Tara said.

Sophie shook her head. 'I can't just up and leave. I have a three-year-old.'

'Why not? Bring Levi. He'll love it. It'll be like old times.' Old times, like when the three of us jetted off to Hawaii ten years ago. I picked up the suntan lotion and popped the lid. 'Smell that and tell me you can't escape for a couple of weeks.'

We sniffed the oil and giggled.

'Come on. Let's get sunburnt, outrageously drunk in Greek bars, and cut loose for two weeks.' I almost had them. 'Please! I can't go without my besties!'

Tara and Sophie were my best friends, but over the past few years, what with us each pursuing different paths, we hadn't spent as much time together as we used to. Even though I was sharing Tara's house, we were like ships passing in the night. I wouldn't go so far as to say we were drifting apart, but we weren't drifting together either. And in the last six months, I'd probably seen Sophie five times. I missed my friends, missed our sleepovers when we'd talk into the early hours, sharing secrets, dreams and ambitions. I wanted to recapture that time, our enthusiasm, our deep friendship.

Tara picked up the photo and examined it. 'We were so young.'

I gazed over her shoulder at the image of us flanked by two strapping Hawaiian dancers in traditional costume. Sophie, with her beaming pixie face and masses of curly hair, was gazing off to the side – from memory, at a gyrating Elvis (circa 1962) impersonator. Tara was front and centre, holding her wine glass and shouting, 'Cheers,' her eyes as wide as saucers. And then there was me, laughing so hard I was almost falling over, despite having my arm wrapped around a gorgeous Hawaiian. This was one of my all-time favourite photos. It didn't hurt that my hair, as dark as Sophie's is blonde, had a carefree wave, and my freckles, usually prominent, seemed to have been airbrushed out. My pale skin was slightly tanned, and, thanks to stilettos, I appeared tall.

'Why Santorini?' Sophie asked.

'Because I've got a tiny bit of work to do in Athens and, as a bonus, Marcus (my boss) is paying for a further two weeks of accommodation on Santorini.'

'Lucky you,' Tara said.

'And lucky you too. With the accommodation taken care of, you two only have to cough up for the airfare. You're always saying we should take another holiday together.'

'I was talking about a weekend in Melbourne,' Sophie said.

'Or Byron Bay,' Tara chimed in.

'Byron, Santorini... come on, guys, what's the problem?'

Tara sighed. 'I've got deadlines.'

'When was the last time you took a holiday?'

No response.

'I'll tell you. Three years ago. You give your all to that magazine. Besides, didn't you say you'd had enough of Melinda?' Melinda was Tara's maniacal boss.

Tara swallowed an olive. 'True, maybe the timing is perfect.'

Sophie smiled as she sipped her wine. 'Has it really been a decade since we went to Hawaii?'

I nodded. 'Yep. It was just after you met Alex.'

Tara was shaking her head. 'And you made us watch all those ancient Hawaiian *Brady Bunch* episodes.'

'The curse of the Tiki!' Sophie yelled.

'Mike's and Greg's frizzy perms.' I laughed at the memory.

'I was terrified about parasailing,' Sophie said.

Tara patted Sophie's arm. 'But you did it. The pineapples, leis, Elvis... it was great.'

'The best,' Sophie agreed. 'But we were younger then. Won't I cramp your style, being the only married one and taking Levi as well?'

'Nonsense,' I said. 'I have very little style, so there's nothing to cramp. What do you say?'

'A break would be nice,' Tara mused.

'Especially in Santorini,' Sophie added.

'So, we're all agreed?'

We clinked glasses and danced around the living room, singing *Dancing Queen* and sloshing wine. The deal was sealed. Ten days from now, we'd fly off on the holiday of a lifetime.

I neglected to mention how this little venture had really come about, and that after our sojourn I'd be looking for a new job.

It wasn't as though I'd been sacked or anything. No, Marcus was too smooth for that. Instead, he'd orchestrated my removal from the office for two weeks so I could get over my ill-advised fling with him by way of an all-expenses-paid vacation in Europe. He'd dropped hints about the difficulty of our working together after that.

I felt like such an idiot. Marcus, a self-made millionaire, had built up one of the largest importing firms (olives, oils, that kind of thing) in Australia. He was good-looking, charismatic, and for the past few months I'd been... well, I hadn't been myself, so I'd been vulnerable to his considerable charms. I'd slept with him once, a while back, even though I'd known it was wrong on so many levels. First, he was my boss; second, he was married – well, newly separated; and the levels went on.

I swear I'm not the sort of person who sleeps with married men, newly separated or not. And after that first time, I promised myself it wouldn't happen again. But it did – a further dozen times. What was I thinking?

Anyway, it was over now, truly over. When Marcus's soon to be ex-wife, Trish, came into the office a couple of weeks ago, I'd felt physically ill. It didn't matter that they were no longer together, our affair felt sordid and cheap. And I was past being sordid... and cheap. Truthfully, my feelings for Marcus had deepened, and there were moments (mostly after watching an old Julia Roberts or Hugh Grant movie, definitely after watching *Notting Hill*) when I believed if I quit working for him, we could have a real relationship conducted openly, sipping champagne at Belle Époque or margaritas at Cloudland. But Marcus wasn't interested. In fact, he'd been decidedly cool the previous few weeks. So before I really fell in love, it needed to end.

True to my good intentions, the day after Trish's visit, I hung around the office until the other staff had left for the evening. 'I can't do this anymore,' I said to Marcus when he swung by my office.

'And what might that be, gorgeous?'

'Don't *gorgeous* me. You know what I mean – you and me. I think your wife knows. She looked at me—'

'You're paranoid, Claudia. Trish doesn't know anything. Besides, it's none of her business.'

'I don't care. I'm not the sort of woman who goes around sleeping with married men.'

Marcus regarded me with his blue eyes, gym-toned arms crossed in front of his broad chest and cocked his handsome head sideways. 'Calm down. We're okay.'

I shook my head. 'I don't think so.'

I mean, how could we be okay? Sneaking around, never going out in public. Tara and Sophie didn't even know about us. It was wrong. If we were truly a couple, I'd have told them, and Marcus and I would be dining at a three-star Michelin restaurant instead of eating takeaway pizza in the boardroom.

He took a moment. Several moments. Marcus likes to deliberate before making decisions. 'I was going to head over to Athens to meet with a new investor, but quite frankly I think you could do with a break. Why don't you go instead?'

'To Athens?'

'For a day or two. Meet this guy, have him sign a slip of paper, and then take a holiday. The Greek Islands. Santorini maybe? Take your girlfriends.'

'You want me out of here? Got your eye on the new sales rep, is that it?' I'd noticed how he'd held Evie's gaze a bit too long at that afternoon's sales meeting.

'I thought you didn't care. Now you mention it,' he said, rubbing his chin, 'she's not bad looking...'

I shrugged. 'I'm so glad I didn't fall in love with you.'

Marcus smiled at me in that provocative way of his. 'Seriously, it's probably best that we—'

'End it?' The *it* caught in my throat.

Marcus nodded. 'Yeah, that's what I was thinking too.'

I willed myself not to cry.

He hugged me and then held my shoulders. 'We good?'

I couldn't speak.

'Go. Have fun. Use the holiday to get over me. I know it'll be damn hard, but you have to try.'

So that was it. Marcus, the Porsche-driving gazillionaire and I were kaput. And to soften the blow, he was offering me a holiday in Greece, all expenses paid. I deliberated over the ethics of the situation for all of five seconds before accepting the deal. He knew I was totally cash strapped. I couldn't afford a holiday in Surfers Paradise, let alone Santorini.

As for romance? From now on, I was swearing off *all* men, for good. I didn't care how charming, good-looking or perfect they appeared. If Jesus Christ himself made a pass at me, I was determined to say NO!

CHAPTER 2

There we were – Tara, Sophie, Levi and me – filling out departure cards at Brisbane International Airport. (Well, obviously Levi wasn't filling out a departure card; he was too busy running around pretending to be an aeroplane. At least he was on theme.) Yes, I had to do a little job for Marcus in Athens en route to Santorini. No biggie, I was used to running errands. But I stopped at the sixth question – occupation – I didn't want to commit my mundane job description to paper. Opera Singer? Fashion Designer? Archaeologist? They all sounded fabulously glamorous, but mine? Not so much. Besides, why did Customs need to know?

'Tough one?' The masculine voice came from behind my right shoulder.

I turned, annoyed at the interruption even though I was holding up the queue. I think I had the only working pen. 'Pardon?'

The man standing beside me smiled, showing off his perfectly straight white teeth. 'You seem to be having trouble with your departure card. Can I help?' As if this was the thirteenth century and helping damsels, whether in distress or not, was a man's everyday business.

I shook my head and shuffled away. I was too hung-over to make idle chit-chat with a man who was wearing an Akubra hat. Where was his stuffed koala?

'Well?' he persisted, moving closer.

I studied his face. Tanned, even complexion, big brown cow-like eyes. Way too attractive.

'I can't remember my passport number,' I lied, instantly regretting my stupidity. My passport lay open in front of me for all to see.

'Well, Claudia Marie Taylor,' he said with boyish enthusiasm, pointing to my passport number. 'MC879045. Enjoy your flight.'

I glared after him as he strolled towards the security X-ray machines, then down at my passport photo. I looked fifty, not thirty-five, three years ago when it was taken. I'd had the flu that day. My hair was a mess, my skin blotchy – and my nose? I looked demented.

I jotted down *Office Manager* in the blank space on my card (boring, but true) and joined Tara, Sophie and Levi outside a duty-free shop where oversized bottles of gin, Scotch and vodka clamoured for attention.

'Where the hell is Claudia?' Tara said. 'Don't tell me she's lost already. That'd be a record, even for her.'

I flinched. That's the thing about best friends – they know all your failings; thankfully, they love you anyway. Tara and I met at school, in Year 10. We were partnered together in biology, and dissecting frogs was our first joint endeavour. When I fainted at the sight of several dead frogs pinned to chopping boards, Tara threw a cup of cold water over me. By the time I came to, she'd made the necessary incisions in the dead amphibian and proceeded to tell me I was 'the reason this country has to put directions on shampoo'. I still can't believe I was the only one of the twenty-two giggling fifteen-year-old girls in the lab who passed out. It's not like slicing open frogs' intestines is an everyday occurrence.

'She was right behind us.' Sophie was too busy struggling with her Prada carry-all, an assortment of stuffed toys, and Levi to notice my arrival. She and I met in homeroom, Year 9. She stood next to me during roll call (Taylor, Turner) and we bonded over our mutual love for Matthew Perry and *Friends*.

Anyhow, Sophie, Tara and I had been best friends forever. Apart from a very long four months in our late twenties, we'd never actually lived together as a trio. We'd come to the mutual conclusion that flatting together was one of those things we shouldn't do, along with sharing boyfriends or razors, doing the Hokey-Pokey and blow-drying our hair in the bath. Despite this, I'd ended up sharing Tara's small Queenslander in Red Hill for over a year.

'Sorry,' I said, making my presence known. 'Stress attack over the departure card. All sorted.'

'I want chocolate,' Levi shouted, as he threw his pink lollipop to the ground.

'Well, you got strawberry.' Sophie sounded as though she'd already flown halfway across the world.

Tara nudged me. 'Twenty hours on a plane with him!'

'Nothing a few long movies and a sturdy set of earplugs can't fix,' I replied.

'And a litre of vodka,' Tara added, only half-joking.

'That's enough, Levi,' Sophie said, but her petite Kylie Minogue frame was no match for her son's theatrics.

Generally, Levi's antics were the kind that led strangers, childless strangers in particular, to believe that someone, in most cases his mother, was beating him. She wasn't, of course. When it came to Levi, Sophie had amazing love and self-control.

As for today's airport display, fellow travellers soon realised it was only a tantrum and tsk-tsked as they hurried by.

'I'm off for a spot of duty-free shopping.' Tara went to abandon Sophie and me to our noisy fate.

'Wait!' I said, frightened she'd disappear into the shiny rows of liquor and designer perfumes without me.

Tara groaned. 'He's started already. How am I going to find peace to write on this holiday? I need space and silence. Instead, there'll be tears and tantrums.'

'Don't be like that.' I wrapped my arm around her. 'Levi's excited, he'll settle down once we're on the plane. Besides, you need us. You steal most of your ideas from Soph and me.'

'As if,' Tara snorted. 'You won't let me write down any of our conversations.'

'You bet. Copyright.'

'What's the point of having friends if I can't write about you?'

One of the things I loved about Tara was her forthrightness. A few years ago, when I'd decided to go blonde in an attempt to win over a potential boyfriend, she'd taken one look and declared, 'Your hair's yellow. You look like a clown. Either fix the colour or shave your head and wear a wig for the next six months.'

Most of the time, I admired Tara's honesty. Sometimes though I wanted to slap her.

Nearby, Sophie was verging on tears as she continued trying to calm Levi. 'I'm insane for thinking I can holiday with this monster. I should just turn around and go home.'

'Don't be silly,' I said, watching Levi spin on the floor. 'Can't we pretend he's not ours?'

She didn't laugh. So, being the attentive godmother, I liked to think I was, I picked up the Chupa Chup (coated in human hair and other vile detritus) and sat down beside him. I held his head still and whispered into his ear. When he grinned, I scooped him into my arms. Tantrum forgotten – at least as far as Levi was concerned.

Sophie ran her slender fingers through her blonde hair, popped her sunglasses back on her head and gathered up Levi's discarded belongings.

'What did you say?' she whispered.

'I told him the reason chocolate is brown is because poo is mixed with it, but the strawberry ones are only ever made out of strawberries.'

'And he bought that?' Tara asked.

'Of course. Kids love hearing an adult say *poo*.'

Levi turned around and giggled.

'Okay, we get the picture,' Sophie said as she fossicked around in her enormous bag in search of boarding passes.

'I won't be a moment,' I said, ducking into the duty-free shop and making a beeline for the Clinique counter.

Waiting in the queue, I saw Akubra guy hovering by the whisky section and I glanced around to see who, if anyone, he was travelling with. I handed over my credit card to the sales assistant and looked down at my purchases. Bugger! How had I managed to spend four hundred and twenty dollars in less than two minutes? (Three Dior lipsticks, mascara and concealer for me; Clinique SPF moisturiser for Tara; funky Mac compact for Sophie.)

That side of me, the impulsive shopper side, would have to cease, I told myself sternly. I needed to be frugal. And I would be. Absolutely, definitely – after my holiday. A couple of weeks wouldn't make any difference.

The thing was, financially, I was in dire straits. My massive debt was one of the reasons I was living with Tara. The other being that I'd had no other option after George and I broke up. It was a long story, also a bit humiliating, and I didn't want to think about that.

But I had a plan. All going well, in two years, maybe less if I got my spending under control, I'd be debt free. Of course, I now had to move on from my job as well. Clearly, I couldn't stay there much longer. Even though I wasn't in love with Marcus, well, not desperately in love, office dynamics would be very awkward, especially if Marcus found a new fling... Besides, my job sucked. I was stuck in an office all day, reconciling olive oil accounts.

Yes indeed, a holiday was what I needed to escape Marcus and the mundane, debt-ridden reality of my life.

CHAPTER 3

The plane was packed to capacity, so we struggled to fit our bags into the overhead compartments. The four of us fidgeted to get comfortable in the middle row of cattle class as the plane took off. I glanced across at the smug travellers lucky enough to have snagged seats in the exit row with the extra leg room. I'm sure they were only pretending to read their safety cards in the unlikely event of an emergency. Through the curved clear plastic windows, I could just make out the endless white clouds stretching beyond the horizon.

'Thanks for the moisturiser,' Tara said, taking the glass jar out of its box. 'It may actually save my skin from getting the life sucked out of it by the plane's air conditioning. But we've talked about this, Claud. However generous, you simply can't afford it. You have to start saving money.'

'It was taunting me—'

'And you had to buy it?'

I nodded and set about taking off my shoes and replacing them with the thin navy airline socks. 'Other than my spending habits, what are you thinking about?' I had a fair idea. *What the hell am I doing sitting next to Levi in economy on a horrendously long flight to Europe?* After all, she wasn't his godmother.

'Looking around for howling children,' she replied, pointing to three in our vicinity before sipping her lukewarm chardonnay. 'That, and inspiration.'

'Ah. Inspiration is a tricky thing. You can search for it everywhere and still come up with zip.' I picked at my peanuts. 'The magazine?'

'What else? I never had any intention of staying longer than three months and now look at me... five thankless years.'

Tara was the senior features editor at *Modern Interiors*, a monthly lifestyle magazine that devoted several pages an issue to the latest cushion colours, fabrics, textures and stuffings from all over the world.

'You're very knowledgeable about... cushions.'

She rolled her eyes. 'I left the office yesterday praying I'd never have to go back.'

'You hate it that much?'

'I'm almost forty. I'm terrified of spending the next thirty years in a tragic state of boredom.'

'That's not going to happen after you write your novel.'

Tara frowned. 'What? Write a Regency romance, a sweeping saga with a handsome hero—'

'But the hero has to die,' Sophie chimed in.

'Definitely, but only after he's saved the baby.'

'Yeah. People love that,' Sophie agreed. 'Or serial killers. People love reading about sociopaths too. Look at *The Silence of the Lambs*.'

Tara sighed. 'There'll be no babies or serial killers in my novel.'

'Maybe you should rethink that,' I said. 'You're running out of time. Although I'm closer to middle age than you, and I don't know what I'm doing with myself. I still act like I'm twenty-two.'

'Mmm,' Tara said knowingly.

'Meaning?'

'Nothing. You're okay,' she conceded. 'Considering you're a bit irresponsible, never exercise and don't have any restraint when it comes to tequila or chocolate.'

'Gee, thanks. And to think we've got two whole weeks to dissect our unsatisfactory careers, tragic love lives and expanding flabby regions.'

'Touché,' Sophie said.

'Peanut?' I held out my handful of nuts.

'God, no.' Sophie shuddered as Tara grabbed a few. 'Just the thought of eating nuts'll add ten kilos to my thighs.'

'You must be kidding,' I said. 'You've always been a size eight. Apart for the week before Levi's birth when you *ballooned* to a small size ten.'

Sophie's fat talk was a familiar tango we'd danced around since high school. Back then, we'd experimented with new diets and reinvented old ones like the Israeli Army diet – two days, green apples; two days, cheese. Not nutritious or smart, but we did it. I usually bowed out after the first day, but when it came to food abstinence, Sophie had amazing willpower. The Lemon Detox was her friend. She could stay on it for days and still not be tempted by hot chips. But come the end of a diet, she could single-handedly start a twenty-first century potato famine.

'Don't remind me. I was the size of an overweight hippo.'

Just then, Levi flung himself across Sophie, directly onto Tara, making her spill wine on her black T-shirt.

She pulled the clinging wet material away from her chest. 'Great. That's just great.'

'I'm so sorry.' Sophie handed Tara several tissues from her handbag. 'Levi, why can't you just sit still?'

He squirmed and propped his head on a miniscule airline pillow against Sophie's shoulder.

'It's okay,' Tara said, even though she looked as though she'd have loved to whack him over the head with a blunt instrument. She stood, pulled her thick dark hair into a high ponytail, climbed over the top of me and stalked as best she could along the narrow aisle to the tiny bathroom.

Sophie leant across Tara's vacant seat. 'See! I told you. I should be at home baking cakes, like all good mothers do, not flying halfway around the world to sun myself in Santorini.'

'It was an accident. We'll have a great time, you'll see.' How hard could looking after a three-year-old be? Three adults taming one child. Surely the odds were in our favour.

'Yeah, you're right. It'll be great. I probably won't want to come home again... not that Alex would notice either way.'

'That's not true and you know it. He's just busy, that's all.'

'Story of my life.'

She had a point. Alex was a decent guy and was happy for her to have this holiday, but he did work long hours and travel frequently. This week, he was in Melbourne. The upside of having a workaholic for a husband was that Sophie had a gorgeous home in Hamilton and a holiday house at Byron Bay, a TV celebrity hangout. She also had magnificent jewels, not to mention the latest designer clothes and accessories. I gazed lovingly at her Prada bag while patting my Furla wannabe (another impulsive purchase – this season's must-have red snakeskin oversized clutch).

'If I didn't come home, I bet Alex would soon be partying with glamour girls and scantily clad women wearing nothing but sequins covering their nipples and nether regions.' Sophie gulped her wine. 'Or worse! What if he went back to bloody Harriet? I still dream of breaking into her house in the middle of the night, shaving her head and cutting up her Ralph Lauren clothing collection.'

Harriet was Alex's pearl-wearing, blonde-bobbed first wife

and mother of Alex's fifteen-year-old son, Ollie. I'd only met her a couple of times but each time, her pretentious palaver left me in giggles. I couldn't take her seriously. She was as elegant as a cold sore.

'Claud, can I get past you?' Tara was pinned uncomfortably next to a dinner trolley in the aisle. 'And the flight attendant wants to know if you want more wine. God knows, I do.' Tara pushed past me and sat down. Her shirt was almost dry, but she smelled like a wino.

Tara buckled her seat belt and gratefully accepted a Sauvignon blanc. 'I should've packed a change of clothes in my carry-on. Everyone tells you to. I even wrote an article, "Essential Travel Tips". Rule number one: always fly with a clean set of clothes in your hand luggage should any unforeseen accidents occur.' She glared at Levi.

I whipped out my Sponge Bob pencil case full of pencils and crayons. 'Look what I have. Colouring books! Which one do you want first, Levi? Batman or Frozen?' I held up both books and he pointed at Frozen. 'Elsa. My favourite too.' I handed the book and pencils to Tara to pass down the line.

Thank you, Sophie mouthed.

I reached across Tara to pat Sophie's arm, then focused on Tara. 'Remember the flight to Honolulu, where we wrote down all our fears and hopes?'

'As we hurtled towards thirty,' Sophie said.

Tara rubbed her eyebrows. 'Please don't tell me we have to play that game again.'

I poked my tongue out. 'Spoilsport.'

Tara blinked. 'I was still getting over my divorce.'

'And I'd just met Alex,' Sophie recalled. 'Working in corporate law, on the fast track to becoming a partner.' Pause. 'So much has happened in the last ten years.'

I'll say. Back then, I was selling media space for an

advertising firm. It would be another four years before I got my dream job as an events coordinator in the food and wine industry.

'And then again, so much has stayed the same,' Tara reflected. 'I'm still writing for magazines, albeit a different one now.'

Different? I certainly thought my life would be different by the time I turned thirty, let alone forty and that was only a year away. As much as I wanted to forget, my thirty-ninth birthday was in a few days' time. Somewhere along the line, my twenties and thirties had disappeared in a murky haze of office jobs (aside from the fabulous stint as an events coordinator), unsuitable shags and superficial spending. When I was younger, I'd assumed that by this stage of my life I'd be settled and have a couple of kids. Instead, I was living with Tara, broke and alone. I didn't even own a cat.

'I always wanted to be a writer,' Tara said.

'You are. A damn good one.'

'But the years are slipping away. It's hard when I'm writing about furnishings five days a week. When I get home, I'm not inspired to work on my novel. Maybe I'm not as keen as I keep telling myself.'

'But you are.' I squeezed her hand. Tara had dreamt of being a novelist since she was at school. 'You've had short stories published. You'll see. Once you get to Santorini, it'll come together. You just have to believe in yourself.'

She snorted before popping on her eye mask and resting back into her seat, crossing her arms in front of her chest.

'I wanted to be a fashion designer,' Sophie said. 'How'd I wind up practising law?'

'Um,' I mumbled into my peanuts, 'I kind of lost my way after the frog thing.' Right up until that debacle, I wanted to be a vet.

After settling Levi, Sophie put on her eye mask as well. How did she do it without completely messing up her curls? Tara's hair was all over the place.

Following my friends' lead, I reclined my seat to maximum (much to the annoyance of the budding *Biggest Loser* candidate behind me) and donned an eye mask and ear plugs. But I couldn't get comfortable. My mind raced, leapfrogging from one thought to another. Truth was, I was pinning all my hopes on this holiday giving me some much-needed direction in my less than scintillating professional and personal lives. I wouldn't go so far as to say I was soul-searching, but I needed to gain some perspective. I didn't want to arrive at seventy and wonder what the hell it had all been for.

You see, my life changed dramatically four years ago when I fell in love with gorgeous George. He was in the navy and I couldn't resist a handsome man in uniform (or out of one for that matter). After we'd been dating for three months, he suggested I move into his luxury city apartment. I was thirty-five and certain he was the one, so I jumped at the chance. Before I knew it, I'd given notice on my flat in Toowong, put my furniture into storage and become happily ensconced in George's magnificent thirteenth-floor apartment with spectacular city and river views. I neglected to pay attention to the finer details of the arrangement: namely that the monthly rent was more than my salary – before tax – and that George expected me to contribute half. But I didn't mind. I was besotted and the apartment was seriously stunning.

The first couple of years were dreamy; so good, in fact, I went off the pill. My biological clock was clanging away, especially as Sophie already had little Levi. I had visions of us basking in the glory of motherhood together. George seemed keen enough – not for marriage, but certainly about the possibility of a baby. However, less than a month after we made the decision, he got shipped out to sea on a naval exercise. 'Only for three months,' he promised.

Well, three months turned into four and, soon after, his rent payments stopped. Not only was I alone, but, what with rental, utilities and George's car repayments (I know, so foolish!) I was paying out way more money than I was earning. When I mentioned the topic of rent in our texts, emails and fortnightly phone conversations, he responded by saying he'd send through his share. And I didn't doubt him. We were in love. We were going to have a baby when he returned.

Still, I was racking up enormous debts and becoming increasingly anxious, especially as I'd only recently started working at Cassoli Imports. My bank even rang Marcus to check I was gainfully employed. I'd taken out several largish cash advances, which the manager blabbed about to Marcus. Talk about privacy issues.

Two days after George arrived back, being away eight months, our relationship ended, and I was left with a massive sexually transmitted debt – and there wasn't anything I could do about it. George may have been a fraud and a swindler, but nobody had forced me to pay his rent and car loan repayments. I was a schmuck.

I was at a low point. But I hit rock-bottom when, not six months later, I found out George was getting married. Despite my debt, I spent even more money.

Then there was Marcus. He seemed to understand, and I came to regard him as a friend, not just my boss. I knew he was married, but until he mentioned it, had no idea he was separated. It suddenly made sense why he put in such long hours at the office; he didn't want to go home to an empty house.

At first, I felt sorry for him, but then I started thinking about him more and getting distracted when he walked past my office or I heard his voice. We started flirting and our relationship shifted. He was charming and the attention was flattering. After the humiliation of George, it was exciting to feel desired and needed again. It sounds crazy, but as much as I thought of Marcus as my protector, I also believed I could rescue him. I couldn't see that Marcus didn't need saving, and that he and George were birds of a feather.

CHAPTER 4

'*D*oes anyone know any Greek?' Tara asked as we dragged our bags through Athens airport in search of signs for the bus terminal.

'*Kalimera*,' I said, confident that bits and pieces of vocabulary left over from Greek Language 101 in a useless Arts degree still resided at the back of my brain. My knowledge also included a partial understanding of Latin; the Mycenaean civilisation; and art history, circa fourth century Athens BC. I optimistically assumed that I'd pick up the local lingo as I went.

Tingling with excitement, I couldn't stand still. Greece! This was the moment I'd been waiting for. We'd arrived in paradise. I intended to immerse myself in the culture, the language, the food. Athens, the Acropolis, Santorini – it was all ahead of us and I planned to make the most of it.

'It's so beautiful,' I said, mouth open and eyes wide, as we walked towards the exit past huge posters of ancient temples; the Greek Islands; and the locals' happy, smiling faces, who'd no doubt welcome us with open arms. I was already in love with the country.

Out on the street, a searing wall of heat slapped me in the

face. The air was thick and hot, the ground grey and dusty. Sweat oozed from every pore of my body. Except for a few grubby buildings in the immediate vicinity, and a couple of dusty mountains in the distance, the airport sat smack bang in the middle of a gigantic dustbowl.

'Just remember, *óchi* means no and *naí* means yes,' I told the others.

'No means yes,' Tara repeated.

'*Naí.*' Despite the clips holding it back, my lifeless hair stuck to my face. Perspiration trickled down my forehead, under my boobs and in the backs of my knees. So much for making a glamorous debut in Greece.

'Is that it? The extent of your Greek vocab?' Tara asked, pulling at her damp shirt.

I shrugged. 'Obviously I know the odd swear word.'

'Obviously.'

'Let's catch a cab.' Sophie's face was hidden by large dark sunglasses and a navy silk scarf. The epitome of movie-star cool despite the wretched humidity, which only made her hair shinier, her ringlets more defined.

Nearby, old beaten taxis sat next to the kerb, their drivers leaning against them, either alone or huddled in small groups, smoking fat cigarettes and twirling worry beads. A couple of heads turned our way as we passed by, mostly to admire Sophie, but no one rushed over to demand our business. Perhaps it was Levi's whimpering that made them wary. Or Tara's snarl.

The stress of over twenty hours cramped together on a plane showed. We were more than ready to be driven by air-conditioned limousine to our opulent five-star hotel and escorted to our glamorous suite where, after the requisite luxurious bubble bath, I imagined draping myself in a fluffy white guest robe and sipping chilled Moët, while Levi played quietly, perhaps sedated, with his roly-poly Greek nanny.

'No,' Tara said. 'I read somewhere that local drivers will rip us off. Three women and a child? Talk about a gift. They'll take us for everything. How hard can it be to catch public transport?'

We traipsed past several taxis to a line of yellow buses. None of their destination signs read *Acropolis* or *Plaka* (the old town at the base of the Acropolis where we'd be staying), or any other words I vaguely remembered from my Lonely Planet guide to Greece, the printed pages usefully hiding at the bottom of my suitcase.

I studied the oversized road map on a nearby information board but still had no idea which bus to catch. Our patience and Levi's sudden calmness couldn't last. Any minute, one of us would explode. I hoped, for dignity's sake, it wouldn't be me.

'Which direction?' Tara asked.

No one answered.

We joined the long queue of fellow travellers at an official-looking yellow booth near the buses. Behind the counter, a diminutive ferrety-looking man handed out tickets at a leisurely pace between cigarette puffs and gulps of coffee.

'*Kalimera. Acropolis?*' I said brightly. He looked at me, grunted, and raised his left arm, in what I assumed was a pointing motion, towards a bus several metres away.

The four of us trudged over, Sophie lugging a bedraggled and grumpy Levi and several pieces of luggage. I should have felt sorry for her, but I found it hard to rouse sympathy. Her monogrammed Louis Vuitton suitcases would hold the latest colour-coordinated fashions, accessorised with the newest belts, hats, bikinis and shoes. Meanwhile, my scruffy red Samsonite contained little more than pea-green sandals (gorgeous but impractical in size seven and a half – on most occasions, I take a size eight), some very expensive duty-free cosmetics and a few Witchery casuals, none of which had been purchased on sale.

Tara's tattered black backpack held essential toiletries,

swimmers, a change of underwear and a few comfy mix and match ensembles, circa 2015. I knew because I'd watched her pack. It took all of seven minutes.

We climbed aboard the bus, hauled our bags into the overcrowded luggage section and sat down.

'Why didn't we just catch a cab?' Sophie asked into the thick air as we stuck to the vinyl seats.

A few unpleasant minutes later, the engine started up.

'I feel sick,' Levi moaned as the bus screeched around the fifth corner in as many seconds.

Fair call. The driver was travelling at speed along congested dirt tracks that passed for roads and overtook other vehicles regardless of bends and oncoming traffic. None of the other passengers seemed to care. They read books, chatted amongst themselves or slept, while we gripped our seats in terror with every screeching brake and blaring horn.

❦

Forty minutes later, we arrived at what could loosely be described as a backpacker's hostel. We were hot, tired and pissed off.

'Fu– fecking feck,' Tara said, hauling her backpack up the six flights of stairs, only pausing reluctantly when it was her turn to cajole Levi to continue his crawl up the steep narrow steps.

Our two meagre rooms had no air-conditioning, no fluffy white robes, no comfy beds and barely enough space to stand in, let alone unpack clothes and other personal items. So much for the 'Grecian decadence and splendour' promised on the hotel internet site.

After showering I climbed into a crumpled denim skirt, white T-shirt and sandals with a four-centimetre heel. I never wear lower. Sensible shoes, like Tara's Birkenstocks, were not my style, though I had to admit they did look comfortable and certainly wouldn't pinch the toes the way my shoes did. Tucking my hair behind my ears, I clipped several loose strands into place under my red Nike baseball cap.

'Shower's free,' I said to Sophie, who'd already pulled out her knitting, despite the heat and her drooping eyelids.

I could always tell when anxiety gripped Sophie. She knitted. She'd taken it up years ago as a form of therapy. 'It's really quite soothing,' she told me. 'It's easy to control and there are no surprises.' If it was good enough for Ryan Gosling and Julia Roberts, it was good enough for Soph. And she was really quite talented. Between them, Alex and Levi had dozens of jumpers, cardigans and beanies, and my hall stand back home (now in storage) had always been overflowing with Sophie's colourful knitted scarves.

'Thanks, but given that he's crashed,' Sophie replied, pointing a knitting needle in Levi's direction. 'I'll sit for a while.'

Levi, bless him, was asleep in a small wooden chair. He looked exceptionally uncomfortable. His arms and head were scrunched in an awkward ball and he was snoring loudly.

'You have to go now?' Tara asked in disbelief as I rummaged through my suitcase.

'As much as I hate the idea of wandering the streets of Athens while I'm exhausted, it's better to deliver this now and get it over and done with.' I unzipped the side pocket of my suitcase and withdrew a substantial yellow envelope. 'Then we can get on with our holiday. Anyone want to come?'

No response.

The errand Marcus wanted me to run, in return for an idyllic Greek Island holiday, was to deliver this envelope to his new investment associate, Con Kafentsis. I had to witness Con's signatures and bring the papers back to Marcus. I also had to give Con a USB flash drive, which was all of three centimetres long and was currently sealed in the envelope with the papers. Con happened to live in Athens, a short plane trip from Santorini and paradise. Simple.

Now all I had to do was track him down – in this sprawling city of over three million people.

CHAPTER 5

Stepping out of the hotel foyer with a complimentary map (Ha! Hotel foyer, my backside. More like a dark narrow corridor) and onto the uneven street, I checked the address on the envelope, read the instructions and consulted Siri and then the map. Joy! Another bus ride was in order.

I headed towards Syntagma Square, pretty sure I could catch a bus from there. Walking the cobbled streets was easier without dragging luggage, but it was still draining in the afternoon heat and high heels. Every couple of minutes, I looked up from my map to cross a street or backtrack. The square was nearby, but jet lag and hunger had joined forces to render my sense of direction completely unreliable.

I spotted a vaguely familiar face in the crowd. The Akubra guy. My departure card embarrassment was still a fresh memory, so in a moment of extreme maturity, I shielded myself from his view under my oversized map and cap.

The map and cap combo worked well because I couldn't see a thing. Therefore, I assumed – incorrectly as it turned out – that no one could see me. (Like I said, I was tired.)

Moments later, my right knee slammed violently into the

side of a cart of sunglasses, the force knocking over several stands. I caught a pair of glasses as I fell to the ground.

Unsurprisingly, the proprietor was not happy. '*Klefti! Klefti*,' he yelled, obviously thinking I was a dim-witted foreigner trying to rip him off.

'I'm not a thief,' I yelled back from the dirty gutter, holding my bleeding knee.

The vendor, spurred on by the growing crowd, continued ranting in Greek.

This would have been a good time for me to charm him with my fluent language skills, if only I'd paid attention in Greek 101 all those years ago instead of doodling Rob Lowe love hearts.

Lamely, I mumbled, 'There's no need to call the police. I'm not a thief,' as a hand reached out and pulled me up.

'Chloe, isn't it?'

'Claudia,' I said as he held out the same hand.

'Jack. Jack Harper.'

Shaking his hand while hopping on my good leg, I briefly wondered whether other women would fall into sunglasses stands at the sight of Jack Harper walking towards them. Probably.

Jack reached across and relieved me of the sunglasses I was clutching in my other hand. 'I think these are what he's upset about.' He asked the irate vendor how much they were. The man held up ten fingers.

'*Entaxei. Efcharistó*,' Jack confirmed, and handed over a ten Euro note.

Pocketing the money, the vendor hastily shooed us away and began reconstructing his display.

Jack helped me up onto the pavement and bent down to inspect my wound. I'd have preferred he didn't. It was embarrassing enough as it was. I didn't need him poking my knee.

'You'll live,' he said finally.

'Thanks.' I sniffed and pointed at several carts cluttering the streets. 'These really shouldn't be blocking the roads.'

'It helps if you look where you're going.'

'I guess,' I said, noticing his perfectly arched eyebrows. I couldn't get mine to do that, and I'd spent years and hundreds of dollars trying. Jack's were perfect male specimens. They were thick but there weren't any strays lurking on the bridge of his nose.

He held my eyes far longer than necessary. 'You sure you're all right?'

'Fine. Thank you.'

He handed me the newly purchased sunnies. 'Okay, see you around.'

'The glasses, wait. I owe you—'

Jack shook his head. 'Buy me a drink sometime.'

I watched as he disappeared into the swarm of afternoon shoppers, before examining my newly acquired Armani rip-offs. Then my swollen knee. It hurt like hell, but my pride hurt worse. I'd made a fool of myself the first time I'd seen him, and I'd just made an utter arse of myself again. Not that it mattered. I usually made an arse of myself when it came to men.

Eventually I found the right bus to take me to Con Kafentsis, and after nabbing a window seat, I stared out at the passing throng. Thick grey clouds had gathered, trapping the smog and humidity below. The people around me fanned themselves with newspapers and hats, probably more to disperse the overwhelming smell of petrol fumes than to keep cool.

Thanks to heavy traffic, the crowded bus ride was tediously slow. I could have walked faster if I had two good legs and knew where I was going. To compensate, the driver sat on his horn, as did all the other drivers in this car yard of honking horns. Hello *chaos*! Now I knew why the English stole this word from the Greeks.

{❧}

Half an hour later, the bus arrived at a block of shabby public toilets in a desolate area and all remaining passengers jumped off. The bus driver turned to me, clicked his tongue and motioned for me to disembark in no uncertain terms. My asking for directions appeared to test his patience. Tired and grumpy, probably at the end of a fourteen-hour shift (not that I'd know), he pointed past the toilet block, away from the main drag.

Once off the bus, I checked my map and instructions again. Where the hell was Marcus sending me?

It was late in the day and the further I walked the more concerned I became. According to the map, I was heading in the right direction, but I quickly got the feeling it was a dodgy area – mostly because men and adolescent boys lurked in broken-down doorways or leered at me from mopeds. Despite the oversized map of Athens, I hoped I looked like any other local gal out for a stroll at the sleazy end of town.

A guy in tight black pants, an unbuttoned shirt and thick gold chains around his neck, breathed in my ear. '*Sighnómi, thelis paréa?*'

The good news – I understood what the creep had said. The bad news – apart from saying *óchi*, I could only respond in English. '*Óchi*. No, I don't want any company. *Óchi, óchi!*'

I stared straight ahead, focusing on my task. The thick grey cloud cover made the air hot, the breeze non-existent. I was tired, sweating profusely and my leg throbbed, but I still managed to speed up my steps as the whistles and stares intensified.

My relief at making it to the given address quickly turned to annoyance when I found myself facing a decrepit disused warehouse – at least, what was left of a decrepit disused warehouse. What remained was little more than a shell of an ugly graffiti-covered grey building with smashed or boarded-up windows and concrete lumps sticking out of the ground at odd angles. Broken glass lay everywhere and syringes littered the ground.

Feigning confidence, I stuck my piece of paper under the nose of a middle-aged woman walking by. 'Excuse me,' I said in Greek.

She shrugged, raised her hands in the air and kept walking.

Heart pumping, I scanned the area. I was in the middle of nowhere trying to communicate with shady-looking characters in limited Greek, nervy and uncomfortable, eyes twitching. I didn't even have a photo to help me find Con. I should have tried harder to get Tara to come with me.

I hobbled to a small convenience store at the end of the street to try my luck there. Several locals – all men – sat outside on old wooden stools, drinking thick Greek coffee and playing backgammon. Without exception, all of them stopped playing and stared at me as I opened my mouth to speak.

The proprietor's name was Con. Yippee! Unfortunately, he wasn't the Con I needed. His ruddy, whiskery face was friendly enough, but his dark eyes narrowed when I asked about Con Kafentsis and showed him the address on the envelope I'd been hugging for what seemed like hours. He lifted his arm and pointed back up the street towards the condemned building.

Before hiking back to the crumbling ruin, I called Con's number, to no avail. Voicemail. Having no option, I walked towards the given address, feeling the shopkeeper and his cronies' eyes on me. I was getting a little tired of this, not to mention a teeny-weeny bit furious with bloody Marcus.

Back at the warehouse, I tentatively ventured around the

side pathway, avoiding jagged pieces of glass and used syringes. There was another building at the back of the property. It too was grey and covered in graffiti, but the structure appeared to be intact. I guess you could call it an office, just. But the Greek signage dangling from the wall was mostly faded and for all I knew, could have read *Drug deals done here.*

I'm not generally a scaredy-cat, but this was pushing it. Cutting a path through the overgrown weeds, I knocked on the front door. It swung open, so I tentatively called out hello. '*Geia sas.*'

Good sense told me to drop the envelope at the door, turn around and run away. But then again, I rarely listened to good sense.

I stuck my nose in the dark hallway. It smelt of rotten wood, mould and cigarettes. Stepping inside, I heard a loud thud followed by a muffled scream. At the end of the hallway, some distance from me, two men, silhouetted in dim light, appeared to be arguing with a third man. One of them held what looked like a long piece of wood.

Not good. I had to get out without being seen. Carefully, silently, I backed out of the hallway, through the open door, and ran as fast as I could towards the street. Surely no one would come after me in broad daylight? Still running, I tripped on the uneven gravel road and crashed to the ground, landing on my already-grazed knee.

Bleeding profusely, I could barely walk. But I didn't care. Though my legs were shaking, I longed to get the hell away from the place. The street was silent as I struggled back to the café. Again, the locals watched as I sat at a table, my face burning, my skin clammy and hot.

Con walked over and handed me a glass of water.

'*Efcharistó*, thank you.' I trembled as I accepted the drink.

Dazed and dehydrated, I downed the liquid in one go, then ordered a short black.

Moments later, he returned with coffee and two wedges of baklava glistening with honey and walnuts. 'Eat!' he commanded, not unkindly.

By the time I'd downed the coffee and finished the baklava, my breathing had almost returned to normal. It dawned on me that I still had Marcus's rotten envelope. So, I called him.

'Marcus, you sent me to a wasteland. Con wasn't even there,' I shouted into my mobile, only to realise it was after eleven at night in Brisbane and he was probably in bed. Awake, as he'd answered quickly, but in bed. 'I also rang the number you gave me for him. Voicemail.'

'Claudia, calm down. All I've asked in return for a two-week holiday is that you deliver some papers to Con and have him sign them. You'll need to go back—'

'That address was a condemned building, not an office. Men were arguing. Big, angry men. It was really dodgy. I'm not risking my life to give some random guy an envelope, even if he does make the best olive oil in Greece.'

'Not to mention organic wine.'

'Marcus!'

'Risking your life? You wouldn't be exaggerating, would you?'

'There were syringes—'

'Okay, okay, I'll ring him and get him to call you. We don't want you imperilling your person again. He'll catch up with you before you head to Santorini.'

'And if not?'

'I guess he'll have to find you there. Make sure you keep your mobile charged and turned on.'

After I hung up, I sat on a rickety wooden stool in the corner of the café, pretending to read a Greek *Cosmopolitan* but thinking about what had just happened. Who were the men in the building and what were they doing? My imagination ran wild, coming up with increasingly life-threatening scenarios involving my being killed or sold into white slavery.

As the shopkeeper cleared away my plate and cup, I decided to have another go. 'Excuse me, do you know Con Kafentsis?' I asked in broken Greek.

He shrugged and made a fifty-fifty motion with his right hand.

I was hoping for more, but this Con wasn't about to shed any light on *that* Con. He did offer to call me a cab though.

In an effort to distract myself while waiting for my ride, I turned my thoughts to Marcus – how he sashayed through the office, bestowing smiles on his appreciative staff and regaling them with anecdotes he'd picked up on breakfast radio on his drive into work. I pictured his hands as they cupped his morning coffee (black, one sugar), his fingers as they hovered over the computer keyboard. I remembered the many times I'd catch his eye and then quickly look away, shy, embarrassed, and more than a little aroused. Then there were those secret times after work – no game playing, no having to be careful because someone could be watching – when it was just the two of us, alone. Alone with our private jokes and intimacies.

I should have forced myself to stop before our flirtation went too far. But I couldn't pull back, even though I knew where it was heading. I tried not to think that I might have been falling in love with Marcus. We were just two work colleagues enjoying each other's company. At least that's what I foolishly told myself.

CHAPTER 6

'No wonder you thought the guys were sleazy, Claud,' Tara said, scanning her phone as we drank a local white wine blend and picked at feta and black olives in a traditional taverna near the hotel. 'You were in the red-light district.'

'That explains a lot.'

'Didn't you read anything about the area before going?'

'Too tired. I just wanted to get there. I was going to read on the bus but...' I raked my fingers through my hair and exhaled. I didn't want to think about it anymore. 'Look at my bloody knee,' I said, peering down at it. 'It's swollen.'

For God's sake, this was supposed to be a holiday. Two weeks in the sun. We hadn't been in Greece a day and I was wrecked already.

Severe jet lag was setting in and I found it increasingly difficult to think straight. I didn't have the energy to tell Sophie and Tara the finer details about my adventure and the dubious characters I'd seen.

I turned my attention to the scenery. Here we were, in the Plaka, gazing up at the Acropolis perched high above us on the hillside. The impressive combination of moon and artificial light showed off the ancient architecture to its majestic best. I'd dreamt of seeing the Acropolis all my life and now I was finally here. I had arrived. It was breathtaking. All around, spruikers did their best to persuade hordes of hungry tourists to sit and sample traditional Greek mezedes and drink retsina.

'Look at that,' Tara said. 'The locals hang out on their mopeds, drinking short blacks, while tourists like us lounge in overpriced cafés and bars, guzzling beer and eating dinner at the ridiculously early evening hour of,' Tara checked her watch, 'eight.'

I nodded, listening to the foreign voices murmuring around us. Nearby, several local lads stood beside a souvlaki stand watching *gyros* kebabs twirl on a stake.

'There are a few locals sitting down,' I said.

Close by, men clicked worry beads between nicotine-stained fingers and played backgammon. Two men at a neighbouring table shouted at each other, gesturing at their backgammon board. One of them slammed his fist on the table, sending several pieces flying. They stood, berating each other and gesticulating madly. Arms swung widely in all directions. Others came to join the fierce debate.

'Feisty, aren't they?' Sophie said as we sipped our wine.

Even Levi, who was falling asleep in Sophie's arms, raised his head.

Moments later, the men embraced and slapped each other on the back. They sat down, repositioned their pieces and got on with the game as though the previous five minutes had never happened.

'Passion,' Tara remarked.

'Imagine if we screamed like that at each other?' I said. 'We wouldn't speak again for days.'

The waiter arrived with more food – garlicky yogurt dip,

steaming calamari, dolmades swimming in olive oil, and freshly baked chunks of bread. Each mouthful tasted more delicious than the last.

'The music, the atmosphere, the gorgeous Greek boys,' Sophie said, her eyes settling on a couple of handsome locals.

'Absolutely.' Tara raised her glass. 'A toast to Claudia for insisting we come along.'

'It's Marcus you should be thanking,' I said as we clinked glasses and sipped our wine.

'Okay, let's drink to him too,' Sophie said. 'And to an amazing two weeks in paradise.'

'I know Marcus is funding this holiday,' Tara said slowly... a *but* was coming... 'But I'd have left the envelope under the door. Then it'd be over and done with.'

Bingo! 'I know you would've, Tara, but I want to do the right thing by him. He specifically told me that the papers need to be signed in my presence.'

Tara eyeballed me. 'Yeah, and he's like the third richest guy in Queensland, but seriously, does Marcus do this for all his staff?'

'No, and that's why I don't want to let him down,' I said quickly. 'He could've done this job himself, and then where would we be?'

'Brisbane,' Sophie pointed out.

'Exactly! And he knows all about the mess I got into with George. Thankfully, Marcus is too busy to leave the office so he's doing me a favour because he's a nice bloke.'

'I guess.'

'All I have to do is watch while some guy signs a piece of paper and collects a memory stick. It shouldn't be this hard.'

Although I hadn't told Tara and Sophie about my liaison with Marcus, I got the distinct impression Tara was suspicious. Marcus would have told me I was being paranoid, so I didn't dwell on it and busied myself hovering a dolmade towards Sophie's mouth.

She pushed me away. 'I expected a call from Alex by now. You'd think he'd at least want to talk to Levi.'

Levi coughed and drowsily looked around.

'I'm sure he's just busy. He'll ring when he can.'

Sophie bit her top lip and sipped her wine. 'Alex is always too busy. Never too busy for Ollie though.'

'I lub Ollie,' Levi said, now wide awake.

Sophie shrugged and turned to me. 'Don't know why, all he does is grunt and eat.'

True. I'd been in Ollie's company a few times and the kid showed a distinct dislike of words. Sophie had tried being his friend; she'd known him since he was little. But the two had never taken a shine to each other. I guess it was just one of those things.

'How about I read your Angel cards?' I offered. 'See what the Goddess Oracle has in store for us?'

Tara looked up from her phone and shook her head in disbelief. 'You've got to be kidding. You brought those things with you?'

'Sure did.' I never travelled anywhere without my Angel cards; you never knew when you might need a little guidance or direction. True, they hadn't guided me away from stuffing up my life, but still. I pulled the cards from my bag, released them from their purple satin sack and patted them. 'We'll stick with the three-card read, hey?'

'How about I read your cards first, Claud?' Tara said.

'Okay, I don't mind.' But secretly, I did. The Goddess wasn't backing me at the moment. I shuffled, picked out three cards and laid them on the table.

Tara looked at the angels and fumbled with the instruction book before shrieking. 'The Angel of Death!'

'That's bad.' Sophie twitched uncomfortably and twirled her ringlets.

'Can't be good, can it? Let me read,' Tara said. 'Says here that choosing this particular angel could represent a preoccupation with death.'

I knew the angels weren't on my side today. I should have listened to my inner goddess, the one that minutes before had shouted at me not to choose any of them.

I looked at the cards again and grabbed the book from Tara. 'Here. Give me a look at that!' After reading and rereading several interpretations, I came to my own conclusion. 'Look, you fool. It doesn't necessarily mean death as in dead. It says, "This angel may also represent the end of a particular cycle or way of life." And as I'm just about to turn thirty-nine and will be job-hunting when I get back home, I think this reading might be very accurate.'

'Jeez, you can put a positive spin on anything,' Tara said. 'But why will you be job-hunting, especially after Marcus has been so generous?'

'I need a change. You know me. I don't stick with things too long.'

'You haven't convinced me,' Sophie said. 'I wouldn't be happy with death being thrown at me.'

'Tara put me off by telling me she wanted to read my cards. I didn't get a good shuffle in,' I said, looking at Tara who was smirking into her wine. 'It's not a game. It's not for laughs. You have to respect the angels. Appreciate the messages the universe is sending you.' Who was I kidding? I was jumping from one landmine to the next.

'Okay, okay,' Tara said. 'You may as well read mine. Can't be any worse than a tap on the shoulder from death.' She picked up the cards and shuffled.

I swished my hands dramatically in the air while Tara laid

out her three cards, then I studied them before consulting my guidebook. '"From now on things are going to be different. At first, you may only notice subtle changes. Forget the past. It's really over. The future is looking rather wonderful."'

Tara spluttered calamari over the cards. 'I ask you. What the hell does that mean? "The past is over." A truly earth-shattering revelation there.'

To placate her, I scanned the book for more information.

There wasn't any.

'I'm more annoyed with myself than you, Claud,' Tara sniffed. 'Please don't read for me ever again. I get so worked up I could scream.'

Sophie picked up the cards, shuffled, and placed three on the table. 'Do mine. Hopefully, the angels will tell me how I should be living my futile life.'

Tara yawned. 'If your life's futile, there's no hope for the rest of us.'

I eyed Sophie's pink Pucci-inspired Maxi and the Tiffany rock sitting on her perfectly manicured ring finger and held my tongue.

After examining her cards, I said, 'There you go. "Be careful today, you are attaching too much importance to something that is ultimately irrelevant."'

'Please explain,' Tara said, glaring at me while Sophie chewed her bottom lip.

'It means that although I'll die in the next couple of days, ultimately it won't matter to Soph. And with me out of your life, Tara, you'll have your house back and your future will be rosy. There. You happy?'

Sophie smiled. 'Interesting.'

'I do believe I'm feeling better already,' Tara said.

'Yeah, well while we're waiting for me to die, let's drink more wine, then hit the Athenian sights tomorrow, for soon we fly to

Santorini.' I dismissed the angel talk with a clap of my hands as a photographer came by to 'take picture of beautiful ladies'.

Twenty minutes later, after parting with thirty Euros, we each held a keyring of the four of us (Levi holding a green dinosaur) with the neon-lit Acropolis in the background. Okay, so my hair was messy, and Tara was pouting, but on our very first evening in Athens, we'd scored an unforgettable keepsake.

It felt like old times, the three of us eating, drinking and nattering about the minutiae of our lives. The team was back together again. That was the beauty of long friendships – we could pick up the pieces of a conversation thread from five, ten, fifteen years ago and know exactly what the other person was talking about. We might not always agree, but we respected each other's opinions and supported one another's choices. Over the years we'd told each other many home truths from dubious boyfriends and less than-stellar career choices to the odd bout of halitosis – no matter how painful. Tara and Sophie could tell me things I didn't want to tell myself. They knew everything (almost everything) and still hung out with me. I stared at my new keyring; it didn't get better than this.

CHAPTER 7

*T*he next day, we walked. And walked. Three women (one with a bung knee) and a cranky child in a worn red Bugaboo Bee stroller.

'He looks preposterous.' Tara was pointing to Levi in the straining stroller. 'He can't be comfortable. He's all squashed and his legs are buckling.'

Sophie glared at her. 'Do *you* want to carry him around all day?'

In the sweltering heat, we strolled through the Plaka towards the Acropolis, distracted every couple of metres by the vast variety of souvenir shops selling everything from plastic replicas of Greek icons like the Parthenon, to T-shirts and jewellery. The cobbled alleyways were colourful, frenzied and loud.

Shopping. I couldn't help myself. Once I started buying presents for friends, I couldn't stop. How could I resist when there were so many kitsch icons to purchase?

'Hey.' Tara dragged me away from a fascinating street stall selling bronze statues of Zeus, Poseidon and Eros. 'You've bought enough trinkets.'

'But they're bargains. It'd be a crime not to buy a few more.' I spotted a marble Zeus paperweight. 'Marcus would love that,' I started – because he collected paperweights, not because I was thinking of him.

'Marcus?' Tara said. 'Why would you buy him a present?'

'Hello! He's the one who made this holiday possible.'

Reluctantly, I left the paperweights and walked over to Sophie, who'd been taken in by a street vendor offering his 'best price' for nuts, strawberries and coconut sticks. She handed over several worn Euros, then saw her purchases for half the price three stalls along.

Twenty metres down the road, Tara succumbed to an outrageously overpriced battery-operated ornament – a dancing Last Supper. 'Mum will have a fit.' Tara smirked. After that, I didn't feel so bad about my impulse buys.

Armed with bottled water, trinkets, T-shirts and enough nuts and strawberries to last several lifetimes, we made it to the Acropolis. We staggered through the grand entrance of the Propylaia and along the dusty winding path leading to the Parthenon and Acropolis Museum. With perspiration trickling down our backs and legs, the three of us grinned. We'd made it! It was a complete travesty that the Acropolis wasn't one of the Seven Wonders of World.

Despite the damage, scaffolding and pollution, the visual impact of the area was breathtaking. I stood in front of the Erechtheion – the most sacred site of the Acropolis – where Poseidon and Athena had had their contest over who'd be patron of Athens. Breathing deeply, I allowed my mind to drift back in time to when this place had been the centre of Greek culture and religion. I found it incredible that these structures still existed thousands of years later. My almost thirty-nine years on Earth seemed insignificant.

I fumbled for my vibrating phone. Con. 'Hello.'

'Clow-di-ah?'

'Yes, is this Con?' I asked, walking away from the group.

'*Geia sas. Me léne* Con.'

Thank God! I knew I was being paranoid the previous day. Everything was fine. I'd get Con to sign the papers, then continue my holiday to Santorini.

'You have something for me. *Naí*?' Con said in Greek.

'Err, *naí*.' *Naí* meaning *yes* in Greek. It was confusing. 'When can we meet?' I asked in broken Greek.

'Not today.'

'Not today? But I leave for Santorini tomorrow. We must meet today.' Could Con have been one of the men I'd seen in the abandoned warehouse in Athens? Looking back, that whole afternoon was a blur. I'd been so overcome with heat and tiredness, perhaps I hadn't been thinking straight.

'No!' His English was perfect. 'I have business now. We meet in Santorini.'

'Okay,' I said without an ounce of enthusiasm as he hung up.

'All good?' Tara asked when I rejoined them.

I nodded.

Meanwhile Sophie was busy with Levi. 'Please stay where I can see you, Leev,' she said, crouching down and unbuckling him from his undersized stroller, whereupon he promptly ran off and disappeared behind a caryatid. Sophie stood, mumbled something about filling out a Prozac prescription, and set off to find him.

Even with sightseers dotting the hill, the Acropolis didn't feel overcrowded. People kept to their own space, which is more than could be said for the roaming cats.

'How do they survive up here?' I wondered out loud.

'I guess people like us throw them scraps of food and they live on that,' Tara said.

'But it's so dusty and hot. See that one.' I pointed to a black and white moggy, only just out of reach.

As Tara turned, the cat pounced on an unsuspecting pigeon and *crack*, the bird's neck snapped. It was over within seconds. The cat dragged the dead bird to his hideout somewhere underneath layers of ancient sandstone.

Within moments dozens of cats appeared as if from nowhere, presumably to fight over the remains.

'So that's why the cats around here look so healthy,' Tara said. 'Pigeon parties.'

'The Angel of Death,' I said. 'Spooky.'

'Coincidence, more like it.'

I stood still, watching and listening, as nearby tourists gathered in clusters taking holiday snaps. Photo after photo featured smiling couples and groups standing in front of the Erechtheion, the Parthenon and temples such as Nike Athena.

Instead of focusing on the famous buildings, I sidestepped camera-wielding tourists. Every time I turned round, someone was snapping, and I'd inadvertently get in their way. I cringed at being immortalised in some stranger's happy snaps, or worse, their Facebook homepage or Instagram post. But beside all that, I couldn't shake a growing sense of trepidation.

CHAPTER 8

'*I* hate these little planes.' Sophie was holding on tight to Levi's arm as the plane took off for Santorini.

'I second that.' My nails digging into the armrest, I peered out the window as the plane accelerated into the wind and lurched from side to side. My stomach heaved. Clearly that wasn't a good idea. I closed my eyes.

The uneasy feeling festering since the previous day at the Acropolis had stayed with me. Maybe it was the Angel cards or the cat amongst the pigeons – whatever it was, I felt weirdly ill at ease. Maybe it was because I hadn't met up with Con. It was supposed to have been a simple exchange in Athens, but now I'd have to hang around waiting for him in Santorini. I wouldn't relax until I had his signature as Marcus had instructed. Marcus. Was he missing me?

'My God! Bumpy, isn't it?' Tara shouted, as the plane hit an air pocket, flinging Levi's crayons into the air.

'Close your eyes and try not to think about it,' I said as much to myself as to Tara.

'Mummy, I being sick now.'

True to his word, Levi promptly vomited all over his tray

table and most of Winnie, Tigger and Eeyore. For the next fifteen minutes, the flight attendants really earned their pay. Even after Levi had been cleaned up, his toys rinsed and bundled into a plastic bag, the stench remained.

I'd been intrigued by Greece for years. It had been a dream destination for as long as I could remember. At university, I'd been struck by Greece's mythical nature, the beauty of the Aegean Sea, and the teachings of Plato and Socrates. But despite all I'd learnt about ancient Greece, my knowledge of Santorini was vague. I'd intended to use the flying time to swot up, but the plane was swaying too wildly to read, and the vomiting incident left me a little nauseous. I knew it was a beautiful island with white homes dotting rugged cliffs. And that it was one of the two thousand islands stretching from the Ionian Sea in the west to the Aegean Sea in the east (I happened to glance at half a page of Greek propaganda as we boarded the plane), but aside from that, I hadn't done a lot of research.

I'd seen *Captain Corelli's Mandolin* eons ago, so was familiar with Cephalonia or as familiar as you can be after watching a ninety-minute Hollywood movie. And of course, I'd seen the musical *Mamma Mia* too many times to count. I also knew Ios was the party island because my younger sister, Sarah Sunbeam, had shown me photos as proof. But Santorini? Everyone said it was the bride of the Cyclades.

Given the ferocious crosswinds during the plane's descent, we all clapped after Captain Kangaroo bounced us to a standstill at the gate.

Our hostess, Marcella, the proprietor of the aptly named Marcella's Hotel, where we'd be staying the next thirteen nights, had arranged for us to be met at the airport. As we were being driven to our villa, I was captivated firstly by the inhospitable rocky outcrops and then, as we got closer to the island's capital, Fira, by the white stucco homes with blinding blue shutters and the bright purple bougainvillea that climbed the walls and snuck onto rooftops.

Marcella's, perched precariously on Fira's granite cliff, with a quaint block of four apartments with an enormous terrace facing the impressive pool below and the Mediterranean beyond, was prettier than I could have imagined. When we arrived, I was further blown away, and not only by the incredible scenery. The fierce wind was so strong it was difficult walking in a straight line.

'Welcome!' Marcella beamed. With her radiant smile and petite features, she could have been anywhere from her mid-forties to early sixties. 'You have a good journey, no?' she asked in broken English as she led us to our apartment.

We all nodded, overcome by the astounding views.

'It may look pretty but it's fucking freezing,' Tara whispered as we followed Marcella.

Unfortunately, she was right. Even though it was the middle of the European summer, it was about ten degrees below zero and the wind was getting stronger. In the couple of minutes we'd been here, a sturdy beach umbrella and several wooden chairs had blown over and bounced along the entire length of the marble terrace.

'Language!' Sophie hissed, and pointed to Levi, who was spinning around in the blustery weather.

'Well, it is,' Tara said, trembling in her chinos and Lady Penelope T-shirt. 'I hardly brought any warm clothes.'

'Don't worry, I've brought an extra couple of pashminas you can borrow.'

'Oh, I'm thrilled,' Tara said. 'I've always wanted my own pashmina but somehow never got around to buying one.'

'Please yourself,' Sophie replied. 'You can be rude and shiver, or you can graciously accept my offer. Take it or leave it.'

We walked, hunched over, to the edge of the terrace. 'Get a

load of this view,' I said, ignoring the appalling conditions and patio carnage. 'It's even more dramatic if you stand on the edge. Absolutely mind-blowing.'

'It would be if it wasn't so freakin' freezing. The travel guides don't mention *that*, do they?' Tara growled. 'Can we hurry up and move inside?'

While Levi twirled in the wind, Marcella unlocked our painted wooden front door (blue!) and lifted the latch so the door swung open.

Downstairs had a kitchenette, bathroom, bedroom off to the side, and a combined lounge and dining room that opened onto the huge terrace with the stunning views; upstairs were two more bedrooms.

'You like?' she asked, smiling.

We all grinned.

'It's gorgeous,' I said.

Finally, we'd have our own rooms. In Athens, we'd shared two tiny rooms, which was fine for two nights, at a stretch, but there is such a thing as too much togetherness. Here, we each had a cosy bedroom with built-in wooden cupboards and bookshelves. Mosquito netting draped elegantly over the four-poster beds. Perfectly romantic – not that any of us would be seeing any bedroom action, but it was nice to know the setting was there, just in case.

Tara and I took the rooms upstairs, while Sophie and Levi chose the downstairs bedroom, close to the bathroom and kitchen. They could access those and have breakfast on the terrace early in the morning without waking us. As we'd found during our short stay in Athens, no matter how late Levi went to bed, he'd still wake before dawn.

Although simply furnished, the apartment, with its polished marble floors and high decorative ceilings, felt comfortable and struck a perfect balance between traditional and contemporary (clearly, I'd spent far too much time reading Tara's magazine).

Marcella gave us sightseeing brochures, the bus timetable and several other useful pieces of information. She handed us the keys and smiled at Levi. 'A gorgeous boy, no? I look after him. You ask me.'

Obviously, Marcella couldn't smell the vomit because of the howling wind, which was just as well. When you got up close, Levi really did stink. The stench didn't seem to bother him, though – he was already playing with his cars and dinosaurs on the floor.

'It does not fill my eye,' Marcella said, opening the front door and walking out onto the terrace.

'Pardon? *Sighnómi?*' I said.

'Here,' Marcella gestured. 'I am not happy with this cloud.' She threw her hands into the air. 'Clow-di-ah, there is nothing I can do. Tomorrow, weather much better.'

Nodding, I walked back inside. The Greek Isles. I didn't care that it was blowing a gale. I was finally in Santorini!

I dragged my bag upstairs to the front bedroom, which Tara had graciously insisted I take. 'Finder's fee for bringing us along,' she said. I didn't argue.

Downstairs, Sophie was saying, 'Levi, wash yourself! You smell. No. Stay in the bath.'

No doubt he was struggling to escape his mother's clutches. I felt a fleeting twinge of sympathy for the poor kid. It wasn't his fault the plane ride had been so bumpy. On the other hand, he did reek.

My bedroom window overlooked the terrace below and further south to the cliffs and water. Rows of dazzling white houses perched on reddish-purple rock. On the southern side were more houses, and to the north, at the other end of the island, another white village, Oia, clung to volcanic cliffs.

According to my map, the island in the distance was the volcanically active Nea Kameni; if we were feeling energetic, we could scale the volcanic cone and crater. And maybe throw Levi in, if he continued vomiting in confined spaces.

I couldn't wait to get out and explore. But maybe I'd wait until the wind died down, the clouds disappeared, and brilliant sunshine returned, as the pictures on the postcards promised.

After I'd unpacked, I wandered downstairs as Sophie walked out of her bedroom.

'He was asleep before his head hit the pillow,' she said, shattered but triumphant. She produced and lit a lime-scented candle and, after exhaling deeply three times, sat down on the lounger and opened her knitting bag. 'Peace at last.' She rummaged around for her wool and needles.

'He's a good kid, Soph,' I said, breathing in the aroma.

She screwed up her face. 'I know, but sometimes I want to strangle him.' Her blonde curls appeared more tightly wound than ever as she twisted a ball of wool until the threads were at breaking point.

'Have a shot of ouzo instead,' Tara said, walking in from outside.

'You ventured out into those conditions?' I was impressed. 'Well done!'

'Yeah, it's enough to freeze your tits off, but my need for sustenance was greater than my need for comfort. Also, I found this,' Tara twirled to show off the bulky aqua parka she was wearing, 'in the wardrobe.'

'You chose to wear that hideous creation,' Sophie said, her nose in the air, 'over my pale-pink pashmina?'

Tara shot me a grin and plonked several bags on the dining room table. 'We have wine, red and white; ouzo, local and imported from the mainland; as well as olives, dolmades and pasta. All the essentials, and a couple of bits to keep Levi going until morning.'

Soph and I gathered around, marvelling at the array of goodies.

Tara held up a can of sardines and a bottle of ouzo that had been shrink-wrapped together, then shrugged. 'Go figure. I tell you, there's everything you could want and then some – honey, candied fruits, sausages, olives. I was overwhelmed with choice.'

She opened a bottle, and we raised our glasses. 'Here's to Santorini and to us,' we said and swallowed our first sip of Santorini retsina.

Sophie spluttered. 'Oh. My. God.'

'A hint of car oil, pig swill and cat piss,' Tara said, taking another swig. 'However, it *is* alcohol.'

True. We all gagged but that didn't stop us drinking the contents dry within ten minutes. Then we placed the empty bottle in the centre of the table, rather like a shrine. A silent reminder never to buy it again.

'It's really stunning here,' Tara said as we sat by the closed window and stared across the bleak Santorini sky.

Sophie shivered. 'It is. But you're right, it's bloody cold.'

'And extraordinarily windy,' I added.

'At the shops, I overheard a couple of tourists say it'll be sunny and wind-free tomorrow.'

Sophie raised her glass. 'I'll drink to that. As long as Levi can manage a full night's sleep, I'll be happy.'

'Full-on, isn't he?' Tara mused.

Sophie nodded. 'Sometimes I think little boys are sent from hell to test our patience and sanity. I can't imagine what poor Colette goes through.' Colette, another friend from our schooldays, had three boys, the oldest of whom was six. The other two were twins, Levi's age.

'No wonder she drinks,' Tara said.

'It's overwhelming.' Sophie picked up her knitting. 'I wonder what my life would be like if I didn't have Levi. I could do anything. Be anyone. Instead, I have to be responsible, twenty-four hours a day, seven days a week. It's never-ending – the screaming, tantrums, vomiting, washing, cooking, consoling, cajoling. Sometimes, I want to run away and never come back.'

'And what better place to run to than Santorini,' I said brightly. This wasn't the time to get maudlin. For goodness' sake, we were staying on one of the most gorgeous islands in the world. Although, come to think of it, now that it was dark, and given the dismal weather, we really could have been anywhere.

'Your life may have been easier before Levi was around, but it wouldn't be as much fun,' I reminded her.

'Fun? I doubt it,' she said after biting into a green olive. 'No, I just have to accept that some women are natural mothers and others, like me, are not.'

'You *are* a natural, Soph,' I said. 'Levi adores you.'

Sophie exhaled. 'I thought being a litigation lawyer was tough, but it was a cake walk compared to this. Most of the time, Levi calls me an angry monster. I'd hoped it'd get easier as he got older, not harder. When he was a baby, I was forever exhausted by sleep deprivation, but it's way more tiring now. His demands are endless. Meanwhile, the TV's blaring. The phone's ringing. The dog's dying because he hasn't been fed for two days. And to top it off, Alex is asking me where his socks, jeans and life have disappeared to.'

Tara laid out a huge bowl of tomato and basil pasta and green salad on the coffee table.

'Need help?' I asked.

She shook her head and pulled out several plates from the sideboard.

'And then there's Ollie. I know it's only one weekend a fortnight, but... Jeez, listen to me. I have a healthy, energetic little boy and a wonderful husband. It's just that...' Sophie took a moment. 'It's hard being married.'

'Ain't that the truth.' Tara piled pasta onto her plate. 'That's why I ditched Anthony, remember?'

'Poor Anthony,' I said, following Tara's lead and filling my plate. 'As a mild-mannered architect, he was woefully unprepared for someone like *you* in his life.'

'I wanted an easy life,' Tara recalled. 'Turns out it wasn't so easy after all.'

Prior to marrying Anthony, Tara's love was Jules, a university girlfriend. But after that relationship soured and Tara declared her fling 'nothing more than a one-off experiment', she fell into the arms of Anthony. After a whirlwind romance, they married... and six drawn-out years later, divorced.

Tara told him she needed to find herself. 'But you're not lost,' Anthony had argued, bewildered. He was devastated. 'I married for life, Tara. I assumed we were going to have children and raise a family.'

'You will,' Tara had assured him. 'Just not with me.'

Sophie rolled her eyes. 'Tara, please don't compare your marriage to my relationship with Alex.'

Tara glared at her. 'All I'm saying is that I know what it's like. The sacrifices, the compromises, the heartache when it falls apart. I've been there.' Tara took a breath before stuffing lettuce into her mouth.

'You weren't together that long!'

'Are you kidding me? It felt like twenty years.'

'We all know why you married, Tars,' I said, ravenously sucking up a spaghetti strand. 'So that forever more you can refer to yourself as a divorcee rather than a wretched spinster like me... and to get over your ill-fated experiment, to prove to yourself you weren't—'

'That's not true,' Tara argued before I could finish. 'I was just young and stupid when I got married.'

'And now?'

'Well, now...' Tara hesitated. 'I feel much more in control of my life.'

At least Sophie and Tara had marriages to bicker about. Here I was, the same age as they were, still feeling young and stupid, without even an ex-husband to complain about.

Right now, though, I didn't much care. We were in paradise and we still had the ouzo to open. Once Con was dealt with, I'd be carefree.

CHAPTER 9

*T*lay in bed mulling over my aimless existence and the similar lack of direction in my friends' lives. Were Sophie and Tara seeing this holiday in the same way I was – as an opportunity to tackle some hard questions about some of the life choices we'd made over the years? Because the more I thought about it, the more I wondered whether any of us really knew where we were heading.

Sophie seemed the most together of the three of us, which was saying something, considering her history. Back when Levi was three months old, Sophie left him with Alex under the guise of buying bananas. She did buy bananas at the local fruit shop, but then she drove to a nondescript café a hundred kilometres away, where she ordered a large skinny cappuccino and a double slice of chocolate cake.

As soon as Alex realised Sophie was taking an extraordinarily long time fruit shopping, he phoned me. We both knew Sophie wasn't coping with the switch from corporate high-flyer to full-time mother, and Alex panicked she might have done something silly.

Tara and I spent the day ringing friends and searching the

suburbs, desperately trying to find her. By the time Sophie arrived home six hours later, Alex was frantic. Unfazed, as if nothing had happened, she explained that the demands of looking after Levi had overwhelmed her. 'I needed time to breathe.'

'But you can't just walk out like that!' Alex shouted. 'Anything could've happened to you. You could've been dead for all I knew.'

'Sometimes I think I'd rather be dead than look after Levi.'

After the café incident, I moved in with Sophie and Alex for a couple of weeks while they interviewed for a suitable nanny. (Over fifty, was Sophie's only stipulation.)

She seemed paralysed with anxiety and wouldn't even hold Levi for fear of hurting him. 'Not on purpose, Claud, but what if I accidentally drop him or tip steaming hot coffee over him? Besides, what kind of mother leaves her newborn son and husband and goes out for the day without telling anyone? A bad and desperate one,' she answered before I could reply. 'I don't want this baby. I want my life back. I feel sexless. There's nothing left of me.'

I can't presume to know what Sophie was going through – she didn't want to talk about the fact that she was most probably depressed, but I gained some understanding of the physical demands of looking after a baby. Even though Alex and I were helping together, it was exhausting – waking in the middle of the night, every night, sometimes more than half a dozen times to attend to Levi. I remember thinking that babies never slept. At least this one didn't. I was beyond shell-shocked. I don't think I've been that tired, ever.

It was a great relief when Alex hired Kerrie, a responsible live-in nanny (ex-nurse, fifty-three, seventy-eight kilos, stayed eighteen months) and I could go home. But I still spoke to Sophie every day. She felt like a failure who didn't deserve to be a mother. She spent most of her time in bed and her health deteriorated. It was a matter of weeks before she collapsed and was taken to hospital.

'It's a huge relief,' Sophie had admitted to me at the time. 'Finally, I have a reason to stop being a mother for a few days.' She seemed at peace in hospital, despite being hooked up to tubes.

During her hospitalisation, Sophie began seeing a psychologist, then a psychiatrist, and the diagnosis of postnatal depression was confirmed. Once discharged on medication, she kept up regular appointments. Three years down the track, she and I didn't talk about it much. I brought it up now and again, but Sophie just explained it away, saying it was a hiccup. I knew things were still difficult but didn't make an issue of it. I was here if Sophie needed me. As for Alex, he didn't talk about it either, at least not with me.

Anyone could see that parenthood, while amazing and rewarding, had its downsides. I felt sad that, in those early months, Sophie experienced more bumps and setbacks than she'd expected. It knocked her confidence. And it made me wonder if it was better to remain unattached and childless.

In some ways, Tara's life was more complex. The question of why she married Anthony so soon after her affair with Jules had played on my mind for years.

Tara's relationship with Jules began when Jules kissed Tara one night after they'd been to see a local band play at some dive in Fortitude Valley.

'I'm sorry if I offended you,' Jules said to Tara, the next day, 'but it seemed like a good idea at the time.' Tara wasn't in the least offended – quite the opposite – and their relationship progressed rapidly, especially after Tara convinced her parents to let her move into a flat in St Lucia. 'It'd really help my grades if I lived closer to uni,' she'd told them.

Those naive Catholics! So, in a flat heavily subsidised by her devout parents, Tara got hot and heavy with Jules. All was perfect until ten months later, on the morning of Tara's twenty-first birthday.

We'd celebrated Tara's coming of age at her flat the night before, drinking and dancing, dancing and drinking, until we could drink and dance no more. Everyone gradually disappeared and crawled back to their rough student accommodation. All except Jules. Apparently, she and Tara fell asleep on a rather comfortable rug on the living room floor. Naked.

Early the next morning, a Sunday, in strolled Mr and Mrs Murphy, cake in hand, to surprise their gorgeous, studious daughter. There they stood in the middle of Tara's lounge room, dressed in sober church attire, clutching a chocolate mud cake and staring at their daughter, who was buck naked and entwined with another girl. Horrified, Mrs Murphy mumbled something about 'not wanting to interrupt', fumbled to put the cake down and fled with her husband.

Tara was beside herself with anguish when I caught up with her later that afternoon. 'What the fuck am I going to do, Claud? I can never face them again.'

'Where exactly was Jules's tongue when they walked in?'

'I'm serious. They're going to kill me.'

'It could've been worse.'

'How?'

'I guess you're right,' I said after some thought. 'It probably doesn't get more embarrassing than that.'

'I can't face them.' Tara clapped her hands to her cheeks. 'And to top it off, Jules isn't speaking to me. She's pissed off because I didn't lock the front door.'

'Well, yes, perhaps you should—'

'I wasn't exactly thinking about that at three in the morning when my girlfriend stripped and offered me my birthday present.'

'Clearly. Happy birthday, by the way.'

Tara's parents were beyond upset. They couldn't have been more disappointed had she confessed to being a serial killer. It was a matter of days before they staged an intervention, which involved repeating the rosary ad infinitum and praying to God for Tara's salvation, as well as the usual tears and recriminations. It went on for weeks. 'Why did you send her to an all-girls school, dear?' was one of Mr Murphy's often repeated but unanswered questions of his wife.

Three months later, Tara was engaged to Anthony, and six months after that, they married. Although it was all over by the time Tara was twenty-five, they didn't divorce until two years later. Tara didn't want to upset her parents, but when she told them, the inevitable tears, accusations and prayers came forth.

Years later, Tara's parents still brought up the fact that she was a divorcee. Not that she saw them often. After her divorce, Tara grew weary of her parents and their values, their perceptions about how she should be living her life. She wasn't exactly estranged, but she didn't head over there every Sunday afternoon for a family barbecue either.

Eventually I fell asleep, but it was a disturbing night punctuated by dreams of boyfriends past, croaking frogs and several faceless people having sex on my favourite navy leather sofa (the one trapped in storage). Throughout the night, though, one face kept popping in and out of my dreams: Jack Harper's. Bloody hell!

CHAPTER 10

*T*he next morning when I woke up and peered out the window, the sky was the brilliant blue the Santorini postcards promised. All my concerns disappeared into the dazzling sunlight.

'Greetings,' I said, walking out onto the patio where Levi was eating a local version of Weet-Bix and Sophie was drinking green tea.

All the outdoor furniture was upright and perfectly placed in the glittering morning sunshine. Bending over, I kissed Levi. He looked up from his bowl and raised his favourite dinosaur to me. After ruffling his hair, I sat down next to Sophie.

'Have you ever seen anything like it?' Sophie asked, looking across the ocean. 'So serene. Cruise ships sail in, cruise ships sail out. And all the time, the water remains calm, a gorgeous azure blue. Hear that?'

'What am I listening to?'

'Bouzouki music.' She lifted her head towards a distant church. 'Over there. Sorry about last night. Just venting. Jet lag and all.'

'Let it go. Don't be so hard on yourself.'

'Yeah, but...' She looked at Levi.

'He's fine.' I watched as he dribbled milk and Weet-Bix down his blue Batman T-shirt. 'How about I make you some toast?'

'I'm not hungry.'

'Yogurt and honey?'

'Really, Claudia,' Sophie said, her voice rising. 'I'm not hungry. Besides if I'm going to wear swimmers and inflict my flab on unsuspecting beachgoers, I'd better not get any fatter than I already am.'

I was about to bark at her when Tara appeared.

'Blimey!' she croaked as she staggered out onto the terrace, shielding her eyes from the blinding sunshine with her left arm.

'Breathtaking, isn't it?' I said.

'How'd you know? It's so glary.' Tara picked up a glass of water from the table and took a sip, before sitting beside me and helping herself to yogurt and cherries. 'So, what're we doing today?'

'We could explore that volcano,' Sophie suggested, looking towards Nea Kameni.

'What? That thing over there?' Tara replied, spitting out seeds and pointing across the ocean to the tiny island a couple of kilometres away. 'Looks exhausting.'

We took the scenic route to Fira, along cobbled pathways and trellised gardens. Every couple of metres, another tourist posed to have their photo taken in front of a postcard-perfect blue door framed by whitewashed houses splashed with hot pink bougainvillea. So far, we'd resisted temptation.

'Hey, you,' said a strong male voice as someone tapped me on the shoulder.

I swung round.

'Wow!' I said. 'Some coincidence. First Athens, now Santorini.'

'Small world. Nice sunnies, by the way.' Jack was minus the Akubra today. Good decision. He had a fine head of thick dark hair and his shoulders were broader than I remembered. And those forearms! Hooley dooley. Tanned, with shaggy growth on his chin and cheeks, Jack obviously hadn't shaved since stepping off the plane.

I'd heard stories about people constantly bumping into the same people on holidays. I guess it really did happen. I was relieved to remember I'd made an effort this morning to brush my hair and clean my teeth.

Tara coughed, and without a hell of a lot of subtlety, poked me in the back.

'Jack,' I said, 'these are my friends, Tara and Sophie. And that's Levi over there.' I pointed to where Levi had wandered to get a better view of the cable cars moving down the cliff.

'I ran into Jack at Brisbane airport and then, when I tripped into a sunglasses stand in Athens the other day, he rescued me,' I explained to the girls.

Tara raised her eyebrows. 'After you tripped into a street stall?'

'That's the one.' Jack smiled.

'I was wearing a baseball cap... my hair was flat,' I babbled. 'Jack helped me up and here we are.'

'The boat, the boat,' Levi said, tugging at Sophie's shorts.

'How about you give me your address so we can meet for a drink?' Jack suggested.

I didn't answer. Too busy examining his eyebrows... then, the whole package. Blushing crimson, I recalled one of my dreams from the previous night of him whisking me away on a donkey.

'Great idea,' Tara said, jotting down our address on an old

64

but clean napkin she pulled from her bag. Totally ignoring my disapproving look, she added, 'Claud would love that.'

'Great.' Jack took the note, folded it, and put it in his shirt pocket. 'See you soon.'

We watched as, sandals slapping, he walked in the opposite direction.

'Spill!' Sophie said after Jack was out of earshot and we'd started on our way again.

'What?'

Tara poked my arm. 'The bronzed Aussie.'

I shook my head. 'Nothing to tell.'

'Nothing, my arse,' Sophie replied. 'All that hair flicking, you looked like you had fleas.'

I kept walking, ignoring their requests for more information. Flicking my hair? As if! Although I must admit, my legs were a bit wobbly. I wasn't sure if it was because my leg was still hurting from the mishap in Athens, or because I'd just noticed how good-looking Jack was. On the other hand, I wasn't used to walking so much, so maybe I needed more exercise. My lack of fitness was a bit unfortunate, as we'd only started down the six hundred stone steps to reach the small port to catch the excursion boat.

A stocky man with burly arms and a jaunty Greek sailor's cap waited at the boat launch and helped us aboard. Sailing away from Santorini, as the ferry rocked and dipped, I gazed back at the imposing granite rocks that rose vertically from the surface of the deep blue waters of the caldera. On the edge of the red cliffs, hanging over the sea, hundreds of white homes, hotels and churches dotted the landscape.

'I can just see Marcella's,' I shouted over the noise of the boat's engine.

'It looks like it's about to fall into the sea any minute,' Tara deadpanned, then returned to her journal writing.

'Best not to look then,' Sophie said, closing her eyes.

When the boat arrived at the small island of Nea Kameni, Levi spoke first. 'Stinky, stinky poo,' he said, as if trying to get rid of a bad taste in his mouth.

He was right. An overwhelming pong of sulphur filled the air, and everyone sat on the boat looking at each other. After some gentle nudging and sweeping hand gestures by the tour operators, we realised we were supposed to leave the boat and walk around the island, perhaps even hike to the top of the volcano.

'Hey, I didn't think this was a walking thing. I thought it was a looking thing,' Tara said as we stood on black stones and stared up at the volcanic cone.

'Come on, you two. Levi's already taken off,' Sophie said, and began sprinting up the hill over the sharp rocky terrain.

'Do we have to?' I stared down at my pretty open-toed red sandals. Not the smartest choice.

'Look at them,' Tara said as a dozen tourists streamed past. 'Some of those guys must be eighty.'

'Yeah. What if there's something amazing up there and we don't see it because we're too lazy to use our legs?'

While Tara doubted there'd be anything worthwhile at the top, she didn't want to risk missing out. So, the two of us, shamed into walking by a toddler and a group of geriatrics, trudged upwards.

'The smell might be better up there,' I said as we heaved ourselves to the top of the volcano. But as we neared the peak, sulphur still hung in the air.

'Do dragons live inside?' Levi asked as we watched hot vapours spew from the crater.

'Maybe,' Tara said. She took Levi's hand and together they went dragon hunting. Meanwhile, Sophie and I sat on a rock and tried not to inhale too deeply.

'Feeling okay?' I asked her.

'Yeah, no. I love being with Levi most of the time, but I think I need something more.'

'What, like going back to law? But you hated being a lawyer – the hours, the stress—'

'The clients, yeah, I know. No, I don't want to go back to that. I've been thinking about a few ideas. It'd be nice to have my own money so I'm not financially dependent on Alex.'

'I can understand that.'

'What about you? I was shocked the other day when you said you might change jobs when we get back home. I thought you liked working for Marcus.'

'Let's face it, my friend, it's not ideal, is it, me working with numbers all day?'

Sophie smiled. 'I guess not.'

'It was only out of desperation that I took the job in the first place.'

'Great timing, hey, just as George stuck you with that massive debt.' Sophie shook her head. 'What a prick!'

'Yeah, and to think I was planning on a future with him.'

Sophie put her arm around me and nodded. 'Do you still want... children?'

'I don't know. I might have missed the boat.'

'You'll meet someone else.'

I shook my head. 'I don't think I want to.' With my track record, it seemed highly unlikely. The best I could manage was being someone's part-time secret shag and that was not what I aspired to.

It wasn't always that way though.

Ben was my first true love. There have been several since him, but Ben was special. We crossed paths in my early twenties. We'd been dating – oh, about forty-two days – before the 'Sweet Caroline' incident put an end to that sweet romance.

After a few vodka and oranges at Goondiwindi Bachelor and Spinsters Ball with 'easy on the eye' Ben, I'd decided I could sing as well as, if not better than, the lead singer of the covers band. So, foolishly – hindsight is a valuable tool – I jumped onstage and sang the chorus to 'Sweet Caroline'.

The lead singer, who, I believed, had taken a shine to me because I had a good voice and an open heart (big breasts had nothing to do with it), invited me to New York to be a rock star with him. And after seven vodkas, I agreed, as you would, if you were a young Ancient History major and relatively unattached.

I decided the lead singer was a better choice of partner than Ben. The lead singer was going places, New York for one, and I was going with him. That night, after I told Ben the facts, he dumped me. *Me!* Even though I was on the brink of stardom and well on my way to becoming the next Britney Spears or at least Baby Spice! You'd think he'd have clung to me for dear life. Instead, he stormed off and out of my life.

The next day, sporting a killer hangover, I was more than a little mortified to recall I'd sung out of tune in front of fifteen hundred people. Not only that, but no amount of begging would stop Ben driving back to Brisbane in his red Daihatsu without me.

That was one weekend adventure I'd rather never happened. (I never saw the lead singer again. And I certainly haven't been back to Goondiwindi.)

As for my career, I should have stuck to my original high school plan of becoming a vet. The frog thing was a turning point for me because I didn't have a solid plan B – apart from working part-time at a department store to get the ten per cent staff discount.

Truth be told, I don't think my not becoming a vet was solely due to my inability to dissect amphibians. I'll admit, fainting at the sight of intestines wasn't a good look for a wannabe vet, but my inability to commit might also have had something to do with not excelling at maths or, in fact, any of the sciences.

Career highlights thus far? After university, I dabbled as an administration assistant for a less than scintillating hardware company. I moved on to selling media space for an advertising firm, which was definitely a step up. And then I landed a job as an event coordinator for Riesling Renaissance, a Brisbane food and wine management company. Jackpot!

I loved it. There was always something new to organise, from wine tastings to celebrity chef demonstrations and country cook-offs. Yes, there was the occasional disaster, à la the well-known chef who, absolutely plastered, attempted a live cooking demonstration in front of two hundred eager suburban housewives. The front row definitely got more than they bargained for when his hand got caught in the electric mixer and he was carted off in an ambulance, sirens blaring. We were front page news!

It was a vibrant and exciting time and I had visions of one day starting my own consultancy. When the company went belly-up, I was devastated. But I'd met Marcus at several events and when he offered me the job as his office manager, I grabbed it with both hands. I promised myself I'd look for something more suitable, but I was already in love with George by that stage and thinking about having a baby. Then George left me in debt, I had an affair with Marcus... and here I was.

I turned my mind to the 'what ifs' of my life. What if I'd never met George? What if I'd never met Marcus? I liked to think I'd have started my own company. I certainly wouldn't be in the mess I was in now.

As an office manager, often I was reconciling accounts. And I was hopeless at it. The figures never added up. It always looked like the company was losing money. But whenever I asked Marcus about it, he just shook his head, laughed, and told me his accountants would take care of everything.

I had to face the cold hard facts. Although my job was boring, at least I was being paid. Still, a couple of things worried me about going back to the office: a) I didn't want to fall back into old habits – i.e. resume my liaison with Marcus, even though the sex was thrilling; b) I liked Marcus as a person. What if he ignored me? Or worse, treated me like any other employee?

'Amazing to think, isn't it,' Tara said, returning from her dragon walk with Levi, 'that this baby could blow at any moment.'

'Like a real volcano?' Levi asked.

'Ooh! What was that?' Tara shouted, jumping up and grabbing Levi around his waist. 'It's the volcano dragon.' Tara and Levi ran around shrieking and laughing, much to the astonishment of the senior citizens.

'Nice way to go three days before my birthday,' I said.

'You just wanted to mention your birthday.' Tara bent over to catch her breath.

The truth was, I wasn't rapt about turning thirty-nine – it was a whisker away from forty. I couldn't get away with careless behaviour like sleeping with my boss for much longer. Being in your forties suggested a level of maturity I had yet to reach, so I certainly didn't want a big fuss made about it.

Two hours later, after our ferryman had successfully manoeuvred past dozens of fishing boats and shiny yachts all bobbing in the water vying for space in Fira harbour, we stepped off the boat and gazed up at the hundreds of steep steps we needed to climb to get back to the town centre.

'I'm buggered,' I said. 'I can't move. I've just spent two and a half hours walking up and down a volcano. My feet can't take any more. I have blisters.' Plus, there was my damaged knee. I looked down at my very dusty sandals and charcoal toes and ankles. 'Damn these beautiful stupid sandals.'

We gazed at the donkeys, then at the cable cars that had temporarily come to a halt.

'What do you reckon?' Sophie was hugging a weary Levi in her arms.

'Donkey?' I suggested. There were no taxis, so a four-legged ride was the only option.

'Look at the poor things.' Tara walked over to pat one. 'They're half-dead.'

'Tara! We're half-dead.'

'They're exhausted. God knows how many times they've already climbed those steps today.'

'Maybe you're right,' Sophie agreed. 'We can walk.'

'It's the donkeys' job. They won't get fed unless they take us up the hill,' I said irritably. 'Besides, they look happy – enough.' An outright lie, but I was tired. I had to look after myself, being middle-aged and all.

Twelve donkeys were lined up in front of us, ready for action, their black saddles decorated with multicoloured blankets and harnesses adorned in coloured beads. The beads gave them a soft glow. Or maybe the hot afternoon sun made the weary tourists see a soft glow. Either way, I won the battle. We chose three relatively friendly and agile-looking donkeys and clambered aboard.

Eventually, they started walking.

Slowly.

'At least mine knows that the stairs are an inevitable part of his job, even if he's gnawing the bit with his teeth,' I said to Sophie when her donkey stopped at the second step, blocking all the others behind him. He seemed content to fling his tail around, swat flies and pick at non-existent grass.

'No doubt trying to bore you off,' Tara said.

A withered old guy with a stick spotted the trouble and came over.

'Please don't,' Sophie pleaded.

He ignored her and gave the donkey a sharp whack on the rump. The old animal took off, practically galloped up the next ten steps, which came as quite a shock to Sophie and Levi. After an initial burst of energy, the donkey settled to a sluggish walk with his four-legged friends.

I was shaky in the saddle at first, but as I got used to the donkey's height and gait, I relaxed, smiling as we strode past foolish tourists who'd chosen to walk the uneven steps. Ha! Bet they were having second thoughts about that decision.

At the end of the twenty-minute journey, we dismounted, and before anyone could turn and give them a thank-you pat, the donkeys had bolted back down the stairs. Obviously, they hadn't stopped to consider that as soon as they arrived at the bottom of the stairs, they'd have to carry some lump straight back up again. Donkey logic.

'My legs won't work properly for a good hour,' Tara grumbled, shaking her legs as she stumbled along the pathway.

A few metres ahead, Sophie and I stepped over a huge turd, evidently deposited by some unusually large donkey with an extremely efficient digestive tract. Even Levi, who was half-asleep, looked down in amazement and giggled.

'Watch out for the donkey—' I called to Tara.

'Shit!' Tara screamed as she slid on the donkey droppings and fell straight onto her bum.

Sophie and I guffawed and Levi bent double.

Tara steamed with fury. 'Shut up and help me. I'm covered in it.'

Unfortunately for Tara, we were laughing so hard we were useless. She kept slipping as she tried to get up, covering herself with putrid brown paste. By the time she finally got up, she was in no mood for chit-chat.

'Just walk a bit ahead of us, Tara, there's a good girl,' Sophie said as she and I fell behind her to escape the stench.

I walked towards the cliff side of the road to avoid Tara's downwind, half-expecting her to shout at me.

And she did. 'Get out! Get out of the way.' Tara was waving her arms. 'Watch your bag!'

A scooter veered towards me so quickly it almost didn't register. The driver reached out to snatch my bag, and I jumped to the side of the narrow road. I almost threw myself over the cliff. Instead, I ended up in a prickly red bougainvillea. My right leg took the brunt of the fall. The same one I'd mangled in Athens.

'Claud, are you all right?' Sophie called as she and Tara rushed over to pull me from the bush and onto my feet.

'I guess so,' I said, brushing myself off before picking up my battered bag. 'Bloody bag snatcher. Ha. Well, he lucked out this time.'

'Why he do that?' Levi asked.

'A filthy thief,' Tara offered.

'He wouldn't have gotten far on twenty Euros and a packet of Mentos,' I said calmly, though my mind raced. Was this just a random attack? There were other tourists around, why was I singled out?

I shook my head; I was overthinking it.

Retrieving my broken sunglasses from the road, I gave them a quick once-over – terminal damage – and tossed them into a nearby bin.

We walked home in exhausted silence. Once there, I politely suggested Tara use the outside tap to freshen up before having a proper shower inside.

'Get fucked,' was her agreeable reply. 'Don't you think I've been humiliated enough? I need a hot shower, so get out of my way and let me in.'

Tara in a foul mood was one puppy not to play with. Sweeping past me, she slammed the bathroom door.

CHAPTER 11

*A*fter an hour checking Insta posts and reading magazines on the couch, watching Levi run over dinosaurs with imaginary motorbikes, and listening to the clickety-clack of Sophie's knitting needles, I ventured upstairs to Tara's room and knocked on her door.

'What?'

'You okay?' I asked.

Silence.

'Glass of wine?'

'No!'

I hesitated. Should I go in and try to soothe the savage beast, or stay outside where it was safe? What the hell! A scooter almost ran me down and I'd survived. How much worse could this be? Opening the door, I found Tara lying on the bed, draped over her notebook, tears rolling down her cheeks.

'It's pointless,' she said, wiping her eyes. 'I've got the first five chapters, but I can't get any further.'

'Maybe your writing style is more suited to short stories.'

Tara shook her head. 'That's not what I want to do. I really thought that being here, away from the magazine, I'd finally find some inspiration.'

'Give it time, it'll happen.'

'You said that days ago.'

'Maybe you need *more* time.'

'I've got notebooks full of ideas and observations, I just wish I could commit to seeing an idea through rather than giving up when it gets hard.'

'Maybe if you reread some of your—'

'You don't understand,' she interrupted. 'I can't concentrate. I need to clear my head but what with Sophie's noisy needles and Levi's shrieking—'

'He's not shrieking anymore. He's playing.'

'Hallelujah.' Tara raised her hands. 'And the clicking?'

'Still clicking.'

Tara sat up and closed her notebook. 'How do you think she is anyway?'

'Not happy, but I'm sure once she's spoken to Alex—'

'Why doesn't she ring *him*?'

'She has.' I paused. 'Maybe he really is tied up with work.'

'Calculated neglect, I'd call it. I did it to Anthony all the time, and most of the other partners I've had. Guaranteed to drive you insane.'

'I'm sure he's not knowingly ignoring Sophie,' I said, wondering if Marcus would do the same to me when I returned.

'True. Alex isn't that much of a bastard.' Tara regarded her notebook and plethora of coloured pens on the bed and took a deep breath.

'Come on, leave the writing for tonight and enjoy the sunset.' I ruffled her hair and she stood.

'You're right. But don't ever play with my hair again.'

We joined Sophie on the patio, where drinks and mouth-watering appetisers – vine leaves filled with rice and raisins, marinated eggplant and artichokes, and briny olives – awaited us. I loved it, loved listening to the cicadas and the church bells in the distance, watching the lemon trees sway gently in the breeze. My relaxed toes tingled, and my head was light. I could easily stay here for the foreseeable future. Santorini, where I didn't have a care in the world.

'Tara,' Sophie said when we'd settled. 'I've read about this sort of thing, it's very common.'

'What sort of thing?'

'Writer's block. You're forcing yourself. Just take it easy. Why don't you write a self-help book? People love those. I'd buy it.'

'It has to be a quirky self-help book though.' I scooped up a cracker of baba ganoush. 'Something like, *My Cat Saved My Life and Forty-Nine Other Sanity-Saving Tips*. It'd be a bestseller in no time.'

Tara shook her head. 'Very funny, guys. You love playing this game, don't you?'

'Are we annoying you yet?' I asked.

'Not overly. Anyway, I don't think it is writer's block. I think it's me not following through. Maybe I'm scared of failure.'

'How?'

'I've been talking about writing a novel for years but never seem to make much progress.'

'That's not true,' Sophie said. 'What about those fantastic murder stories you wrote?'

Tara sighed. 'Yeah, that was then. Besides, I told you, I'm not writing a serial killer novel.'

'We didn't say you have to,' I said. 'But you were prolific at school and uni – short, gripping, edge-of-your-seat murder mysteries.'

'Maybe you could change jobs, so you're not exhausted when you get home?' Sophie suggested.

'True. When I think about working for Melinda *I'm-a-self-styled-visual-publisher* Mason for the rest of my years...'

'Yeah, getting out from beneath her should be inspiration enough,' Sophie said.

I agreed. 'If I were you, I'd have killed myself by now.'

'You're a fine one to talk,' Tara said. 'What about that place Marcus sent you to?'

'That reminds me, I should call him.'

I moved inside and dialled his number. 'Marcus?'

'Claudia, you like ringing me in the middle of the night, don't you? How's the holiday going?'

'Fine, but after Con called me in Athens, I haven't heard anything more. Should I be worried?'

'He's a busy man. But he knows you're in Santorini, he'll call when he gets there. Just make sure you don't give the information to anyone else, okay?'

'All right. And Marcus...' I hesitated.

'Yeah?'

'Nothing. Speak to you soon.' I clicked the end button on my phone, muttered 'calculated neglect' under my breath and resumed my seat on the terrace.

I hated that I liked him so much. But I couldn't help myself. He was charming, kind and generous. What wasn't to like? Oh yeah, that's right. He was married. Separated, but still married.

'Claud, how's your knee?' Sophie asked.

'Sore.'

'We should've reported that guy,' Tara said.

Sophie peered over her knitting. 'How? His scooter had no licence plate, and he was dressed helmet to shoes in black.'

'It was an accident,' I said, not wanting to relive it again. 'He probably didn't see me.'

'I saw the way he was riding, Clauds, he was gunning for

you,' Tara said. 'He purposely accelerated into you to steal your bag.'

'It was a scooter. What harm could it have done?'

'Doesn't it bother you?' Sophie said. 'What if Levi had been standing next to you? That guy could have run him over.'

It crossed my mind to tell the others about the dubious characters I'd seen at Con's 'office' in Athens, but I knew Sophie and Tara would go ballistic if they heard even the barest details. Besides, if I started talking about Con, it would inevitably lead me to telling the girls about my affair with Marcus, and they'd never approve. I needed to keep that little nugget all to myself.

CHAPTER 12

'*B*ugger.'

Wrenched from a peaceful sleep, I realised I'd forgotten to switch off my phone and now it was ringing at the ungodly hour of – I raised my arm to check my watch and squinted – nine! In the morning. Who rang at this hour? On holiday?

Fumbling, I groped for my mobile lying on the bedside table. 'Hello.'

'Clow-di-ah?'

'Yes.' I sat up on the edge of the bed, pulling hair away from my face and glanced at the caller ID. 'Con?'

'*Geia sas. Me léne* Con.'

'Hi.'

'*Fira ávrio. Énteka. Nai.*' Con was all business and talking so rapidly I had difficulty understanding. When I sat the oral Greek exam at uni the examiners spoke V... E... R... Y slowly.

'*Edó?* You want to come here?' I asked, clutching the sheets around me. Stupid, Claudia! Mentally, I whacked myself on the forehead.

'*Óchi.* The café opposite the bus terminal.'

Thank goodness. '*Simera?*' Today? I hoped so. I wanted this matter dealt with as soon as humanly possible.

'No. Ávrio! Tomorrow,' Con said, irritation rising in his voice. He continued to give me instructions in Greek, which I did my best to interpret.

'Eleven tomorrow at the café opposite the bus terminal?' I repeated.

'*Naí.*'

'How will I recognise you?'

'Marcus sent me your picture. I will – how you say? – recognise you.' Con disconnected before I could say anything more. My brain was spinning. All I wanted to do was get those papers signed and hand over the flash drive.

I clomped downstairs to the bathroom, determined to put my niggling concerns about Con to one side. By the time I'd finished showering, I was feeling more philosophical about his call and had even devised a charming scenario of how my meeting with him would play out. We'd meet at the café for ten minutes, tops, knock back a grainy Greek coffee with a side order of baklava, then I'd hand over Marcus's documents, Con would sign them, and it'd be over. *Finírisma!*

What did Con look like anyway? Perhaps he was a swarthy-looking Greek who'd roll up to the café on his Vespa, dark curls twinkling in the sun, bod firm and tanned from years spent fishing out on the ocean and dragging nets ashore. Those guys looked incredibly laid-back when I'd seen them propped up in bars, smoking cigarettes and downing ouzo. Hitch: from the brief conversation I'd had with him, Con didn't strike me as the laid-back type.

Maybe he was more the suave and slick man about town, wearing a sharp designer suit with the obligatory heavy gold chains dripping from his neck and arms (and maybe a couple of thick gold rings on his fingers). He'd saunter up to the table, engage me in flirtatious chat, while all the time leering at my breasts and legs. Plausible.

Scenario three, he'd look like any of the hundreds of nondescript blokes I'd observed since my arrival in Greece. Though I doubted Con would be wearing an *I'm with stupid* T-shirt and loud, red board shorts.

I walked out onto the terrace, where Marcella greeted me with freshly baked *koulourakia* – sweet biscuits – and yogurt.

'Eat,' she said, imploring me to sit with her. This morning, she'd pulled her hair back in a colourful headscarf and was wearing a peach-coloured dress with faded navy apron. 'Your holiday, it is good?'

'Very. Thank you,' I said, taking a scoop of yogurt.

'But you here alone? No husbands?'

I shook my head. 'Sophie is married but Tara and me...' I shrugged.

She nodded. 'Men. Too much trouble.'

I studied her for a moment, taking in her strong arms and worker's hands. She didn't wear a wedding ring, not that that meant anything. Plenty of married women didn't wear jewellery. However, she did seem to run this business by herself.

'Are you married?' I ventured.

'*Óchi!* No!' Then she softened. 'A long time ago, yes.'

I felt embarrassed. I hadn't meant to pry.

'I am happy woman. But you girls work too hard.'

I looked up, inviting her to continue.

'Tourists come from all over world to Santorini. All year work so you come here for two weeks, get sunburnt. Go back home. Work again. What kind of life is this?'

Was she angry that we were being disrespectful to her country? 'We're having a wonderful time here,' I said. 'It's very beautiful.'

She shook her head. 'You could live like this too.' She threw her hands into the air. 'My life is simple but good. Here,' she picked her picnic basket up off the ground, 'take these.'

She handed me a basket of limes, strawberries and oranges. 'Enjoy life.'

I marvelled at her vitality. In the air I could smell the sharp sweet scent of lemon blossoms and all I could think was that in my next life I wanted to be just like Marcella.

CHAPTER 13

*A*t Kamari, we positioned our deckchairs on the black sand beach underneath huge blue and white striped umbrellas so our bodies were in the sun and our heads in the shade. Then I fixed my beady eyes on the beautiful people strolling the beach to see if they flinched walking barefoot on the unforgiving hot pebbles.

'Does my bum look big in this?' Sophie asked after she'd discarded her new clothes to reveal a burnt orange crocheted bikini sitting on her lightly sun-kissed frame. Yeah, and her blonde curls bounced around her shoulders too. Surprise, surprise, she looked stunning and was fast attracting envious glances from passers-by.

Meanwhile, I was wearing one-piece miracle swimmers, basic black, which, according to the promotional information, were made of a patented fabric blend delivering three times the holding power of ordinary swimsuits without inner linings or control panels. Whilst wearing them, I apparently looked five kilos lighter. Ha! Anyway, they were comfortable. (Isn't sporting comfortable clothing one small step away from accepting your body isn't what it used to be and never will be again?)

Sophie persisted. 'Does my bum look big in this?'

'What bum? You don't have one,' Tara said.

'Yeah, your back is the width of a Marlboro Light,' I said, shaking my head. 'You wouldn't know the first thing about the pain of buying new swimmers every season.'

'Don't know why you bother,' Tara replied flatly. 'I've had these for years.' She pulled at the worn navy Lycra that used to be a shoulder strap.

I laughed. 'Yeah. I remember them from our Hawaiian holiday.'

'Hmm. I guess they have had their day.'

'Day? Try decade.' I felt a bit catty, even though it was true. Tara's style, if you could call it a *style,* was minimal, simple. No tizz. No fuss. She was the type of person who wore clothes until they fell off, then went and bought an exact replica of the clothing that'd died.

Tara was still smarting over the swimmers comment when she took off with Levi to the water's edge. They splashed in the sea and played on the black sand.

'Her swimmers *are* atrocious,' I said to Sophie when Tara was out of earshot.

'Preaching to the converted, luvvie. You don't need to convince me.'

As much as I hated to admit it, because it sounded ridiculously parochial, the Greek beaches I'd seen so far didn't do it for me. This long stretch of beach didn't compare to the shorelines back home. Sure, the fine black sand was a novelty, but what about the uncomfortable pebbles? Try lying against your towel on those without succumbing to serious stone bruising. The good news was that there weren't any high-rise hotels shadowing the beach.

Away from the shore, a rock rose out of the sea. Further down, three elderly Greek men fished on an ancient pier. They lived the good life, in the midday sun, laughing and smoking hand-rolled cigarettes without a care in the world. Obviously, lung and skin cancer didn't factor into their thinking. Those guys probably guzzled ouzo until the early hours, then were up the next day, fishing, smoking and drinking strong Greek coffee. What a life.

'Tell me about Jack,' Sophie said, after several minutes' lazy silence.

Jack? Perfectly charming Jack. 'He's okay,' I said.

'If you want my two cents' worth, I think he's delish!'

I squinted into the sun.

'What?' Sophie continued. 'I'm married. I have to live vicariously through friends. So far, you and Tara have offered very slim pickings.'

'Yeah, well, I didn't come all this way to hook up with an Australian.' I closed my eyes and lay back in my chair.

What was I saying? I didn't come here to hook up with any man – Australian, Greek or Icelandic!

I was asleep when Levi tapped me on the shoulder with two fistfuls of pumice. 'You were snoring.'

'Pardon?' I yelped as his cold little paws pressed against my warm skin.

'Snoring like Daddy.'

'Was not.'

'Yes you were. Wasn't she, Happy?'

'*Happy?*' I opened my eyes to find a small boy about Levi's age standing in front of me, completely nude, nodding and playing with his penis. I hoped he was wearing full body sunscreen.

'See. Happy says you were snoring.' Levi who was also nude and tugging on his own penis.

He wasn't making any sense. 'Where's Mummy?'

'Ober dare.' He pointed to where Sophie, Tara and another

woman were chatting. Thankfully, when they saw me, the three of them walked over.

'Claudia, meet Angie. Harry's mum,' Tara said.

Harry. Okay, so Levi had articulation issues.

Angie was thirtyish, English, pretty and tall, with honey-blonde shaggy hair and an olive complexion. She had a small red heart-shaped tattoo on her left shoulder, inscribed with the word *Harry*. I soon found out she was a lawyer and that she and Harry lived in London, just off Marylebone High Street, near a fancy cheese shop.

'Harry and I are here on holidays,' Angie was saying. 'In fact, I'm celebrating the first anniversary of my divorce.'

It wasn't long before Sophie began quizzing her about why her marriage had broken down. Angie was remarkably candid.

'Peter was a complete shite,' Angie said after Levi and Harry had released their penises to start flinging pebbles into the ocean. 'I came home from work early one day and found him banging my neighbour in the shower. Harry was in the next room watching *The Tweenies*. Poor love.'

'Then what happened?' Sophie asked.

'I stood there watching them – only fog, soap lather and a shower screen separating us. When he saw me, he asked for a towel. Wasn't even embarrassed. Banging bastard.'

'Then what?' Sophie asked, mesmerised.

'I said a few choice words, then kicked them both out, yeah.'

'Yeah,' the three of us repeated.

I was distracted, trying to place Angie's accent. She sounded a bit like the Queen, but then my experience with English accents boiled down to *Billy Elliot's* working class and *Mary Poppins*, posh, with not a lot in between.

'Was the neighbour married?' Sophie questioned.

'Nah, she was a singleton, keen to bang a married man—'

'Why would you say that?' I asked.

'Why wouldn't I?' Angie replied. 'What self-respecting woman goes around shagging other women's husbands? Can't they find their own?'

'I... maybe she was lonely,' I ventured.

Inside, I was shaking. That's what most women thought about other women who slept with married men, even if the man was recently separated. And they were right. I had no excuse. To his credit, Marcus never told me he was lonely, or that his wife didn't understand him. He simply said that they'd stopped being lovers years ago and, though friendly, had stayed together for the sake of the kids. I actually got the impression he quite liked his family. Not that Trish and his kids were a hot topic of conversation between us, but whenever Marcus mentioned his sons, his eyes lit up, confident and happy, like *life's great and I'm having a ball.*

I listened silently to more stories about Peter the banging bastard, followed by Alex the workaholic. Even Tara threw in her two cents' worth about Anthony.

'At least you lot have had husbands,' I said. 'Why are all the men I meet happily committed to remaining single and then they marry as soon as I'm out of the picture?' (Okay, I wasn't talking about Marcus.)

'Marriage is outdated,' Tara said. 'No offence, Soph. But men can have sex without marriage. They can enjoy the benefits of having a wife without actually getting that little piece of paper that says you're bound for life.'

'Yeah, I know,' I said. 'I probably won't end up getting married, much to my mother's horror.'

'You'll find the right person eventually,' Sophie said. 'Besides, they're *all* the right person until the lust wears off. And then they're like an annoying flatmate who hogs the shower, won't put the toilet seat down, and comes home from work late expecting dinner on the table.'

'Gee, when you put it like that...' I said.

Sophie sighed. 'It's true. Alex doesn't even pick up his socks.'

'But he didn't pick them up before you were married either, did he?' I said.

'My marriage might have been a disaster, but I'm so glad I have Harry.' Angie looked over at Harry and Levi who were licking pebbles and giggling. 'He's worth every ounce of unhappiness I went through with Pete. Harry brings a love and contentment to my life I can barely describe. And now we have the freedom to do what we like. No one will ever again tell me what to wear or when to come home, and I'll never have to lie about the two new pairs of shoes I buy in my lunch hour.'

My most recent shoe purchase – outrageously expensive maroon suede boots – sat on display underneath my dressing table at home, gorgeous but unworn. Half a size too small. I swear my feet grew by the week. 'Sounds like prison.'

'It was,' Angie said. 'I just didn't realise it at the time, more fool me.'

'I was lucky to escape from Anthony when I did,' Tara said.

'But don't you think your soulmate is out there somewhere?' Sophie asked.

'Maybe, but when I find him, I certainly won't need to sign a contract to tell me I have,' Angie said.

'I thought Alex was my soulmate. We used to have so much fun together.'

And they did. Even though their weekdays were manic, with both working long hours, every weekend without fail they'd head to the beach or go sailing or drive to the mountains for a day's hiking. They were always busy together, focused on enjoying each other's company. Sophie and Alex were an ideal couple – apart from the fact that Sophie didn't like being Alex's second wife.

'What went wrong?' Angie asked her.

'Life, I guess. Growing up. The pressures of Alex's work, not falling pregnant. Falling pregnant. Having Levi.' Sophie stood and dusted sand off her legs.

We watched as she strode down to the water near a couple of fishing boats that had just motored in.

'Come on.' I grabbed Levi's and Harry's hands. 'Let's see what they've caught.'

A large crowd, including Tara and Angie, gathered around the men, who proudly held up octopus, moray eels and mottled brown flying fishes before carefully arranging them in crates with dozens of other fish I'd never seen before. After a quick inspection, locals bargained over prices, loud and frenzied.

Deals completed, several locals took their purchases to the water's edge and, squatting on the pebbly shore, expertly scaled and cleaned the fish in the sea.

After a few minutes, I'd had enough of blood and guts and turned away, but the others remained.

Some distance from the fish entrails, I waded into the crystal-clear freezing ocean and caught up with Sophie.

'Before you say anything,' she said, holding up her hands, 'I'm sorry. It's just that sometimes I hate Alex for taking my baby's love from me and I hate Levi for loving Alex more. I know I'm not supposed to say those things but that's how I feel. Alex is so affectionate with Levi. He's never that loving with me. I'm jealous. The way Levi smiles at him and loves Alex. The way their faces light up when they're together, I feel totally excluded. There, I've said it! It's like I don't exist. I don't get what Angie was saying about Harry. Of course I love Levi, he's my son, but I don't feel an overwhelming passion for him.'

Sophie exhaled. 'As for Alex, at the end of the day we want different things. He comes home to get away from people talking to him, but I look forward to him coming home so we can chat. We're never on the same wavelength. I end up going off at him for some minor irritation like leaving his shoes in the hallway and we have a massive fight. It's much less hassle for me to go to bed. When I'm finally alone, I breathe a sigh of relief. I'm sure Alex does too.'

'Soph, I'm so sorry.' I hugged her in the icy water. 'What can I do to help?'

Sophie shrugged. 'You've helped by bringing me here.'

'But it's—'

'Given me breathing space to think about my life and what I want from it.' She kissed me on the cheek. 'Thank you.'

I wasn't sure that was exactly what I'd been going to say, but I kept quiet and nodded.

'Sometimes I wake up in a cold sweat in the middle of the night with the words *Alex doesn't love you* screaming inside my head and I'm terrified. Terrified of him leaving me, of being alone.'

'You'll never be alone. You have me.' I plastered on a huge smile.

Being alone was one thing I wasn't frightened of. Yes, I was concerned I'd never have a child of my own and I'd never stop spending money long enough to save any, but not being in a relationship? I'd been alone before and, to all intents and purposes, I was alone now. It didn't bother me, except when I was required to take a 'plus one' to social events. I think Tara was getting sick of being my date. But maybe it wasn't my destiny to go the traditional route and have a husband, a mortgage and 2.2 kids. I did want a kick-arse career though, and on days when I was feeling confident and enthusiastic, I really believed I shouldn't have given up so easily on starting my own events management company.

'True. And of course, I love Alex and Levi.' Her voice faltered. 'I can't imagine my life without them, but I want more.'

'Sophie—' I began, but she disappeared under the water before I could badger her further.

'I'm worried about you. I've seen this happen before,' I said when she reappeared.

'That's the problem with lifelong friends; they know too much.' Sophie gazed out to sea. 'Come on, Ms Doom and Gloom,' she said, snapping back to her old self and glancing over at Levi who was standing at the water's edge, calling out to her. 'It's no big deal.'

'Okay but promise me you'll eat all your lunch.'

'You make me sound like one of those people who take themselves off to a Swiss treatment clinic four times a year to be re-educated about what constitutes a calorie-controlled meal.' Sophie rolled her eyes, then flicked sea water in my face. 'Race you to the shore!' With that, she was off and paddling in the calm water towards her son.

CHAPTER 14

*L*ater that afternoon, having caught the bus back to Fira, we walked slowly home to Marcella's, stopping every few metres to window-shop. At least Tara and I did. Sophie on the other hand...

'You're taking this peasant look seriously, aren't you?' Tara said to Sophie, who walked out of the fourth clothing shop clad in a tiered white cheesecloth skirt and an embroidered lace-up blouse with bouffant capped sleeves.

'Who are you? My personal style icon?' Sophie was indignant. 'And this coming from a woman who's wearing ancient black shorts and a white T-shirt that's gone dirty grey from years of washing.'

'Take it easy. I'm just saying we've been here two minutes and you're already hopping on the boho bandwagon.'

Despite *Marie Claire* urging us to have a boho spring, I wasn't feeling the vibe either, but I kept my mouth shut.

'What? It's the quintessential Santorini look,' Sophie said.

Granted, Sophie's new top was groovier than your average peasant would wear, but it had a definite gypsy edge to it. The whole ensemble looked fabulous on her, but I doubted she'd wear it once she left Santorini. Possibly to the beach, but even then, I wouldn't take bets. She'd been sucked in like the other tourists, embracing new looks in foreign lands – torturing and twisting their hair into thirty-six tiny plaits while confidently embracing the grass skirt and scooped-out coconut-shell bra – only to arrive home and discover they look a smidge silly. No matter how thrilled one is with one's new shark-tooth necklace or sari, chances are, people back home will stare.

'You look great, Soph,' I said. 'Wish I could wear that garb.'

Sophie and Tara looked at me, puzzled.

'Boobs! I couldn't get away with wearing clothes like that.'

'Oh,' Tara said. 'I thought you meant it was an ugly look at best only attempted by two-year-olds and nannas who don't know any better.'

Sophie sniffed. 'At least I don't wear tatty clothes from five years ago and try to pass them off as vintage.'

'My clothes aren't vintage, and I don't feel the need to dress in the latest fad because it happens to be trendy.' Tara was getting cranky.

'Trendy? Who are you, my mother?'

'All right, all right, let's simply enjoy, hey?' I said, taking a deep breath. 'We're on holidays remember.'

Just then, I thought I spotted Jack and upped my pace. After several metres, I slowed again, obviously mistaken.

As Sophie had already bought several pieces of clothing and Tara had zero interest in island fashion, we walked in and out of a few more shops without opening our purses. But the temptation was too great to resist when we stopped in front of what had become my favourite jewellery store, from the outside at least. I had no intention of popping in and trying on rings, bracelets and other fancy trinkets, but Nikos, the jeweller, was very persuasive.

'Come, lovely ladies,' he said as Tara, Sophie, Levi and I

hovered outside. 'I cannot be drinking my special home-made wine alone. Please! Join me.' Nikos's deep voice, a heavily accented mix of English and Greek, was too irresistible to refuse.

'You are all so beautiful,' Nikos continued as we accepted glasses filled to the brim with red wine. 'I bet you get offered goats all the time.'

We laughed. I'd read about the traditional Greek custom of shepherds offering goats to women as a declaration of their love. No doubt Nikos paid this compliment to every female over seventeen who walked into his shop. But we didn't mind. Not only was he charming, he had a gorgeous smile too.

Next thing you know, I'd blown five hundred dollars on an exquisite silver and ruby ring. (Gorgeous, stunning and all mine!)

'Are you sure you can afford that?' Tara asked after we'd walked out.

'An early birthday present from Mum and Dad,' I lied.

In the distance, late-blooming almond trees scattered their pink blossoms in the sea breeze.

We arrived home to find a freshly baked baklava sitting on the kitchen benchtop and all our laundry washed, dried, ironed and, in Tara's case (her shorts), mended! We examined them for over fifteen minutes. Marcella's handiwork was impeccable. We really were in paradise.

CHAPTER 15

I almost bounded out of bed – almost, that is, until I remembered that today I was meeting with Con. I didn't want to. I wanted to hang out, laze by the pool, catch up on the latest Twitter feuds and slurp strawberry smoothies. Really, that should have been the beauty of being on holidays – not having to think about Con. I should have been basking in the Santorini sunshine pretending I always led this rich and luxurious life. Instead, I was only on pseudo-holidays until the delivery of Marcus's precious package.

Finishing my yogurt, I sat quietly in the sun, pushing thoughts of Con aside and focusing on my make-believe glamorous life. On holidays and living in 'Claudia' world, I didn't have to worry about the ugly sunspots forming on my shoulders or the crow's feet multiplying with every eye squint from baking in the sun sans sunscreen.

It was Santorini sun after all. Each new wrinkle materialising on this holiday would be a permanent reminder of my island sojourn. In years to come, I'd point to my furrows and say, 'I got those reclining on my banana lounger drinking fresh orange juice and gazing out across the Mediterranean.' It would be worth it.

Besides, didn't international sun authorities claim that Mediterranean sun was less harsh than Australian sun? Couldn't I sit in the European sunshine for a full two weeks and only do the equivalent of four days' worth of Aussie sun damage? I convinced myself that, yes, indeed, I could.

Sophie peered over the top of me. 'Pardon?'

An extra set of wide little eyes stood beside her, glaring at me.

'Just chatting to myself.'

'Obviously. About anything interesting?'

'I'm justifying why I'm baking in the sun. I'm also trying to remain calm about meeting Con.'

'Con?'

'Marcus's envelope, remember? Hey, Levi,' I said, sitting up as Levi clambered onto my lap, 'if you could have a bowl of chips or a block of chocolate, which would you choose?'

Sophie glared at me. 'Why are you asking him about chocolate so soon after breakfast?'

'It's just one of those questions that pop into your head.'

'Your head, maybe.'

'And I want a three-and-a-half-year-old's perspective... so,' I said, turning back to Levi, 'chips or chocolate?'

'Both. I want both.'

'You can't have both, you have to choose.' Clearly, he hadn't been paying attention.

'I want chocolate *and* chips.'

'I don't have them, Levi. It's a hypothetical question.'

'Yeah.' Sophie snorted. 'Good luck. Like he'll understand *that*!' She toddled off to shower, leaving me struggling to explain to her child that it was only a game. Unsurprisingly, I failed. Big time. Within seconds, Levi was on the floor screaming for chocolate and chips. A perfect morning in tatters. All of my own stupid doing.

'Steady on.' Tara yawned as she ambled down the stairs. 'What's up?'

'Claudie not giving me chocolate.'

'Give the kid chocolate, for God's sake.'

'Can't. Sophie'll kill me.' To which Levi responded by flinging himself on the floor and screaming even louder.

'Listen, I'll kill you. Give Levi some chocolate.' Tara turned, strode into the kitchen and retrieved an unopened family-sized block of Dairy Milk. Back outside, she waved it in front of Levi's nose. Almost instantly, he stopped, stood, and reached for the chocolate.

'No more tears, okay?' she said, handing it to him.

He nodded, before ripping off the paper and foil and cramming the chocolate into his enormous toothy mouth.

'Did you give him chocolate, Claudia?'

Tara and I swung round to see Sophie's cranky face. Levi, meanwhile, was sucking his chocolate-covered hands in the corner of the lounge room.

'No, she did.' I pointed to Tara.

'Only because he was screaming,' Tara spluttered.

'And we're on holidays,' I added.

Sophie tapped her foot. 'I can't trust you, can I? I have to do everything myself.' She turned to look at Levi and then back at us and shrugged. 'Anything to keep the peace.' She disappeared again, presumably to get dressed.

That was easy.

'Do you ever think about having kids?' I asked Tara.

'Heavy topic. Where's this coming from?'

'It's been bubbling in my head since Angie mentioned it yesterday.'

'Angie?'

'Yeah. She said that Harry brought a love and contentment to her life she could barely describe.'

'So now you want kids?'

'I used to think I might have one or two by now.'

'Is this because of your impending birthday?'

'Maybe. Parenthood seems so time-consuming, doesn't it?'

'I'll say.' Tara paused. 'Anyway, I don't think it's on the cards for me.'

'Why?'

'Because, as I've said to my mother on those rare occasions when we're speaking, I don't really like children – and then we go back to not talking again for six months.' Tara laughed. 'You really think you'd like to have a couple of kids? You'll be a pensioner when they're teenagers. You'll be one of those "older" mothers in the maternity ward, with the words *elderly primigravida* emblazoned on your bedhead. You'll be—'

'Okay, I get it.' I put up my hands to stop her. 'I'm old. It's not a good idea.' Besides, I wasn't smart enough to have a child. I didn't know how planes stayed in the air or why flies had 4,000 lenses in each eye. And I certainly didn't know why the number eleven wasn't pronounced onety-one.

I glanced at my watch and my stomach squelched. It was almost time to meet Con. I walked inside to retrieve the envelope, but it wasn't on the dining room table where I'd left it with my keys, phone and purse. I could have sworn I'd put it there. I looked underneath the table.

'Levi!' I screeched, as he clenched his chocolate-covered hands tighter around the package. I snatched it away from him.

'Gib it back,' he hollered. 'My dinosaur.'

'No, Levi, you can't draw dinosaurs on this.' I stuffed the yellow envelope, crumpled and covered in black marker ink and chocolate, into my daypack. 'Have this instead.' I handed him a tattered paper scrap. More crying. So that's why you don't give kids chocolate in the morning.

'Come on, Leev, there's a good boy, shush,' I said, trying to distract him from the chaos he was about to create. Why is it that when you shush a child they tend to scream, cry and fling themselves about with all the passion of a teenage girl? 'Play with your dinosaurs out on the terrace.' I put the paper and pens aside and cajoled him out onto the terrace. Levi followed, but his temper didn't improve. He screamed louder. Where was the child's mother? Tara also seemed to have conveniently disappeared.

I worked out that Levi's screaming was because one of his beloved dinosaurs was missing. So, while he bawled on the patio, no doubt to the annoyance of guests trying to enjoy the church bells and gentle strings of bouzoukis in the distance, I crawled around on my hands and knees in the lounge room looking for the missing stegosaurus.

I reached behind the sofa cushions. Ah. So that was where my new Dior lipstick had disappeared to. I pocketed it. Sadly, there was no sign of the reptile.

'I want my steg—' crying '—aahh—' high-pitched squealing '—sawrrrrus!' Huge racking sobs. Levi was oblivious to my attempts to placate him.

'Look, Levi.' I clutched my leg dramatically. 'Something's got my leg.' It was as much for my own amusement as his.

He stopped crying for a millisecond.

'I think it's a legasaurus,' I screamed, then laughed hysterically.

Levi cried hysterically. He couldn't see the humour. How he could possibly tell the difference between a stegosaurus and a regular dinosaur was beyond me, but he was adamant that the couple of stray relics I'd found were not the ones he was after.

It was ugly. My head ached from the screaming, not to

mention I'd bonked it against the concrete walls a couple of times as I crawled around on the cold marble floor. I offered Levi everything I could think of; not chocolate obviously, he'd scoffed it all. In the kitchen, I searched for chips. There weren't any. Fizzy drinks? No. However, there was fresh strawberry juice, which he vomited up on the outdoor table. Ghastly.

I wanted to pour apple schnapps down his throat and be done with it, but I knew Sophie, the killjoy, would never approve, even if it meant that her son would quietly slumber for the next ten hours. So I resisted the urge. Although, retrieving the bottle from the kitchen bench, I thought maybe if I drank the liquid, the pain of this nightmare would go away. I was rapidly losing my remaining self-control.

No wonder Alex worked incredibly long hours. I would too if I lived with Levi. Maybe I could gag him. What a good idea. I grabbed a tea towel and was so lost in my own thoughts I didn't notice Levi had stopped screaming.

Tea towel in hand, I walked out onto the terrace and saw Tara comforting him.

'Don't you remember, Leev? You said your stegosaurus could go home with Harry last night.' More sobbing, this time gentler, certainly not the ear-piercing, rip-your-heart-out screaming that had been going on five minutes before. 'You gave Stegosaurus to Harry and said he could give it back the next time he saw you.'

'Oh yeah,' Levi said, his tears dissolving. 'I dib, dibn't I?' He hugged Tara, then galloped over to where I'd lined up his other dinosaurs.

Jeez. No 'Thank you, Claudia', nothing. I was the one who'd found all the bloody reptiles and it turned out the bloody stegosaurus wasn't lost to begin with. I was outraged.

Levi and I didn't speak after that. Truth be told, I should have been happy. After all, I'd found my new lipstick and Levi had remembered where his stegosaurus was, but I'd had enough of him. The child was spoilt, wilful, obstinate, petulant, irritating, exasperating, recalcitrant and really annoying. Seriously, I wanted to pinch him. Before I gave in to my inner spoilt child, I picked up my bag, popped on my sunnies and stalked out the front door. Without doubt, motherhood was not for me!

CHAPTER 16

I arrived at the café just before eleven, sat at an outside table, ordered a coffee and pulled out the local Santorini newspaper. Peace and quiet at last. I gawked at the spectacular views of the cliff and islands. Then I turned towards the streets, searching for a man who could be Con. Mopeds and taxis zoomed up and down, their horns beeping and engines in desperate need of a tune-up, but at least it wasn't irritating child noise.

There were plenty of scooters around. They all looked the same. Any one of them could have been the one that tried to run me down the other day. I was making an effort to ditch my paranoia, so I chose to believe it had all been a mistake. The rider hadn't seen me. That's why he'd accelerated into me, rather than swerving and hitting the brakes. Who said it was a male anyway? It could have been a woman, or a newly qualified driver for that matter. Perhaps it was a teenager who'd only held their licence a couple of days.

While I drank my coffee, I listened to the donkeys' tinkling bells as they climbed up and down the stairs to the port. Annoyingly, Jack sprang into my mind. Had I seen him the previous day? He was in Santorini, it wasn't unrealistic. Maybe, if asked, I'd go out with him. It might be fun. At least he might take my mind off Marcus for an hour or two.

Half past eleven. Exactly how long was I supposed to wait for this Con character? I'd already downed my coffee and eaten a huge slice of spanakopita, and although the view was stunning, I was growing increasingly agitated. Not even the lively games of backgammon being played at nearby tables – complete with loud language and insulting hand gestures – held my interest.

I checked my watch for the umpteenth time. As I was preparing to leave (I have a mobile, Con could have rung), I remembered an earlier conversation I'd had with Marcella.

'Why wear a watch?' she'd asked with genuine concern.

'So I know the time,' I'd replied.

'Time!' Marcella threw her hands in the air. (I'd noticed a lot of hand throwing in Greece.) 'Why? Time is – how you say? – like a rubber band.' She held her hands apart before bringing them together and pulling them out again, several times. 'Clocks are not the boss.'

Maybe she had a point about time being elastic here. The locals I'd met didn't seem to be in a hurry for anything except coffee, ouzo, backgammon and a robust shouting match with friends and family.

'*Proí*, Clow-di-ah?' A man was standing next to me.

I jumped, then stood. 'Yes.'

'Con!' was all he said. His lips twitched and he didn't look me in the eye. In fact, his eyes darted in every direction but mine.

I shivered a little before extending my right hand in greeting. He didn't take it. Instead, he pulled out the chair opposite me and sat, motioning for me to do the same. As I did so, he called to the waiter to bring him coffee.

He was big, far too big, for the dinky plastic chair he sat in. As much like a Con as the next bloke, he was not overly tall, not overly fit and not overly attractive. He had a dumpy square face, beaky nose, rough voice and dark skin, eyes and hair – not only on his head. Coarse black hair sprouted in tuffs on his arms, neck and on what I could see of his chest and back. His teeth were crooked and yellowing, and a rolled-up cigarette hung limply from the right side of his mouth.

I didn't recognise him as one of the men I'd seen in Athens. But then again, I'd only seen those people for a few seconds, and it had been very dark inside the building. Plus, I'd been shit-scared.

Polite as I tried to be, I wanted to give Con the flash drive and get him to sign the damn papers so I could leave. His eyes continued flitting feverishly, unnerving me. Hence, when he gulped his coffee in one go, I was pleasantly surprised.

His mobile rang. Con mumbled two indistinguishable words into the mouthpiece and, completely ignoring me, rushed off to a waiting car.

'Hey? What about this?' I called after him, shaking the envelope.

'*Ávrio*,' Con barked as he slammed the car door and the driver sped away.

Bloody tomorrow!

As if that wasn't enough, I also got stuck with his bill. Hello? I was trying to stick to a budget!

'Marcus,' I said into my phone moments later, 'I've had it. I'm not waiting around for this guy anymore. He was half an hour late and when he did turn up, no apology mind you, he got a phone call and took off before I could show him the papers.'

'I'm sure it was just a misunderstanding. Thanks for ringing me at a civilised hour by the way. I'm still in the office.'

'Misunderstanding or not, I don't trust him. There's something shady about him—'

'How would you know?'

'I just do, okay. He has funny eyes. He couldn't look at me straight.' As much as I tried to ignore my inner voice, I couldn't. Con unsettled me. I didn't want anything to do with him. 'And he doesn't look like a businessman or entrepreneur. He looks shifty.'

'Shifty?'

'Shifty. This oil and wine he's bringing to the company had better be special.' Was Marcus talking to someone? 'Who's there with you?'

'No one,' he said as a door closed in the background. 'Don't tell me paranoia's followed you to Santorini?'

'I'm not being paranoid. Con's creepy.' Maybe that was an exaggeration, but I was annoyed he'd scooted off without finishing our meeting. I'd wasted my whole morning.

'Aren't you having a good time?'

'Yes, but I can't relax. There's the envelope business here and when I get back to Brisbane, my relationship with you—'

'Whoa! Back up, Claudia. We don't have a relationship, I thought we decided—'

'I know what we decided!'

'Look,' Marcus said, softening, 'if you do this job for me properly and get creepy Con – he who has the most superior oils, vinegars and wines in all of Europe – to sign the papers, I'll wipe your debt.'

'What?'

'I can afford it. Twenty-five grand, isn't it?'

I totalled the ring and duty-free cosmetics I'd splashed out on. 'Twenty-six.'

Marcus sighed. 'Okay, twenty-six.'

'A holiday in Greece and twenty-six thousand dollars? You must be feeling very guilty.'

'You're right, it's too much. I'll give you twenty.'

'Really? I couldn't, Marcus. I—'

'Gorgeous, you've had a hard time over the last couple of years and maybe I've taken advantage of the situation.'

'Oh.'

'Do we have a deal?'

I wiped a couple of rogue tears from my cheeks. 'Okay, but Marcus—'

'Before you say anything more, it might be best if you start looking for other work.'

'You're sacking me?'

'Not at all. I'm just suggesting you might be more comfortable working somewhere else.'

Great. This was all I needed. Not only was I a spendthrift who went around shagging married men, I was about to become an unemployed shagging spendthrift. Excellent.

I played with my coffee cup, remembering the first time I slept with Marcus. I hadn't seen it coming. Okay, I sort of had. We'd flirted before then, but Marcus flirted with all the women in the office. I'd like to say that the evening's scenario didn't include a tired cliché about working late until we were the only two people in the building. But I'd be lying. He had a tender due, and I was frantically trying to get all the necessary documentation together. At seven thirty, when he ordered Thai food and offered me a drink, we were about three-quarters of the way through. Until then, I hadn't known he kept bottles of vodka, rum and whisky tucked away in his cabinet drawer.

I was drinking my second vodka and tonic when he brushed some hair away from my face. Alarm bells went off in every part of my body, but I still let him kiss me. And kiss me again. It was wrong from the beginning. I felt guilty but excited and nervous as well. It fed my ego, right up until the last month or so.

As I wiped more tears away, I looked up, taken aback at seeing Jack standing a couple of metres away staring at me. He mouthed to ask if it was okay to sit. I nodded, finding it hard to speak. I was pleased to see him, if a little embarrassed.

'Claud, are you there?' Marcus was shouting into the phone. 'I'll transfer the money into your account. I really do care about you, gorgeous.'

'I guess I can meet Con one more time. But,' I lowered my voice, 'I don't have a good feeling about him—'

'Let me worry about Con. You just wait for the call.'

I nodded, despite the fact that Marcus couldn't see me. 'Okay.'

'And Claudia? Have fun over there. Consider the twenty grand a bonus.'

'It's a bonus all right.' I pushed the end button on my phone and momentarily thought about bursting into full-on raging tears. While I was ecstatic that Marcus was wiping most of my debt, the flip side was that he wanted me gone. I wanted to quit on my own terms, in my own time. I didn't want to be shoved out the door like a houseguest who'd overstayed her welcome.

'You okay?' Jack asked, pulling me back to the present. 'Looks like you're carrying the weight of the world on your shoulders.'

'Not at all.' I turned my attention to him. He looked casual and relaxed, in faded navy shorts and a worn khaki T-shirt. Suddenly I felt nervous. 'This is a nice surprise,' I said, then smiled broadly.

'Sophie told me I'd find you here. You want to answer that?' We both looked at my phone, which vibrated on the table, trumpeting 'The Toreador Song' from *Carmen*.

Bloody hell, every time I heard my phone ring in public, I wanted to toss it. 'The phone only plays that tune because I was fiddling with the options when I first got it. I don't know how it got stuck on that,' I explained and switched it off, before glancing at the caller identification. Con.

'Lunch?' Jack suggested. 'I know a great little place just up the road.'

'Why not?' I said, even though I wasn't the slightest bit hungry, having gorged on spinach pie.

٭

A short stroll later, we came to a tourist shop and I popped inside to buy Levi a cute blue T-shirt with a Santorini dinosaur on the front. 'I had an argument with him this morning,' I said to Jack by way of justification.

Jack flashed his killer smile. 'He's three, right?'

I nodded. 'I'll just buy these sarongs while I'm here,' I said, gathering up several sarongs in different colours.

We left the cobbled pathways of Fira and headed on foot up the dirt road towards Firostefani. 'This walk's killing me. Where are the donkeys when you need them?' I shouted to Jack, who was practically jogging up the steep rocky hill.

'It's not much further,' he said, barely glancing behind.

Jack was obviously a fitness freak. I did my best to keep up, wheezing and puffing as I walked. Not the most attractive start to lunch with a handsome man.

After another excruciating fifteen minutes, we arrived at Aktaion, one of the oldest tavernas on the island, so Jack told me.

Sitting at a table in the sunshine, overlooking the Mediterranean, I presented a picture of calm and confidence, despite the perspiration dripping from my face. Marcus had just promised to pay off most of my debt, yippee. But he'd also told me I should look for another job, sigh. He was right, but I couldn't do much about it until I got back to Brisbane. In the meantime, I was in Santorini and really needed to lighten up.

It wasn't as though this was a date. I'd sworn off that sort of thing. I was just having lunch with a fellow traveller. I needed to go on a date like I needed another pair of shoes. Besides, first dates were tricky, even if they occurred in idyllic settings like this. Some were immediate disasters and left me dying to escape. Still, I was pleased to say, I'd never run out on a man before the entrée. That'd be plain rude. But as I watched Jack, I also knew I didn't want this to be another rung on my long ladder of luncheon disasters.

I took a deep breath and forced myself to relax, recalling the single yoga lesson I'd taken a hundred years ago. It had something to do with breathing in, breathing out, and the *ohm* sound. I couldn't quite recall how it worked. At any rate, the vague memory didn't help me calm down. What a waste of twenty-two bucks that class turned out to be.

After we'd ordered – grilled swordfish and salad for me, smoked mackerel for him – we set about finding out more about each other.

'Here on holidays?' Jack asked. 'Sorry, stupid question, of course you are.'

'Yes. And you?'

Jack nodded, frowned and stopped while the waitress set down our complimentary antipasto platter and a decanter of red wine. 'How long you here for?' he asked as he poured two glasses.

I flicked my hair. 'Two weeks.'

'Me too.'

It was a dying conversation, no doubt about it. I wasn't being witty and couldn't think of anything interesting to say. I was asking inane questions, feeling frumpy, foolish and boring. I couldn't talk about my work and didn't want to get into a long-winded conversation about how I came to be living with Tara. So what did I have to fall back on? The beauty of Santorini? We'd already covered that.

I put it down to being stone cold sober. To be honest, I'd met most of my first dates (not that this was a date) in dark places with loud music, after the consumption of several bottles of wine. Hence, the confidence factor was way up. Sadly, the mystery of the first date evaporated around the second or third date under the weight of that niggling little inconvenience called reality. By the fourth date, I'd notice subtle flaws, like the guy was a mummy's boy, an arms dealer, a dentist, or simply dull and boring.

'Olive?' I held the antipasto plate out to Jack.

His youthful unlined and ringless left hand reached out to choose an olive. Then I looked at his other hand. Not a freckle on either of them (mine were freckly and dry). I glanced up at his earlobes – they were generous, not small and mean.

'Claudia,' he said, drawing me back to the conversation. 'What are you thinking?'

I flinched. His expression while waiting for me to answer was boyish and enthusiastic. I'd even go so far as to say he looked interested. I could hardly say, 'I was admiring your generous lobes.' He'd think I was odd. What next? Checking out his nose hair? Not that he had any visible strays.

I said, 'About how beautiful it is here and how lucky I am to be enjoying this day.' No doubt about it; I was a moron.

'With a gorgeous girl.' Jack raised his glass, clinking it with mine.

That took me miles away. 'Gorgeous girl' was what Marcus called – used to call – me.

Jack was a nice enough bloke, but really, what was I doing here? I didn't want any complications, and I had an unnerving premonition that this was going to turn into a complication. Besides, there had to be something wrong with him. A good-looking bloke like Jack didn't ask a girl like me out to lunch. I tapped my fingers absent-mindedly on the table.

'How do you, Sophie and Tara all know each other?'

Ah! It wasn't only me who was struggling for conversation.

'School. The three of us have been best friends for years. We've known each other so long it's almost like we're one person at times. We know what each other's thinking, can finish each other's sentences.'

'Scary.'

I nodded. 'Yeah, but I'm not sure Tara and Sophie would be friends if not for me. I'm the glue.'

A moment or two of silence.

'The glue?'

I clasped my hands. 'Holding it together. We don't see as much of each other these days, what with Tara's hectic work schedule and Sophie being busy with Levi.'

'And your work?'

'Yeah.' Discussing Cassoli Imports was the last thing I wanted to do. 'We're all busy. That's why it's been good to catch up on this holiday. It certainly beats a weekend camping at Straddie.'

Jack smiled.

'Anyway,' I said nervously. 'We're all different, but somehow our threesome works. Tara's a writer. She carries around a notebook and jots down snippets of conversations she eavesdrops on.'

'Has she written anything?'

I nodded. 'Besides her magazine articles, she's published a few short stories. Now she's working on a novel. I think she's finding it tough going, but once she gets into it, she'll be fine. She has an amazing imagination.'

'Impressive. And Sophie?'

'Used to be a litigation lawyer.'

'And now?'

'Looks after Levi. It's a full-time occupation.'

I sat back in my chair, momentarily fearful I'd revealed too much.

'How about you?' Jack leaned across the table toward me. 'What's the Claudia Taylor story? I know you can't remember your passport number. What else should I know about you?'

Loaded question. Jack didn't need to know I was a closet karaoke tragic, that I hated using public rest rooms and that I had a shocking history with men.

'Not a lot to tell,' I said, my hands sweating. Heart pumping. 'I've got good friends, a great family and I'm fairly happy most of the time.'

'Is there a *but* in there somewhere?'

I shook my head. I was happy. It's not like I cried into my pillow every night. Jack didn't need to know any more.

I distracted myself with the olives and Jack's good looks. He looked like one of those rugged jackaroos from the outback I'd seen in magazines. Manly, virile and a bit scruffy around the edges. Tanned and muscular with broad shoulders and a great face. He wasn't a chiselled work of art; Jack had a lived-in face brimming with character and expression, and he had a fantastic smile and a cute gap between his perfectly white front teeth.

And so far, he hadn't done anything offensive. He'd been nice to the waitress, made eye contact when talking, eaten with his mouth closed. He hadn't dribbled fish down his T-shirt, hadn't belched or farted. Didn't appear to be chauvinistic, too try-hard or so charming that he was weird. He seemed, well, he seemed normal. There had to be a catch.

I licked my lips... couldn't feel any lipstick. It must have worn off. I checked my glass. Red rimmed the edge. What happened to the supposedly stay-fast formula? The lipstick that only an efficient sandblasting would remove? Apparently, not that stay-fast, because I was sitting at lunch with nude lips.

When he excused himself to go to the bathroom, I picked up my phone and found a message from Con.

'Crazy busy. Double booked. We meet soon.'

I shook my head. This was getting ridiculous. '*Entáxei*. Okay,' I messaged. 'Please don't leave it too long.'

Jack was back.

'What about you?' I asked. 'You live in Brisbane?'

He nodded. 'Though I started out in Yackandandah.'

That sparked my interest. With those arms, I could imagine Jack growing up on a magnificent cattle property, with stables, and maybe a show-jumping arena, and enchanted landscaped gardens... spending his days bareback on a stallion, mustering cattle in the wild and untamed Aussie bush.

'As a jackaroo?'

Jack laughed and shook his head. 'Where'd you get that idea?'

'You're from the country, so I assumed...' It sounded foolish now I'd said it out loud.

'Surprisingly, not all of us country folk are farmers or jackaroos.'

Touché! I was a nude-lipped idiot.

'I moved to Sydney when I started high school and boarded at Kings. Then studied engineering at Sydney University.'

An engineer! 'You like maths?'

'Yeah. Working with formulas, solving problems, logical thinking.'

Strike one. I wasn't a maths fan.

I wanted to ask him about his personal situation. Was he married? Divorced? With a significant other? But I didn't want to be too nosy. Didn't want him getting the wrong idea. I wasn't looking for a new boyfriend. 'Have you been to Santorini before?'

'Never. But the opportunity came up and I thought, *Why not?*'

I smiled. 'Same here. So, are you here alone?' I couldn't help myself.

He nodded and suddenly I was more than a little interested. What had I told yours truly minutes ago? I could have slapped myself.

'Tell me more about you,' Jack said. 'Any family?'

'Only parents and two sisters,' I said, trying to flutter my lashes, which probably looked more like an involuntary twitch.

He nodded, seemingly unaware of my wonky eyes.

'I'm the middle of three girls. Lizzie, the eldest, is a podiatrist,' I said.

'Likes feet?'

'Yeah. Go figure. And Sarah, well Sarah's a bit of a misplaced hippie. She lives in inner-city Sydney but calls herself Sunbeam and pretends she's living in Nimbin. Your average run-of-the-mill suburban family.'

'You sound disappointed.'

'Nah, it's just that we've never really had any dramas.'

My parents weren't religious zealots, like Tara's parents. My father wasn't a maniac, like Sophie's dad. Mr Turner's temper tantrums were legendary. Sophie said it was because he'd fought in the Gulf War. Whatever the reason, I was terrified of him. He yelled all the time for no apparent reason. She told me she'd lost count of the number of times she'd fainted or vomited during one of his tirades.

'Looking back on my teenage years, my family was incredibly normal. Not that you'd think it considering some of our awkward family photos.' A framed portrait of the five of us wearing matching high-waisted denim shorts sprang to mind.

'And now?'

'Normal. I have my friends, my work. Sometimes I find

myself asking, "Is this it?" and I feel like doing something crazy to inject a bit of excitement into my life.'

'Like skydiving?'

'Not that crazy.' Maybe I wasn't explaining myself clearly. 'You know the movie *As Good As It Gets*?'

Jack nodded.

'Sometimes I find myself asking the same questions as Jack Nicholson. "Is this as good as it gets? Is this all there is?"'

Heavy conversation for what was supposed to be a getting-to-know-you lunch. I needed to lighten up. Either that or slow down my wine intake. I glanced at my phone. No more messages from Con, but where had the afternoon disappeared? Marcella was right. Why was I so fixated on the time? What did it matter? I was on holidays in Santorini and time was fluid.

'No skeletons in the closet?'

Odd question. 'Not that I know of, though as I said, my sister calls herself Sunbeam. Who knows what she gets up to.' The last time I'd heard from her she was squatting in a terrace in Newtown and protesting about melting glaciers in the Antarctic.

Jack nodded and stood. 'It's getting late. I should see you back to your apartment. Your friends will be worried.' Suddenly he was all serious and businesslike.

Friends? I thought absent-mindedly. *What friends?*

I pulled myself up sternly. This was not allowed to happen. I'd sworn off men. There was no way I was about to fall for another handsome man's charms. He said he was here alone, but for all I knew he had a wife tucked away at home. That would be just my luck.

CHAPTER 17

By the time Jack and I meandered back to Marcella's, Sophie, Tara and Angie were sitting on the terrace enjoying pre-dinner drinks. The sun was warm, the breeze cool, and Jack was incredibly good-looking. And that wasn't the wine talking. So what if he wasn't a jackaroo? I was happy enough hanging out with an engineer. At least he wasn't a dentist.

I expected he'd stay for dinner, but he hesitated. 'I really should be going.'

'You sure? My friends don't bite.'

As we stood awkwardly on the stairs, he seemed reluctant, preoccupied. But quickly the cloud lifted, and he broke into a huge smile. 'Okay. That'd be great. Thanks.'

While Jack and I retrieved chairs from inside, Tara poured two extra glasses of rosé. Good, I thought hazily, just what I needed, more wine.

'I bought you both sarongs,' I said to Sophie and Tara, tossing them one each.

'Very nice,' Sophie said. 'Thanks.'

Tara unfolded her gift. 'Hey, there's a baggage limit... Having said that, this is quite stunning. Thanks.' She held up the green and blue piece of cotton for everyone to admire. 'I'm not normally into sarongs.'

After introducing Angie to Jack, we joined the conversation, which unfortunately was about work, careers and generally making something of your life... topics I was desperate to avoid in public, given I'd generally not made anything much of my life thus far.

Still, Marcus's offer of a 'bonus' posed an irresistible opportunity to reinvent myself. I hated being confined to an office eight and a half hours a day. I didn't want to push papers around for the rest of my life, bound by four walls and a tiny window overlooking a dark back alley in Fortitude Valley. But the looming reality terrified me. As long as I was trapped by debt, I had an excuse as to why I wasn't moving forward with my life or embracing new opportunities. Once I was debt-free, I'd have no excuses and nothing holding me back.

'At least you have a job, Tara,' Sophie was saying.

'Yeah, but I hate it.'

'Why? Apart from working for maniacal Melinda, it's fascinating. Seeing the inside of those amazing homes and writing about them, being on the cutting edge of interior design.'

'I've done it to death. There are only so many ways you can describe a pink wall. After all, pink is just pink, isn't it?'

Sophie looked horrified. 'There's light verona, coral, poppy, starfish glow, sorbet, lipstick, watermelon, Priscilla, cherry, cranb—'

'I get the picture,' Tara said.

'Rose, plum, Persian red, bloom, Indian rose, parrot red—'

Pink was Sophie's favourite colour. Clearly she knew all the subtle variations.

'I'm sorry I even mentioned it. Either way, I'm sick of writing about it. I want to write my own stories.'

'Like a novel?' Angie asked.

Tara nodded. 'I've written a few short stories, but my aim is for something longer. I wrote a lot today.'

'That's fantastic,' I squealed. 'See, I was right. I knew you'd find the energy and inspiration here.'

'It's early days,' Tara said, looking a little shy. 'But I'm more motivated than I've been in a very long time.'

'We've been giving her advice,' Sophie told Jack and Angie, as if we were Tara's interfering parents.

'Here we go,' Tara said, theatrically rolling her neck.

'For example,' I said. 'I'll say, "What about a cookbook? *MasterChef* is huge." And Tara will say...'

'I don't really cook,' Tara replied on cue.

'In London, it's all about vampires and zombies,' Angie said.

Tara grimaced. 'Hmm, I don't think they'll make it into my novel either.'

'But the main thing is you're making progress,' I said.

'Yeah. I had a real breakthrough today. Who knows, if I'm still feeling enthused in a couple of months, I might take more time off work to concentrate on it. I'm owed a lot of holidays and I'm sick of being a wage slave.'

'Right on, sister!' I said confidently, trying to embrace a more adventurous spirit. (Someone with less spirit would have fretted that she – i.e. me – was destined to remain chained to a desk in a cramped overpopulated sweatbox.) 'Go for it.'

We raised our glasses and toasted Tara. She looked suitably mortified.

Then Angie turned to me. 'And what do you do, Claudia?'

I knew eventually the conversation had to shift to me, and were my ears deceiving me? Was Angie talking with a Hyacinth Bucket lilt? (Though I generally tried to avoid watching repeats of *Keeping Up Appearances*, it was one of Mum's favourite shows. She had every episode on DVD.)

I shouldn't have sat down. I should've gone straight inside and joined Levi and Harry who were happily watching *Frozen 2* for the tenth time.

'Yes,' Jack said. 'What *do* you do with yourself when you're not holidaying in Greece?'

'I'm an office manager,' I said dismissively. 'But I'm thinking about changing careers.'

Tara sipped her wine. 'I'll miss the free oils and vinegars.'

Jack raised his eyebrows.

'I work for a company that imports food, oils mostly. Most of it comes from Greece. But I want to make money. I'm sick of being in debt—'

'You do spend a lot of money,' Tara started.

'Yes, and I don't want to feel guilty about it.' Everyone was silent. 'I know it's not politically correct in these difficult economic times, but the truth is, I don't want to be a pauper, living in your house, Tara, for the foreseeable future. No offence. And I don't want to be stuck in an office for the rest of my life. I'm not suited to that job. I'm usually asleep at my desk by ten thirty every morning.'

'That's true,' Sophie said. 'You ring me just to keep yourself awake.'

'It was only ever meant as a stopgap. It was never supposed to be a career. I want to do something exciting, work outdoors, travel, see a bit of action.'

'And don't forget, earn wads of cash doing it!' Tara snapped her fingers. 'You'll land a job like that in no time.'

'Maybe, but I liked my job as an events coordinator, and I was good at it.'

'True,' Tara said. 'And you did get us great freebies at fancy restaurants.'

Sophie held up her glass. 'Wine too.'

'I'll look into something like that again when we get home,' I said, thinking aloud.

'Sounds like a plan,' Sophie said. 'I know I need to get out more. Since having Levi, I've been defined by him. What happened to me? I can't even remember the person I was before Levi came along. It seems like a lifetime ago.'

'What *did* you do before Levi came along?' Angie asked.

'Corporate law. Litigation.'

'Snap,' Angie said, clearly impressed. 'I love it. I love the drama, the pressure-cooker atmosphere, thinking on my feet.'

'I don't miss that so much.' Sophie wrinkled her nose. 'I couldn't handle the stress, but I miss the freedom. That, and eating lunch with adults. I miss the independence, miss having my own money. I miss having contact with people who aren't mothers, you know, normal people who aren't defined by how many children they have.'

'You're bored,' Tara said. 'Is that it?'

'I could hardly be bored with Levi around. It's just I'd love to do something creative like you, Tars. Not writing, but maybe decorating—'

'Huh?' Tara said, taking in her words.

'I've even looked into doing a six-month interior design course at TAFE, two days a week. It's doable if I put Levi into preschool one more day a week.'

'Really?' I asked.

'Why? Does that make me a bad mother?'

Tara jumped in. 'Not at all, but you haven't mentioned TAFE before.'

'Because I don't want everyone thinking it's a stupid idea.'

'It's not stupid,' I said. 'You should definitely give it a go if that's what you want.'

Tara turned to Sophie. 'Remember Bryan, the stylist you met the day we did the "New Glamour" piece on your home? He's always looking for willing victims to be his work-experience slaves. If you're interested, I could text him and see what he says.'

I clapped my hands. It sounded like a great idea. As far as I could tell, stylists were people who got paid an obscene amount of money to shop. Perhaps it wasn't that simple, but Sophie looked the part. This evening she was wearing a groovy purple kaftan (another Santorini purchase) and skinny jeans. If ever there was a person crying out to be a stylist, it was Sophie.

'I don't know,' Sophie said.

'Stop! You've already said you're going to start an interior design course,' Tara said.

'That might be the wine talking. Besides, I said that I was *thinking* about it.'

'Not listening,' Tara said. 'Let me send him a text. It can't hurt.'

That settled, we watched as the sun disappeared into the Mediterranean before tuning into Jack and Angie's conversation.

'So, Jack, Claudia mentioned you're from Yackandandah? Is that how you say it?'

'Most people don't believe it's a real place when I tell them.'

'Like when I lived in Woolloomooloo a few years ago,' Tara said. 'Try saying that after a few drinks.'

'It must have been fascinating growing up in the outback,' Angie continued.

'Bit quiet. Although we do have the annual toad races. That always brings the punters to town.'

'Oh, Jack.' I giggled as I leant back on my chair and almost toppled over.

'And that's tame compared to friends of mine up north who travel hundreds of kilometres to attend the annual Hog 'n' Dog pig-hunting gala day,' Jack continued.

'Imagine if ants were as big as tigers,' Levi was saying to Harry as the two boys walked out onto the patio to join us.

'Yeah and... and tigers were little as ants.'

'Or worms were huge like elephants. Mum?' Levi asked, 'What would happen if ants *were* as big as tigers?'

'I'm not sure, darling,' Sophie replied patiently. 'But I do know it's dark and that means it's time for bed.'

Despite the boys' protests, Sophie and Angie wrestled them into submission in Sophie's room. Meanwhile, Tara and I rustled up sourdough, a variety of dips, salad and a freshly baked moussaka that Marcella had given us earlier in the day. Made from her grandmother's secret recipe, it was tradition that every visitor to the villas received at least one of Grandma Marcella's moussakas during their stay.

'The Greeks certainly know how to make good wine,' Tara said after Jack had opened another bottle.

'Except for that foul retsina,' I said.

'True,' Tara agreed.

'And some of the fashion over here,' Angie said. 'What the eff happened? I mean, are we seriously meant to wear those clothes?'

'Thank you,' Tara was saying. 'We were having a similar conversation the other day.'

'I've had enough of the whole gypsy thing.'

Tara smiled, Sophie fidgeted in her kaftan, and I pulled self-consciously at my comfy cheesecloth shirt.

'I tried on one of those floaty white skirts this morning,' Angie continued. 'I'd have to say there's no place on anyone's body, especially mine, for a white horizontal-panelled skirt.'

'Exactly. You'd look like the back end of a truck,' Tara said.

Sophie gasped in horror.

'No, Tara's right,' Angie said. 'It was gross. I don't know how I got sucked into trying it on in the first place.'

'Vanity,' I answered. 'Vanity will get you every time. I had a pair of white stilettos once.'

Jack raised an eyebrow.

'Unless you want to look like a twenty-dollar hooker, white stilettos should be avoided at all costs,' I explained.

Jack fidgeted in his chair. 'You women have bizarre conversations.'

'You don't chat about hookers and stilettos with your friends?' Angie purred.

Excuse me, but was Angie flirting with Jack? I was not impressed. Flirting with Jack? It wasn't on. Not that he was exclusively mine, but it showed particularly bad form and her behaviour was giving everyone (well, me) the impression she was desperate and man-hungry.

❦

'I've got to tell you,' Angie said after we'd finished our meal, 'these have been the best couple of days Harry and I have had in a long time.'

I could have sworn Angie's eyes were planted firmly on Jack's crotch.

'Didn't you go on holidays when you were married?' Sophie asked.

'Hardly! Pete couldn't stand being out of his carefully controlled environment. Holidays made him anxious. He preferred spending his time making sure he knew exactly what I was doing, who I was seeing and where I was going. Sodding toxic. In contrast, this past year's been exhilarating. You know,' Angie said, twirling her wine glass, 'it wasn't only our neighbour Pete was banging. He loved the conquest and control. There were others. I'm just lucky I found out when I did.'

'That's shocking,' I said, feeling truly sorry for her. Perhaps she hadn't been flirting with Jack, just making conversation. 'You must've been devastated.'

'I was initially, but it's okay. I never could picture Pete and me on the porch growing old together. I never had that image in my head.'

I could see the cogs churning in Sophie's mind before she spoke. Nodding, she said, 'I can see Alex and me clearly. He's much older than me, of course, and his hair is white and thinning, but I'm still sitting beside him.'

Can't say that vision had ever popped into my head, not even with George. But then, I never thought much about the future. I lived in the present, or at least I tried to. I was of the Albert Einstein school of thought: *I never think of the future – it comes soon enough.* Planning for my old age wasn't high on my agenda, except when I was feeling maudlin and lonely. Maybe that's why I'd ended up where I was. I'd always gone with the flow, instead of pushing to take charge.

Tara looked up. 'What if you don't have a porch?'

Sophie sighed. 'It's a metaphor.'

Tara's sarcasm was lost on Sophie.

'I still fancy Alex, but I don't think he's interested in me anymore.' Sophie poked around her ribs. 'Too much baby flab.'

'Sophie!' I yelled.

'All right. All right,' she sulked. 'Maybe he's just bored with me.'

'But, Sophie,' Tara enthused. 'He won't be once you're a fabbo stylist. That'll put the oomph back into your lives.'

'So you reckon he *is* bored with me?'

Tara sighed. 'I didn't say that. So, Jack, what draws you to Claudia, other than her cute freckles and large breasts?'

I almost spat out my wine. I knew buying a cheesecloth top was a fashion faux pas. I looked enormous.

'What?' Tara said. 'I assume he's drawn to you, Claud, or he wouldn't be sitting here listening to our ramblings.'

'You're quite right,' Jack said. 'And I'd have to say that it's the ease with which Claudia handles awkward situations.'

Jack was so sure of himself and full of easy charm, I was almost hyperventilating. But I wasn't venturing down that track again. Jack could ogle my breasts all he wanted, there was no way he was getting anywhere near them.

It was late. We were tired. It was time for bed.

Still, when Jack called it a night and offered to flag Angie and Harry a taxi to make sure they got back to Kamari safely, I felt somewhat disappointed. I'd assumed this late into the evening Jack might have asked to kiss me. Either that, or he fancied Angie. A distinct possibility and probably not a bad idea. If he tried anything, I'd have to reject him anyway. Still, a little harmless flirting was always good for the ego.

Licking my lips, I noticed how dry and in need of balm they were. I was thinking about that when, after walking Jack along the cobbled walkway up the hill to the road, he turned to me, reached for my face and planted his lips on mine, leaving them there for what seemed like minutes. It was probably closer to five seconds.

'You were licking your lips and I couldn't resist.'

It came as an even bigger surprise when Jack took my hand, pulled it around his waist, and guided my mouth to his again. He was forceful without being overly dominant. And strong. I couldn't have escaped his clutches even if I'd wanted to. It was all very exciting. Exciting but over within minutes.

'Sorry,' he said, standing back a little shyly. 'I shouldn't have done that.'

At that moment, Tara, together with Angie carrying a sleeping Harry, arrived. Moments later, the cab did. As Tara and I stood on the street waving them off, I secretly cursed Angie.

Not that I was jealous. The three of them made a nice little family.

Heading back downstairs and inside, Tara pinched my arm. 'Love is in the air.'

'God, I hope not.'

'But I thought you liked him?'

'Not so soon after Mar—'

'Huh?'

'George. Not so soon after George.'

'That was years ago. You and Jack have got chemistry, sweets! And you have to climb back on the pony sooner or later.'

'Whatever.' I gave Tara the brush-off and headed to my room, heart still pounding. Close call.

Chemistry! Ugh! That's all I needed. Thank goodness Jack hadn't tried to seduce me. It had been a long day. I doubt I'd have had the strength to resist him... I couldn't put myself in that vulnerable position again. So I focused on finding things about Jack's personality I mightn't like. Maybe he had some peculiarity that prohibited him from having intimate relations. Or he'd want me to howl like his childhood cat or bark like his fifth-grade teacher. I made a mental list of the many perverse activities Jack could be involved in. He seemed quite fond of fruit, for example.

CHAPTER 18

I peeped over the sheets. Light. Threw the covers back and basked in the morning sunshine. I was thirty-nine. Well and truly an adult. Technically, I had been for years, but sometimes I still didn't quite believe it.

And this year I was celebrating in Santorini. What a gift! Now that I was a woman of mature years, I'd behave in a dignified manner. In my mind, I compiled a list of what it meant now that I was entering my fortieth year:

• no more one-night stands, or affairs with married men, in fact, men, period;
• no more getting drunk in bars and singing bad karaoke tunes;
• no more frivolous spending – I had enough clothes, cosmetics and costume jewellery to last a lifetime; and finally,
• no more running around nude clanging saucepans at three in the morning.

Now that I was of a certain age, it was all about moderation and respect for oneself. And another thing – I needed to diligently apply an SPF moisturiser during the day and wash my face clean of make-up at night, every night. (Until now, I'd been notoriously bad at this.)

I climbed out of bed and padded over to my empty suitcase. Empty, that is, except for the neatly wrapped (hot pink tissue paper, complete with magenta bow and ribbon) solid rectangular parcel from my sisters. It had to be a book. And indeed it was. *Things To Do Now That You're... 40.*

Inside the front cover was the inscription, *Clauds, we can hear you squealing from here! Okay, we know you're not forty (yet!) but we thought you might like a head start as to what to expect from here on in... it's a slippery slope. Love, your ever-thoughtful sisters, Lizzie and Sunbeam xx*

Opening a random page, I spotted this gem: 'Mix your own cement and build a stone wall.' Useful.

I threw the book on the bed, walked over to the dressing table and confidently faced myself in the mirror. Hmm. Not so good. I could almost see the huge *thirty-nine* tattooed across my forehead. Make that *thirty-nine, single, confused and penniless though hopefully not in debt too much longer.* Too many words. Etching the word *loser* on my forehead would get the message across just as well. Damn. I'd vowed not to wake up depressed this morning. Add that to my list: no more feeling sorry for myself. It was my life, and I was in control. I was living.

I studied my reflection and counted the pimples on my jaw. Too much Santorini baklava. I felt the wrinkles around my eyes. Too much Santorini sun. Was I the only person who used both wrinkle and pimple creams? It didn't seem fair. Why couldn't I have had a few years where I didn't need either?

I smeared on both creams as well as a day cream, eye cream, sun cream, body lotion and hand lotion. Yes, I owned all these potions, but I hardly ever used them. Nevertheless, if I didn't make an effort on my birthday, when would I? From today, I promised myself, I'd be more diligent in their application.

I did a quick swing around to check out my backside and caught a fleeting glimpse. I really needed to lose the stray kilos that had attached themselves to my frame. Strictly speaking, I should have exercised the extra kilos away last week, because from today onwards, they'd be doubly hard to shift. An article in *Marie Claire* specifically said that once a woman (me) turned thirty-nine, she (me again) had to work twice as hard to lose excess kilos. Exactly how my body knew I was into my first eight hours of being thirty-nine was a question only the gods could answer, but apparently that was the case. Sagging skin and sunspots were also about to feature in my ageing exterior. So much for life beginning at forty!

I checked my messages. There were three. One from Mum and Dad and one from Lizzie. *Happy birthday to our favourite daughter*, Mum and Dad's text read. They said that every year to the other two as well. All three of us were our parents' favourite.

The third was a text from Marcus telling me he'd transfer twenty thousand dollars to my savings account in the next couple of days. *Call it a birthday bonus. Hope it provides you with enough incentive to be civil to Con when you meet up with him again.*

Twenty thousand! I could hardly believe it. I'd be rich! Okay, I wouldn't be rich, but at least I'd be well on my way to breaking even. Still, I wasn't about to jump for joy until I clocked the money in my bank account.

'Happy birthday, Claudie,' Levi sang and clapped when I walked out onto the patio. Wow! Balloons, streamers, presents and many exotic cakey treats and chocolates greeted me.

'You remembered,' I said, feigning surprise.

Tara handed me a glass of birthday champagne.

Levi was the first to give me a gift: a picture he'd painted of me falling in donkey poo and crying.

'Levi, that's the best present ever,' I said, hugging him. Sure, it was Tara who'd slipped on the excrement, but he'd gone to so much effort I wasn't about to quibble.

Then he gave me the second-best gift, a silver and diamond encrusted tiara (well, plastic actually) which I quickly popped on top of my head. He thought it was hilarious.

Tara and Sophie cheered. 'Come on, Claud, open these,' they said, handing me two more gifts.

I unwrapped the first parcel, a delicate gold and turquoise necklace. 'You shouldn't have.'

'We got a special deal from Nikos.' Tara beamed.

'We're easy targets,' Sophie added.

'Thank you. I love it. It's divine.' I put the necklace on then opened the next one. 'Neck cream! Great.' I wasn't sure whether to be thrilled or insulted.

'Not just any neck cream, it's made from caffeine! All the rage in Paris,' Sophie said, her tone serious. 'Use this every day and you won't have the merest hint of turkey neck.'

'Err. No.' I caressed my skin before stretching out my chin as far as it would go.

'Lolly bags?' Levi asked hopefully.

I shook my head. Obviously, this wasn't the kind of birthday he'd had in mind. He looked expectantly at the chocolates beside me, then together we ripped the cellophane, opened the box and began devouring them.

CHAPTER 19

'Happy birthday, Clow-di-ah,' Marcella trilled a few hours later as we headed up the stairs and past her office. She kissed both my cheeks and presented me with a delicately etched blue bottle of ouzo.

'Thank you, *efcharistó*, Marcella. You shouldn't have.'

'No problem. *Kalimera*, Levi,' she said, kissing Levi's forehead. 'I look after this gorgeous boy while you party tonight, okay, *entáxei?*'

After much arm twisting, Sophie agreed to let Marcella mind Levi for the evening. At five, we'd be heading into Fira, child-free. Yippee. Could this day get any better?

That sorted, the four of us skipped up the road about sixty metres to a quaint little taverna with superb views and plonked ourselves at an outside table. This was the life. Levi happily picked at his kebab and cheese and played dinosaurs in the sand and gravel while we worked our way through a carafe of red wine and a mountain of souvlakia and salad.

'Sitting here, drinking this lovely little Santorini red, reminds me of the time you were going out with that crashing bore, Claud,' Tara said dreamily.

'Which one was that?'

'The boring wine buff. What was his name again? Stan? Simon?'

'Samuel,' I offered. I'd met him at a winter wine tasting I'd coordinated.

'That's right. Remember that dinner party at your place, Soph? It was so bad.'

'Please don't remind me,' I protested, knowing full well they were about to relive the whole horrid evening in vivid colour.

Samuel was in the wine trade, which made him perfect... to begin with. Initially, I was impressed, if slightly embarrassed, by the way he swirled the wine around his glass somewhat furiously before almost inhaling the liquid through his nose as he smelt the bouquet in an exaggerated manner. However, the euphoria soon wore off in the middle of the second date when he insulted a waiter by sending back a Pinot Gris three times! But by then we'd already made plans for our third date, to attend Sophie and Alex's anniversary dinner, and I was too gutless to uninvite him.

Tara laughed. 'He was a tosser.'

'A wine connoisseur, I think he liked to be called,' Sophie chimed in. 'He was impressed with Alex's *stemware* as I recall, the Riedel glasses.'

'Had a huge honker, didn't he?' Tara said.

Funny the things that pass you by on a first, even a second date. These days Samuel was a big wine critic and wrote a regular piece in a national newspaper. Whenever I glanced through his columns, he still sounded like a pompous wanker. I was happy knowing he hadn't changed.

'Come on, it's my birthday. How about we talk about someone else's failed romances?'

'Don't look at me,' Sophie said, flicking dust from her Moroccan-inspired espadrilles.

I tried my luck with Tara. 'What happened to Jules after you dumped her?'

'Come on. That was years ago. I've been married since then, and, had my share of lovers.'

'Do tell,' I enthused.

Tara grimaced. 'I wasn't very nice to her, was I?'

I waved my hand in the air. 'She's probably living happily ever after with her gorgeous Natalie Portman-lookalike girlfriend in New York, leading a wild and exciting life.'

'Hopefully,' Tara mused. 'But straight after we broke up, she joined a bizarre religious order.'

'Pardon? How come you've never told us this before?'

'Because I felt responsible, Claud. We were so young. It was horrible.'

'Horrible maybe,' I said, refilling everyone's glass, 'but it's an excellent basis for a story. Find out what happened and write about her adventures and how religion helped heal her broken heart. Ha. The very thing that caused you two to split became her ultimate saviour. How about that? People love a good spiritual memoir.'

'Even better if there's a bit of romance in there as well,' Sophie added.

'Exactly, but you need a death too. People love tragedies. Tragedies and titillation. Think *Jesus Christ Superstar*.' I laughed. 'I never tire of this game.'

'You'll have to invent a new one when I actually write a book.'

'We will,' I said. 'Especially when yours is on the bestseller list.'

Tara rubbed her chin. 'That was a crazy time, wasn't it? Falling in love with Anthony, marrying him, falling out of love with him, the divorce. What the hell was I thinking?'

'I don't know. What were any of us thinking back then?'

'What about the egomaniac I went out with – that Luke guy?' Sophie said. 'The *I'm six foot one and built for fun!* fool. Let me tell you, Luke was never six foot one despite the rubber lifts he wore. I fixed him when we broke up,' she said, smiling. 'Made sure he'd have to refit lifts inside all his shoes. Talk about a tosser!'

From the outset, Luke picked at Sophie's weak spot, her weight, so she got her revenge by destroying his. Let me tell you, getting on Sophie's bad side is never a good idea.

She turned to Levi, who'd weaselled a bowl of water from the wait staff and was now sitting in the dirt making mud pies. 'Then I fell straight into Alex's arms. Although, why did I have to fall in love with a divorced guy who already had a child? Harriet still blames me.'

'But she was the one who had the affair!'

'She conveniently glosses over that part. Says she was lonely because Alex was always at the office. Maybe I should've listened to her.'

'Soph, you're talking rubbish. Are you going to eat any of that?' Tara pointed to the uneaten food on Sophie's plate while the attendant hovered, waiting to take it away.

'Nah. I'm not hungry.'

Tara and I looked at her.

'Don't scrutinise me like that.'

'Rather than make circling motions in your taramasalata, why don't you eat it?' I asked.

'Yeah, the pink swirls are making me sick,' Tara said.

Sophie stood. 'Would you two get off my back, and could you watch Levi for a sec?' With that, she stalked to the bathroom.

The first time I noticed Sophie's obsession with food was at school when I stayed at her house on weekends. In the morning, she'd drink two cups of coffee, followed by four cups of water, which she'd sip over the course of an hour. Instead of the toast and Vegemite I'd wolf down, she'd absorb a tiny Petit Miam yogurt very slowly, only licking the teaspoon. As for lunch, she'd have a couple of tablespoons of grated carrot. But then for dinner, she'd pig out on meat, potatoes with gravy, and eat buckets of chocolate-chip ice cream for dessert.

'Do you do this every day?' I asked her and she shrugged non-committally, refusing to acknowledge what I was talking about.

In the space of six weeks, Sophie's weight plummeted from a healthy size ten to a skeletal size four. One afternoon, when I accidentally found laxatives in her bag, I confronted her. But instead of screaming and telling me I had it all wrong as I'd desperately hoped, she collapsed. I was so terrified I could barely manage to dial triple zero.

Sophie was rushed to hospital.

Later, she confided that the only power she had over her life was to starve herself or to go to the other extreme and gorge before vomiting. 'My parents control everything else.'

Because of his time in the army, Sophie's father was wary of outsiders. Her parents were notoriously private people who kept Sophie, an only child, on a short leash. I was surprised I was allowed to visit as often as I did. To deal with Sophie's illness, her parents became even more strict and controlling.

A few weeks after her hospitalisation, not long after Sophie broke up with her first 'real' boyfriend, Craig, I found her sitting inside her bedroom cupboard stuffing her cheeks with Snickers bars.

'Sophie!' I screamed, yanking the chocolate from her hands. I also grabbed at the discarded wrappers.

'Get out of my house and leave me alone,' she shouted as she scrambled on the floor, reaching under her bed for other chocolate she'd stashed.

'Stop it! Stop doing this to yourself.'

'What? I'm hungry. Stop being so judgemental. You're not so perfect yourself,' Sophie said, tears streaming down her face.

'I never said I was—' I tried as Sophie rushed past me to the bathroom.

'You're a fucking bitch,' she said, and slammed the door.

I couldn't handle it. It was scary. I imagined having to phone for an ambulance again.

'Sophie,' I called out to her, but she wouldn't come out of the bathroom. 'I don't think I can be your friend at the moment.'

'Good,' came her muffled reply.

I went home to my safe little world and assumed the spat would blow over if I gave her some space.

It didn't.

Sophie didn't talk to me for six months. She wiped me as though I didn't exist. When I tried getting Tara involved, all she'd said was, 'Give her time.' So Tara and I had a huge blow-up too. (Come to think of it, Year 11 was extraordinarily intense.)

Tara said it wasn't our problem, and that she had enough hassles, what with having to attend Mass every other day with her parents, failing economics and only just averaging in English.

What I didn't realise until a few weeks into our feud, was that without me, Tara and Sophie barely spoke to each other. They did initially, but after about a month they stopped hanging out together.

'Why would I?' Tara said when I quizzed her about Sophie, whom I'd assumed she was keeping tabs on. 'She's okay, but if we're not gossiping about you, we have little in common. We're a threesome or nothing at all.'

At the start of Year 12, I got our friendship back on track by doing a hell of a lot of grovelling. That, and by presenting Sophie with a one metre by one metre 'sorry' card featuring the floating handsome heads of Matthew Perry, Matt Le Blanc, and

Rob Lowe, all pleading my case as to why we should be friends again. It worked! We also came to the understanding that Sophie's weight loss had been temporary, due to her intense relationship and subsequent break-up with Craig. I didn't want to get on her bad side again. The three of us resumed best-friend status and, ever since, Sophie had maintained her perfect petite frame, never fluctuating (apart for the pregnancy and early baby weeks).

Even though Sophie's eating disorder was under control, I occasionally thought back to that time and how harrowing it was. Right now, I was worried about Sophie being so anxious that she might fall back into bad habits.

I wouldn't let that happen. And I'd start by insisting she share a baklava with me – it was my birthday, after all.

It was late in the day when we wobbled back to Marcella's.

In between changing clothes and reapplying lipstick for our night on the town, we downed several glasses of water on the terrace. (Okay, we also drank Marcella's ouzo.) I felt on top of the world.

Happy with my red and cream slinky wraparound dress, I added the beautiful necklace the girls had given me, my divine new ring, and then, the final touch – gorgeous pea-green sandals. Gorgeous but uncomfortable. Totally unwearable. I loved them.

'What do you think?' I said, doing a twirl for the girls.

'Too high, you'll fall over in a heap.' Tara was wearing brown Birkenstocks.

'An evening shoe, in this instance an evening sandal,' Sophie in her moderate four-centimetre heels said, 'has to be high, very high, especially given it's your birthday. Besides, flats are for librarians. No offence, Tars.'

We left Marcella and Levi curled up on the sofa watching a show about dinosaurs, and off we trotted.

'Be having fun,' Marcella called out as we disappeared up the stairs.

As we walked along the cobbled alleyway leading into Fira, Tara said, 'Are you *really* sure you want to wear those shoes tonight, Claud?'

'Too bloody right I do,' I said, hobbling towards the setting sun.

CHAPTER 20

We arrived at the magnificent Sunset Bar in Fira and sat on stools overlooking the caldera. The list of exotic drinks was beyond anything I'd ever experienced – mysterious concoctions with ingredients such as tamarillo, lychee, and pomegranate. Martinis infused with basil, lemongrass and rosemary. The choice was overwhelming. We kicked off the evening with a Rude Cosmo.

'It's her birthday!' Tara shouted when the waiter delivered us our next round – poached pear and cinnamon daiquiris with a rhubarb schnapps chaser. Within minutes, he was back with complimentary Oriental Mules.

'This could get ugly,' Sophie said.

Nodding, we sipped our drinks.

'Come on then,' Tara said. 'As is your privilege, you get five minutes to reminisce about birthdays gone by.'

'I thought you'd never ask.' The deal was the girls shouted out random birthdays and I had to sum them up in less than ten words.

Sophie raised her eyebrows. 'Sixth.'

Too easy. 'Fairy party, pink Barbie, *A Bug's Life*.'

Mum and Dad threw me a fairy party and surprised me with a Labrador puppy. Being addicted to *A Bug's Life*, and given I was allowed to name him, we called him Hop, affectionately known as Hoppy, and sometimes Mr Hopper! when he dug up the garden or defecated on the driveway.

'Eighteenth,' Tara said.

'Bomber,' idiot boyfriend of the time, 'crash tackling the chicken coop.'

'At least he wasn't nude,' Sophie said. 'The injuries could have been a lot worse.'

'Twenty-first!' Tara shouted.

'RIP Hoppy,' I said, and we all clinked glasses.

Hopper died the night before my twenty-first and we buried him the next day. Mum wanted to put it off until after my birthday but, it being unseasonably warm, Dad worried that old Hop would start to smell. Unfortunately, the hole Dad dug for him near the orange trees wasn't quite deep enough and Dad had to keep lifting him out of his grave to dig out more soil. In the end, he bent Hoppy's legs to make him fit. My birthday was a write-off. The family was in tears all day, even Dad, once he'd recovered from the shovelling.

'Twenty-fifth,' Sophie yelled.

'Gamine crop. Drunken boat cruise. Never again.' I shuddered at the memory.

'Thirtieth?' asked the waiter, who was delivering Santorini Slings and a round of dips.

'Dud. Bed. Flu. Louise Brooks black bob.'

'Thirty-fourth any better?' He was clearly amused.

'Much. Blonde. Sex on the beach.'

'Well done!'

He returned to the bar and Tara shook her head in disgust. 'Blonde! What were you thinking?'

My five minutes of reminiscing went on for a good hour and

a half. By the time we left the Sunset Bar and had stumbled into Santorini Swings, the crowd was well-primed.

'Karaoke!' I shrieked as we crammed into the smoky dimly lit club. 'This is the place to be!' I'd consumed enough alcohol to consider myself an expert on relationships and was not afraid to give advice, wanted or otherwise.

'See that couple over there,' I said to Sophie when Tara disappeared to the bathroom. 'I bet you anything they've only just met tonight and are minutes away from going back to his place to shag like rabbits.' Sophie was in awe of my ability to read body language.

'And those two over there,' I pointed, 'are totally bored with each other. Look at them. This holiday's a last-ditch effort to save their doomed relationship.'

'They don't look happy, do they?' Sophie agreed.

'Who? What?' Tara asked, arriving back with three mineral waters and a huge bowl of chips.

'I was just telling Soph that the couple over there are doomed because they're not in love.'

'You're an idiot.' Tara sighed. 'They're brother and sister.'

'How can you tell?' Sophie said.

'They look exactly alike for one thing,' Tara said. 'For another, they moved into one of Marcella's apartments this afternoon. I met them briefly.' Tara turned to the side. 'Jack!'

By this stage, I was a little tipsy and convinced I was the best singer and dancer in the world. Not only that, but I was wearing the most fabulous pea-green sandals ever created. Jack would be super impressed!

Next thing I knew, it was 8am and I was lying in my bed. It was quiet, serene almost, except for the thumping inside my head. I felt underneath the covers. I still had my bra and knickers on. Sleeping in my bra? I felt again. Yes.

If only I could open my eyes. One would do. It was my lids. Or rather the lashes on top of my lids. They were too heavy... my new mascara, that was the problem. I couldn't have forced open my lids with a crowbar. I was blind. I'd never see my family, the ocean or those gorgeous maroon suede boots again. And what about my cute little sweater with the flowery embroidery that everyone hated but I loved?

I felt a flicker of a lid and eased myself onto the floor beside the bed, moving very slowly for fear of throwing up. My foot landed in something squishy and wet. After a struggle that seemed to last days, I finally opened one eye properly. A packet of mushy peas! I thought about the peas for a few moments while making an awkward attempt to scour the area. Surely if I'd done something perverse with frozen peas, I'd have remembered.

After staggering to the dressing table, I shrieked in horror at my reflection. I was hideous. I'd been so glamorous the previous night and now I looked like the hunchback's ugly sister. Smeared lipstick, mascara running down my face.

I touched the dark bruise on my right cheek. A hazy memory of snatching a microphone out of an American frat boy's hands, the force of which driving said mic into my cheek, came to mind.

I glanced over at the corner of my bedroom. Flung against the wall were my completely impractical, impossibly high, unwearable pea-green sandals, not looking quite so fabulous now.

I staggered out onto the terrace.

'I love the night life,' Tara sang as she danced over and tried to hug me.

My head exploded. 'Don't touch me!' I said, clutching at a chair and easing myself into it. 'And for God's sake, stop singing.'

'What's the matter? You're the karaoke queen. Sorry, the karaoke birthday dancing queen.'

Tara... her smug, clean, unblemished face, her wide Cheshire grin and her loud booming voice. I wanted to wring her annoying little neck. And I would have, had I the energy and balance to get up.

'You gave an outstanding performance,' she continued.

'Morning.' Sophie handed me a vile concoction. 'Here, drink this.'

'What is it?' I spat the words out after inhaling the stench.

'Eggs with a bit of tomato juice thrown in.'

I pushed it away. 'Err, no thanks.'

'Drink it. You'll feel better.'

'The only thing that'll make me feel better is another day's sleep.'

'Should have stuck to the one alcoholic drink, one water principle,' Sophie said.

'Does anyone do that? Maybe for the first two drinks, but after a few cocktails, forget it.'

'I don't,' Tara admitted. 'Though I did buy mineral waters at one stage.'

I nodded. 'Pity I didn't drink mine.'

'You'd feel a lot better this morning if you did,' Sophie said.

'Okay, Mother. I'll remember that next time,' I said, feeling my face ache every time I spoke. 'Now then, I have a vague recollection of dancing...'

'Well, honey,' Tara said, 'you were on the dance floor, but you weren't actually moving in time to the music. As for the karaoke—'

'How is your cheek, by the way?' Sophie asked and peered closely at it. Too close. 'You can still see the indents where the microphone slammed into the side of your face.'

'I take it that packet of peas you took to bed with you is dead?' Tara said.

'Trod on it.'

'There's no stopping you when you want to sing. I reckon you could've thrown that kid to the other side of the room.'

'The look on his face!' Sophie said.

'It was one of my favourites,' I said, remembering my enthusiasm for 'Sweet Caroline'. Then I remembered the Goondiwindi ball. Argh.

Sophie shrugged. 'Drunk people really don't have any idea how appalling their singing voices are.'

'Yeah, maybe you need a few voice lessons.' Tara patted me on the shoulder. 'For next time.'

I buried my head in my lap. I vaguely remembered singing 'Macarena' complete with all the actions.

'The difference between you and us is that we had the good sense to get off after one song.' Tara chortled. 'You, drinks and microphones, Claud, the three of you must stay apart.'

'Nudie rudie, nudie rudie.' Levi squealed as he ran outside and around the table.

I grimaced. 'I didn't, did I?'

'What?' Sophie asked.

'Run around in the nude, dancing.' I pointed to where Levi was shaking his bare bottom in time to some awful screechy music.

Sophie laughed. 'Not when I was with you.'

'Thank goodness. I thought he might have been re-enacting a scene from last night.'

'Wow, Claud, that mic really did hit you hard,' Tara said.

'Understatement. Look at me!'

'Thanks, but I'd rather not if it's all the same.'

'And Jack?' I asked, almost as an afterthought.

'Soph and I were just discussing Jack. He seemed to disappear amid all the singing.'

'That's a relief.'

'He did get to see a bit of the Claudia Show though.'

I sighed. 'The Claudia Freak Show more like it.'

❧

I slumped against the open fridge door, wanting to throw myself in. I settled for looking for something to eat, anything that'd make me feel better. Water? Tried that, still felt like shit. Strawberry juice? God, no.

I was devouring chocolate ice cream when I felt a pair of eyes zooming in on me. Levi. At least he had his swimmers on. With my mouth full of ice cream, I stuck my head in the freezer and pretended he wasn't there. Then I made kicking motions in his direction. There was something enormously humiliating about being caught by a three-year-old gobbling ice cream from the freezer.

'Go away,' I moaned.

I crawled upstairs and slammed my bedroom door shut. I shouldn't have. The impact sent a searing pain through my brain. I struggled into bed and climbed under the sheets. Safe from the world at last.

But it was no use, I couldn't get back to sleep. My mind raced. Regarding the list I'd made twenty-four hours earlier, I'd failed on every account; okay, so I didn't have a one-night stand or race around the apartment naked, clanging saucepans together, but my behaviour was still shabby and immature.

I climbed out of bed, thinking a cup of tea might help me focus, and limped slowly, hesitantly, down the stairs, only to be confronted by a bemused Sophie, Levi and Tara... And Jack?

CHAPTER 21

*D*ishevelled. Mascara down around my chin. Bruised cheek and wearing a very short T-shirt that read *Bad Girl*. I wasn't looking my best. Then again, I hadn't been expecting company.

While I was in the bathroom, trying to rectify some of the damage with a hot shower, Tara slipped me two magic headache tablets and fifteen minutes later I felt much better. Alive, at least.

What was *he* doing here? Through my bedroom window, I could see and hear Jack laughing on the patio as if he hadn't a care in the world. Didn't he know I was in the middle of a crisis?

No one should ever make an impromptu visit to a person's house the morning after a huge night out. A night out where said person had been partying and now just wanted to recover by lying in the sun and feeling sorry for herself. It wasn't fair. On top of everything, Marcus had been texting about his precious bloody package.

I brushed my hair over the bruise on my face, but I couldn't figure out what to wear. I had absolutely no clothes. All I knew was that I had to wear flat shoes, but that was silly, because I didn't have any apart from the thongs I'd bought at a street stall. I glanced into the cupboard. Thongs it was.

Stay calm. Think rationally. What could I wear, given that I was feeling fat, untidy and unwell? The shorts? No. They'd expose too much thigh. Singlet? No. That would emphasise my upper arms. Skirt? Definitely not. Skirts cut my waist in half and made me look short and pudgy—

Tara flung open the bedroom door and barked, 'What the hell are you doing in here?'

I jumped. 'What are *you* doing in here, more like it? You scared the bejesus out of me.'

'Speed it up, girlie. Put this shirt on.' She tossed a white T-shirt at me.

'It's crumpled. Besides, I'm too pasty to wear white.'

After rummaging in the cupboard, she threw some long pants on the bed. 'Shut up and put it on with these culotty type things.'

'Culottes? These are not culottes.'

'Whatever you want to call them, put them on and get downstairs now.'

It would have been far better had Sophie burst into my room. At least she would have thoughtfully advised me about what to wear, rather than throwing anything into my wretched puffy face.

Finally, I was ready. As ready as I'd ever be this morning, considering that today was up there with one of the worst days in recent memory. I edged down the stairs, holding the handrail for support.

'Hi, Jack,' I said in a bright voice when I'd finally made it to the lounge room.

He didn't turn around. No one did. All four of them were glued to the TV watching yet another report about Ivanka Trump. Why wouldn't she disappear? I slouched against the wall and closed my eyes, waiting for a fresh wave of nausea to pass. Then I jumped to the sound of an ear-piercing cymbal clanging. Bloody Levi!

Jack didn't look like he'd had a rough night. His clothes didn't have that slept-in look. In fact, his well-proportioned tanned face was freshly shaven and alert. The Jack pack scored a big thumbs-up.

'Good morning,' he said, walking across to me. 'Just catching up on why Ivanka wants to be the first reality star female President.'

'I would have thought one President Trump was enough.'

'Shush,' Sophie said, pushing the volume button on the remote control.

'And?' I whispered as we walked outside to the terrace. Rather, Jack walked, I stumbled, clutching at the walls for support.

'Some shit about her father, the usual.'

It was far too early in the day for me to concentrate. Besides, the bruise on the side of my face was throbbing.

'Is it hot out here or is it just me?' I said, sitting down carefully. I was on fire – and not in the good way. I was sweating liquor. Jack watched, waiting for me to speak again. To say something that made sense.

'It's really hot, isn't it?' I waved my hand in front of my face like an imaginary fan.

'Sophie and Tara have been filling me in about how your night ended,' Jack said as Tara and Sophie joined us.

'Not the toilet thing,' Sophie mouthed. (I had no idea what she meant by that.)

'Good night, was it?' Jack grinned. 'You've certainly got a good set of lungs. I'll give you that.'

They all laughed. I didn't. 'Yes, laugh all you want, traitors...

I'll remember this the next time you're hung-over and feeling sorry for yourselves. I too will show no mercy.'

'What happened to your face?' Jack said, his eyes zooming in on my cheek. Did Jack have a sensitive side? I liked that.

'Nothing.' I dismissed my injury with a casual hand wave. 'Slight slip with a microphone, that's all.'

He examined me closer than I'd have liked. He'd be able to count every enlarged pore on my nose if he got any closer. 'Or Botox gone wrong?'

So much for Jack being sensitive. 'Do you mind? I'm in pain here,' I snapped.

'You don't look too bad considering the huge night you had.'

I glared at him. How did he know?

I caught a whiff of my hair. Ugh. It stank – cigarettes, alcohol and sweat. Another wave of queasiness washed over me. *Off you trot*, I thought, *so I can collapse in a heap on the floor*. But Jack wasn't moving.

'How about a late breakfast?' he suggested.

'Gee, I'd love to, Jack,' I lied, suppressing the urge to vomit, 'but I've got things to do today. I promised Levi I'd take him to the beach.'

After I mumbled something vague about seeing him tomorrow, Jack finally departed.

'I thought he'd never leave,' I said to the others later as we sat on rickety wooden stools outside the local shops.

Tara shook her head. 'I don't get it. I thought you liked Jack?'

'She does,' Sophie said. 'But she's scared of getting her heart broken again, aren't you, Claudie?'

'No, I wanted him to leave. I look atrocious.' I didn't want Sophie to be right, but she was. I couldn't go through another heartbreak so soon after Marcus. I was happy to have fun with Jack as long as my feelings for him didn't deepen. But I'd come to learn that my feelings pretty much did whatever they wanted. I had no control over them and that frightened me.

'And?' Sophie persisted.

I glared at her. 'And nothing! End of story.'

The last thing I wanted to do was venture out into the public, but my desire for a Coke Zero and grease was stronger than my urge to lie by the pool and wallow. Besides, Levi had overheard the beach remark and, as a bribe for not taking him, we'd reached an agreement whereby I'd buy him a block of chocolate. A big block.

I looked like death and wasn't feeling much better. My cheek throbbed and my feet were a mass of blisters. So much for being a mature woman.

After wolfing down a kebab and guzzling a Coke, I didn't feel any better. In fact, I felt much worse.

'I think I need to lie down,' I said to the others.

Tara stood. 'No argument from me.'

'Me either,' Sophie agreed. 'Levi and I will read some stories, won't we, Leev?' Hearing that, Levi shook his head and ran on ahead. We watched as he sprinted along the path. None of us was in any condition to catch him, but Sophie's shouting finally pulled him up.

Reaching Marcella's, we began the long descent to our apartment.

'Soph, did you leave the door open?' Tara asked as we neared the bottom of the stairs and saw the front door to our apartment wide open.

'Don't think so,' she replied. It usually fell on Sophie to lock up, as she and Levi were normally last out.

No one could remember who'd left the apartment last that

morning. Two hours seemed like days ago. It could have been any one of us.

I stepped off the stairs onto the terrace. Sophie held Levi's hand and we caught up to Tara who was peeking inside.

'Fuck,' she said, as we gathered around her. 'Some arsehole's broken in.'

In the living room, drawers had been wrenched from cabinets and thrown onto the floor, as had books, magazines and sofa cushions. Chairs lay overturned. It was a huge mess, but nothing appeared broken.

'Aarrhh,' Sophie shrieked from her bedroom. Tara and I rushed in. Drawers lay on the bed and floor and her clothes from the cupboard were strewn about the place. Even Levi's toy case had been opened and tossed about.

After giving Soph a quick hug, Tara and I raced upstairs. My room was as messed up as Sophie's. Tara's room looked pretty much as it had that morning.

'My notebooks, my notebooks,' Tara screamed, before finding them and flipping through the pages to make sure nothing had been ripped out.

'*Óchi*! No! *Syngnómi*. I am so, so sorry,' Marcella said when she arrived soon after.

'It's not your fault, Marcella,' I said.

'Nothing seems to have been taken.' Sophie held up her passport.

'*Óchi, óchi,*' Marcella said, verging on hysteria. 'I call *i astinomía*, police.' She rushed back upstairs after telling us not to touch anything.

For the next hour, we waited out on the terrace until the police arrived. Together with Marcella, they walked from room to room making notes.

'Surely we can have a cup of tea while they're here,' Sophie said, walking outside armed with a tray of tea and chocolates.

I hadn't even noticed she'd disappeared inside to put the kettle on, but the tea was very welcome.

'Maybe the gods are trying to tell us something,' Sophie said after a while, her words hanging in the air. 'First the scooter and now this.'

I'd been thinking the same thing. A rush of guilt coloured my face as I debated whether to tell the girls about the Athenian incident. But the more I thought about it, the more confused I became. Maybe I was letting my imagination get the better of me. Still, my heart pounded as I double-checked the daypack I'd taken to the café. The yellow envelope was still in the side pocket – crushed and smeared with chocolate, but safe. Imagine what Marcus would have said if that had gone missing.

'What are you mumbling about?' Tara asked.

'Nothing,' I said, finishing the last of my tea.

When Marcella walked outside onto the terrace with the police, she apologised again. 'Kids,' she said, throwing her hands into the air.

The consensus was that the break-in had been done by skylarking juveniles, who'd probably done it as a dare and were no doubt looking for loose change and jewels. Thank goodness I was still wearing my necklace and ring.

'It's okay, no real harm done,' I said as Marcella was leaving.

I'd convinced myself that telling Sophie and Tara about the incident in Athens would only lead to unnecessary hysteria. But five minutes later, I took a deep breath, and said, 'I don't want to alarm you guys, but maybe this isn't a coincidence.'

'What exactly do you mean, Claud, not a *coincidence*?' Tara said.

I took another deep breath and told them everything. Sophie and Tara didn't say a word during my admission. They did *not* look happy.

'Why didn't you tell us?' Sophie asked when I'd finished.

'Because I didn't want to upset you. I didn't want the incident ruining our few days in Athens.'

'No, of course not, you bumbling turnip,' Tara snarled. 'Did it occur to you that the two events, now three, might be connected?'

I shook my head. 'Not at the time, no.'

'Explain to me how this has all happened. First, you witness a beating—'

'I couldn't really see—'

'A black scooter almost runs you down—'

'A learner driver who couldn't see the bend in the road properly.'

'And now our apartment has been shredded.'

'The police said it was kids—'

'You're kidding, aren't you? You don't believe a bunch of kids would trash our place for fun, do you? What next?'

'Nothing, I hope. Look no harm's been done. Nothing was stolen or broken. I'm probably just being overly dramatic. Marcus always accuses me of being paranoid and maybe I am a little.'

'Claudia, that's so typical of you. *No harm's been done!* What are you thinking?'

I silently cursed myself for opening my big mouth. I wanted to talk about it calmly, but in the back of my mind I knew Tara would get all high and mighty. Sophie went back inside to attend to Levi.

'You don't have the excuse of being young and crazy

anymore,' Tara continued. 'Not only are you being reckless with your own life, you're messing up ours as well.' Tara pointed inside towards Sophie and Levi. 'Wake up to yourself, for Christ's sake. The things you do have consequences. You should've told us.'

'Jesus, Tara!' I said, my voice breaking. 'I *am* telling you.'

'Look around you. Is this okay? What is it with Marcus and this goddamn envelope? Marcus shouts you a luxury holiday in Greece in exchange for handing some guy an envelope – couldn't he have done it via courier, or the internet?'

I didn't look at her.

'Don't tell me.' Tara was fuming. 'You're sleeping with him, aren't you?'

'Why would you say that?'

'Because you've been acting peculiar all holiday. *Marcus this* and *Marcus that*. So, are you?'

'No, I'm not.'

'Oh.' Tara took a moment. 'I'm sorry. It just sounded suspicious. I thought—'

'At least... not anymore.'

'I knew it!'

'Tara, please don't tell Sophie. She'd never forgive me.'

'Forgive you for what?' Sophie said, walking back outside.

'If the guy on the scooter had swerved and hit Levi,' I said, thinking fast.

'But he didn't. Levi's safe. Nothing happened to him.'

Tara clocked me. 'Maybe you should call Marcus,' she said, then stomped back inside.

Tara had a point. It was one thing to deliver an envelope. Completely another if all these disasters had something to do with it. I was sure I was just being paranoid, but now I'd dragged Sophie and Tara into it.

I took the phone out of my bag and considered the time in

Brisbane. Close to 11pm. Marcus might be asleep, but too bad. I dialled his number.

'It's Claudi—'

'Do you have any idea what time it is? This had better be good. Have you met with Con?'

'That's what I'm ringing about—'

'Have you given him the envelope?'

'No, and don't snap at me. Weird things have been—'

'Weird? What's weird?'

'When I went to see Con in Athens and he wasn't there, I could have sworn—'

'Claudia, do I really have to listen to this? It's late and I've had a busy day. I've told you before, you're being paranoid.'

'I'm not. A scooter almost collided with me, today our apartment was broken into—'

'And the envelope? Because that's why you're in Greece, after all.'

'The envelope's still here.'

'So what's the problem?'

'I'm freaking out, that's what.'

'You're a tourist. The locals are razzing you. Grow a backbone, for God's sake. I'll ring Con. Meanwhile, stay out of trouble. I'm going back to sleep.'

'Okay, well if—' But there was no point continuing. Marcus had already hung up.

CHAPTER 22

*T*he next morning, I woke up and rolled around in bed. I wasn't about to lose my cool. Okay, on the downside, the apartment had been broken into. But on the plus side, nothing had been stolen.

The previous night, Marcella had again spoken with the local sergeant and she'd relayed the news back to me, as I sat on our terrace, reading the silly book Liz and Sarah had given me for my birthday.

I'd already mastered 'a cartwheel across the dance floor in a nightclub' (many years ago). But I'd yet to 'find a pair of sunglasses that make you look really cool'.

Marcella had said that because nothing had been taken, there was little action the police could take. 'Tourists are targets,' they'd told Marcella.

On hearing that, I'd felt calmer. If anything, it was our own fault the apartment had been ransacked – we should have made sure all the doors and windows were properly locked. When Tara had slept on it, she'd see the incident for what it really was – an unfortunate holiday mishap, unrelated to my other unfortunate holiday mishaps.

I pulled back the sheets, climbed out of bed and padded over to the dressing table mirror. The bruising on my cheek had gone down significantly. The fact that my face was red from sunburn helped; it disguised the yellow-purple tinge. Things were on the up and up.

Content I no longer resembled anything to do with a Picasso painting, I changed into navy shorts and a white cheesecloth shirt, brushed my hair and wrapped it in a tiny nest on top of my head. I wandered downstairs to the kitchen and flipped on the kettle before making a huge bowl of yogurt and honey.

Out on the terrace, I adjusted the sun lounger, sat down with my coffee and yogurt and contemplated the view and the hope I'd soon no longer be living in poverty. Sweet!

Sophie shattered my serenity, her usually quiet voice booming over the phone. 'Yes he's good. Having a great time, despite our apartment being broken into by some madman. Although I know you're too busy to concern yourself with such triflings, Alex.'

I tried not to listen, but it was impossible given that Sophie sounded like a cat being strangled. Not only that, but I caught sight of the pile of knitting on the sofa. She must have been hard at it for hours. At the rate she was going, she'd be able to open a jumper shop by the time we left Santorini.

'Congratulations. I am *so* happy for you, Alex, but doesn't that mean you'll be working even longer hours?' Silence. 'I said I was happy for you. Aren't you listening to me? That would be a first... I'm selfish? Yeah, well, screw you.'

Poor Sophie. I looked up from my magazine to see a mobile phone flying across the living room. Moments later I walked inside and stood in front of the locked bathroom door. 'Soph, you okay?'

'Go away,' she said, over the flushing toilet.

A few minutes after I'd retreated to the terrace, Sophie joined me, her face streaked with tears.

I walked over and hugged her. 'You'll work it out. I don't know how you do it all. You're amazing.'

It was true. Until this holiday, Tara and I hadn't realised how wasteful children were with toilet paper, nor did we appreciate how much they ate, how much attention they demanded or how loud they were – all the time. And not only did Sophie have to be on mummy duty twenty-four hours a day – which would be enough to kill a lesser human being (i.e. me, whose biggest worry was whether there was enough milk in the fridge for a cup of tea) – but she also had to be a wife and partner.

'He's just won another huge contract,' she volunteered.

'That's good, isn't it?' As soon as the words had escaped my mouth, I knew they were the wrong words to say.

'Yeah, and who am I? The little wife at home, looking after the kid.'

'Not at all,' I back-pedalled. 'I meant that it's impressive. Alex's business is going so well.'

I looked around, wishing Tara would materialise – she was much better at handling these situations.

'And I'm selfish because I want him to spend more time with me.'

'What did he say?'

'He said that he was doing this for us.'

I took it she meant Sophie and Levi, not her and me.

'That, because of this contract,' Sophie continued, blowing her nose on a wet tissue, 'we'll be able to pay off the mortgage sooner.'

'That's good, isn't it?'

'Would you stop saying that!'

'Sophie, I don't know what to say to help you feel better. I'm not married, or a parent. I don't have anyone relying on me. I'm in awe that you can do it all.'

'But I can't. That's the point. I'm failing as a mother, and as for being a reasonable and supportive wife, I know I give Alex a hard time. He doesn't deserve it. It's like I have this black stormy cloud hanging over my head. I don't see how Alex can be so positive and enthusiastic all the time. It makes me want to scream.'

'Maybe he's trying to show you that it is possible to be happy and satisfied with your life?'

'That would just make me angrier,' Sophie said, bursting into loud sobs again. 'I don't know who I am anymore. Sometimes I wake up in the middle of the night tearing my hair out and wanting to scream, "How the hell did I get here?"'

Now was not the time to jump in with 'courtesy of Qantas and Olympic Airlines', so I said nothing.

Finally Tara, Levi and Jack appeared on the terrace in front of us.

'What's going on?' Tara asked after Levi ran into his sobbing mother's arms. 'I leave you two alone for five minutes and come back to this.'

'Nothing,' I said quietly as Sophie led Levi inside.

'I've come at a bad time,' Jack said.

Hmm, understatement, but Jack was a good diversion. I gave him the sly once-over, checked out his arms, teeth, eyebrows, butt, that sort of thing.

'Not at all,' Tara said. 'Claudia's been waiting for you to arrive.'

I glared at her. It was so obvious I hadn't. I was make-up-less apart from obligatory lip balm and concealer. But at least I was looking better than the same time the previous day.

'That's good,' Jack said, jumping in before I could protest. 'Because I thought we might ride up to Oia.'

'I don't know. Now might not be the best time.'

'Don't be silly, Claud. Go! Have some fun.' Tara smiled. 'Soph'll be fine. I'll look after her.'

'I said, *I don't know*,' I repeated through gritted teeth. I couldn't work out whether Tara was trying to punish me for my Marcus confession, or whether she'd forgiven me and was trying to help me out. But I was scared of being alone with Jack. I didn't want my feelings bubbling to the surface and breaking free.

'You bloody well need to purge Marcus from your system,' Tara whispered to me before saying loudly, 'Either you go with Jack or I will.'

'We can all go,' Jack suggested.

'No, it's all right, I'll go. I'll just change my shirt.' I didn't want to sound overly keen, but obviously I needed to spruce myself up.

I whizzed off to the bathroom and set about making myself beautiful – well, at least passable. A bit more concealer. But no foundation, thank you. It looked silly in the bright Santorini sunshine, and twice when I'd worn it, the make-up had slipped off my face within minutes, leaving my skin with a shine factor not unlike tinfoil. I slapped on what lipstick and blush I could find, then threw on a floaty little sundress I'd bought at the Southbank markets a few weeks before. It was tolerable, although my upper arms needed serious attention. Maybe I could take up tennis... although I hadn't played for fifteen years. I'd add it to my 'to-do' list when I got back home. But for now, I hoped Jack wouldn't notice.

As Jack helped me onto his scooter, I tensed. It reminded me of the one that had almost knocked me down the other day.

'This scooter...' I started.

'Small, isn't it? I ride a bigger one at home.'

'It looks like—'

'Every other scooter on the road here?' Jack laughed. 'I know. They're everywhere.'

I said no more. After the sunglass mishap in Athens and the mic incident on my birthday night, he probably thought of me as an accident waiting to happen.

I glanced around as Jack threw his leg over the seat. He was right. His scooter looked the same as the hundreds of others I'd seen in the past few days.

'Got your swimmers?' he asked as he started the engine.

I smiled awkwardly. Although I was wearing my swimmers (they doubled as a girdle), I was hoping I wouldn't be diving into the ocean today. It was one thing for Sophie and Tara to see me in my miracle swimsuit. It was quite another for Jack to get a gander at it.

I clung to Jack's hips as the narrow coast road veered past hillsides dotted with olive and cypress trees swaying in the breeze. Zooming around slower drivers and only just avoiding goats grazing by the roadside, we finally arrived in Oia on the northern tip of the island. I knew the ride had to end at some stage, but I very much enjoyed clutching his firm waist. I could have stayed in that position longer. I checked my hair. My new silk scarf was a beauty. Not a hair out of place. Locals stared as Jack parked the scooter and helped me off.

In the blazing sunshine, we walked around the town, counting the blinding white houses with red pebbled walls that clung to the rocky cliff face. Every so often, we'd stumble upon a blue-domed church, or some locals merrily sipping ouzo on the steps of their home.

'According to legend, this town is haunted and has vampires,' Jack said as we wandered the cobbled streets.

'Really?' Then, for the briefest of seconds, I felt somebody watching me.

'What's up?' Jack asked, noticing my unease.

'Nothing... it's just that for a moment... It doesn't matter.'

'For a moment what?'

'I thought someone was watching me—' I pointed to the corner ahead of us '—from around there. It's silly.'

Jack puffed out his chest. 'Not if it's going to stop you from enjoying the day. I'll go look.'

With that, he disappeared around the corner.

When I caught up with him moments later, he was patting a motley-coloured donkey.

'Okay, my imagination,' I said, reaching out to the animal.

'Not at all. This particular donkey obviously took a shine to you.'

'Very funny.'

We continued walking, watched closely by middle-aged women dressed in black, standing in doorways, scarves tied around their heads and well-worn aprons wrapped around their generous girths.

After we'd walked twenty metres or so, Jack asked, 'Why would anyone be following you?'

'Exactly. No one would. I guess I'm just tired.' And paranoid.

I picked a leaf from an oleander bush and Jack put his arm around me. 'Come on,' he whispered in my ear.

Eventually, we reached Amoudi fishing village, which lay at the foot of Oia, and strolled along the water's edge to a black stony beach.

'Fancy a swim?' Jack asked, dipping his toes in water that was busy with boats. It didn't look enticing.

I was watching his tanned muscular arms from behind my

dark glasses when, without warning, he ripped off his shirt. *Oh God.* Suddenly I was mere centimetres away from his bare chest and strong shoulders. Very smooth. Very handsome. Very sexy. There was no way I could disrobe in front of him. I was seconds away from hyperventilating with not a paper bag in sight. Thankfully, he didn't whip off his board shorts. Jack in Speedos might have been a little hotter than I could have handled.

When he dived into the water, I was faced with two options. I could stay on the sidelines, twitching and making up excuses as to why I couldn't get into the water – too cold, too hot, too shallow, too deep, too many fish, no towel, just had my hair permed – or I could do the adult thing and quickly undress the next time Jack dived under the water. That way I could jump in before he had a chance to glimpse my exposed flesh.

So while Jack was doing what appeared to be laps beside fishing trawlers in the freezing, jagged, rock-infested water, I disrobed, closed my eyes, held my nose, sucked in my stomach and jumped under the nearest ripple. I couldn't dive, so I did a feeble half-leap half-bellyflop into the sea. The water was glacial.

Normally, I'd have screeched, screamed an expletive and run out of the water at lightning speed. But not this time. It mattered not that the sea temperature was too cold for polar bears. I dunked myself before Jack saw my body – any part of it.

When I resurfaced, Jack was right in front of me. Almost touching me. We smiled at each other and I tried not to think about my modest, almost Victorian, swimmers. Everything was perfect. I was freezing and had purple lips to match my bruised cheek, but other than that, everything was perfect.

Until I stepped on a large sharp rock and cut my foot.

The pain.

The bleeding.

The embarrassment.

I screamed.

Swiftly picking me up, Jack carried me out of the water. Not only did he see my boring-but-practical swimmers up close and personal, he got a good indication of my weight and the undeniable fact that I was a wuss when it came to blood and pain. Carefully, he placed me on some red-hot pebbles and examined my foot.

My feet aren't my most attractive feature. Hair growing out from the toes, second toe bigger than the big toe. Chipped nail polish, ragged nails. An indulgent pedicure wouldn't have gone astray, but it was too late to worry about that now. I was on the verge of fainting and could do little but suck in my stomach and sit awkwardly on the uncomfortable pebbles while Jack examined me.

'Looks okay,' he said after he'd applied pressure to the skin to stop the bleeding. 'A flesh wound.'

Flesh wound? Was he blind? There was a huge gaping hole in my left foot.

'It hurts,' I yelped pathetically.

'Nothing a shot or two of ouzo won't cure,' Jack replied as he expertly wrapped my vibrant new scarf around my bloody foot.

Jack was right. After climbing inelegantly back up to Oia, we found a hipster bar near the ruins of the Venetian fortress where we relaxed on a comfy chaise longue and watched the sunset over a plate of grilled octopus and skewers of lamb and several shots of ouzo.

A couple of hours later, after even more food – a candlelit dinner of mussels, prawns and swordfish – I was feeling decidedly more chipper. Not smart, not proud, but not in agonising pain either.

CHAPTER 23

*I*t was late evening by the time Jack escorted me back to the apartment. I fumbled to open the door. All was quiet. Conveniently, everyone had gone to bed. Most considerate of them. It was just as well because, despite my bandaged left foot, I really wanted to jump Jack's bones. I was determined not to, but my resistance was waning.

'Kiss me,' he said in a strong and steady voice.

The words made me go weak at my good knee. How could I resist? I closed my eyes, reached up and did as instructed. He smelt of the ocean, fresh and intoxicating.

Jack drew me into his chest, returning my kiss. A weird but thrilling, tingling sensation took over as I held his hand and led him up the stairs to my room. We were heading towards a situation – a scintillating situation, no doubt, but a situation all the same. It could be stopped, even now. Hesitating for a moment, I considered Marcus. I really did need to get him out of my system. Even Tara had said I should. Really, I was doing myself a favour.

There we were on my four-poster holiday bed – a queen-sized one with crisp white sheets and casually draped mosquito netting – giggling like a couple of teenagers. Quite quickly, the situation intensified. Kissing, gasping, bodies intertwining. Then Jack reached behind my back and found the zipper to my dress. Smoothly, he unfastened it and, quite unlike me, I sat up on the bed and allowed it to fall away.

Thankfully, I'd had the foresight to dump my swimmers and replace them with my only pair of matching bra and knickers. If Jack and I were ever to have a second encounter, I'd need to invest in new underwear. I pulled Jack towards me and slowly unbuttoned his shirt and cast it aside. I took a sharp intake of breath as his shorts hit the floor. He was as keen as me.

Jack unhooked my bra and my breathing quickened as he cupped his hands around my breasts. His whole body hardened as he pressed against mine, our legs interlacing. And you really don't need to know any more than that, except that for the next three hours, bare limbs touched... frequently.

Suffice to say, Jack Harper was masterful in the bedroom. He was king of the boudoir. After it was over, I lay in his arms while he slept. Okay, so no surprises there. I'd yet to meet a man who didn't fall asleep straight after sex, but I didn't mind. At least he didn't turn away from me and roll across to the other side of the bed, or worse, leap out of bed feigning an early-morning appointment. Jack spooned me. It was nice. I felt safe.

Truth be told, it felt a little too good. George had seemed wonderful at the start too, until he left me with a mountain of debt and lasting trust issues.

Slowly I removed Jack's arm from around my waist and slid out of bed. I wandered downstairs to the bathroom and noticed somebody on the terrace.

'Tara?'

She jumped.

'It's the middle of the night. What are you doing?'

'Writing. Sorry, did I wake you?'

'Err, no.' I wrapped my towel more tightly around my torso.

'Oh! I see.' Tara grinned and looked me up and down. 'You are looking rather hot and bothered. Jack?'

I nodded.

'Good. Let this be the last I ever hear of Marcus.'

'Marcus? Marcus who?' Despite my bravado, I felt a twinge of sadness when I thought about him. No doubt he had a new secret girl by now, but I hated thinking about that possibility. It forced me to realise that, for him, our relationship had been purely physical, merely sex.

I shivered slightly, taking in the cool air and glancing down at Tara's notebook. 'Going well?'

'Yeah. I can't stop.'

'That's such good news.'

'It's amazing. I don't feel tired at all. I've been sitting out here in the moonlight, writing pages and pages.'

'About?'

'Anything. Everything. I've been clogged up for so long, but now words are tumbling out faster than I can write them down.'

'So, Santorini really has given you a kick along,' I said, yawning and pulling up a chair. 'Tell me all about it.'

'I will, but you should go back to bed now.'

I smiled lazily. 'Okay, but you're not getting off that easily. I want to know everything.'

'Yeah, yeah. Go on. Get your naked butt back to bed.'

I drifted off, leaving Tara to her writing, thrilled she'd finally made a real breakthrough. If she could sustain it, I had no doubt she'd be published. The woman had serious talent.

Creeping back into bed, I cuddled up to Jack. In the moonlight, I could just make out the freckles on his tanned shoulders. His messy hair flopped against the pillow. Listening to his heavy breathing, I pushed myself against him harder, tighter. Then I flung myself around, made some noise, ruffled his hair and finally, in desperation, called out his name. But it was no use. Jack was sound asleep.

CHAPTER 24

*D*uring a fitful night's sleep interspersed with hours lying in the darkness listening to Jack's heavy breathing, I had time to consider my fizzled relationships. They'd all ended up in the garbage; so really, I asked myself, why would this one turn out differently?

The rapture I'd felt hours earlier faded rapidly as I slipped deeper into a lonely and gloomy depression. Call it postcoital remorse, but I didn't see the point in Jack being in my bed anymore. Eventually, and the odds were that it'd be sooner rather than later, he'd turn out to be one untrustworthy species of cad or another and I'd be left broken-hearted, again. As soon as Jack woke up, he'd see me for the person I was. A rather shabby middle-aged woman with a gammy foot, a bung knee and a bruised cheek. Not exactly a prize catch.

I wasn't about to let myself be left broken-hearted. I'd put an end to this liaison before it had a chance to do any more damage.

By seven in the morning, I was lying in bed desperately wishing Jack would stay asleep long enough that I could edge out of the bed, retrieve my clothes and make a hasty escape to the bathroom. I'd had my chance last night. Why hadn't I done the sensible thing and put my pyjamas on then? Because I was still in la-la land, that's why. Still trapped in a fantasy where Jack and I were on the fast track to happily ever after. What the hell was I thinking?

Last night we'd been perfect together. Too perfect. The conversation was great, the sex unbelievable. I didn't want him to wake up and face 'morning' Claudia. The real one. The one without make-up. Puffy eyes, dull skin, lifeless hair. Such a contrast to last night's sexy wanton Claudia.

I stared at myself under the sheets. Less than toned thighs, rounded belly, cellulite. Last night I'd obviously been delusional. I edged further and further to the side of the bed, stopping mid-motion at the slightest change in Jack's breathing. Finally, my left big toe touched the floor. Soon enough both feet had connected with the ground. Breathing easier, I crawled around picking up clothes and underwear and a towel.

Bottom in the air, on all fours with assorted clothes in my mouth, I finally reached the closed door. Carefully, I reached up and turned the handle. Overriding the need to keep quiet, I got out as quickly as I could. In the process, I gave the door a tap as it closed. No matter. It was done and I was free. Relief. Relief tinged with sadness, but mostly relief. I stood, wrapped the towel around myself and slowly made my way downstairs to the bathroom.

Amazing how therapeutic showers can be. Under the warm spray of water, my heart rate calmed to its normal pace, and while washing my hair, I was able to rationalise my fling with Jack. He was a good bloke. It wasn't his fault that the relationship hadn't worked out.

'Tara, have you been to bed?' I asked when I saw her surrounded by empty coffee cups, lying on the sun lounger in exactly the same position she'd been in six hours earlier.

'Nope,' she replied, bug-eyed and clearly in the grip of some Mediterranean fever. 'Too busy writing.' She looked up from her notebook. 'Jack.'

'Ah, Jack.' I sat down facing her and ran my fingers through my wet hair. 'Well, it's like this. I didn't come all this way to shag an Aussie bloke – I mean, where's the Greek Adonis? He's the one who's supposed to be in my bed right now loving me up!' Tall, tanned, with curly dark hair and muscles from here to Sunday. Whatever the hell *muscles from here to Sunday* meant, I wanted it and wanted it wrapped up in the form of a virile Greek boy, thank you very much. Not some boy from Yackandandah.

'Um,' Tara said awkwardly. 'I meant that Jack,' she pointed behind me, 'has made you a cup of tea.'

'Oh,' I said, wondering whether I shouldn't just saw off my foot now it was so firmly jammed in my mouth. I swung around to face him. 'Jack, you're awake.' I caught his eye for a millisecond before turning my attention to the marble floor.

'Here's your tea,' he said with forced politeness.

Shit. What had he heard? And if he'd been listening, why hadn't he coughed or done something to let me know he was here?

And he still looked bloody handsome. And fresh. Fresh and perky.

Why'd he have to be so nice and bring me tea anyway?

'I'll leave you to it.' With that, Jack walked inside and retrieved his keys and wallet from the dining table.

'Please stay and eat breakfast with us,' I croaked when he returned less than a minute later.

'Better not, your Greek Adonis might arrive. I'd hate to get in the way.'

I wanted to die, for a sniper to shoot me. But snipers appeared to be few on the ground in Santorini that morning. I wasn't struck by a bolt of lightning either. Nor did the volcano across the water erupt and send boiling lava in my direction and swallow me up. No, sir! I had to face the humiliation on my own, had to look Jack in the face. All alone, I might add, because Tara had rudely excused herself and scurried back indoors.

'I didn't mean anything by it.'

'That's okay.'

I didn't believe him. It wasn't okay. It was insensitive and cruel of me and I told him so.

He shrugged. 'So why say it?'

Good comeback. You win. Because I'm an insecure and pathetic idiot? I shook my head. 'I don't know. Sorry.'

'So am I.'

⁂

'He's gone?' Tara asked when she came outside some time later.

I didn't answer, just sat curled up in an uncomfortable position on an even more uncomfortable deckchair staring out across the azure blue ocean.

'What the hell were you going on about? I thought you liked Jack.'

'I do.' I sulked. 'It's your fault. Why didn't you say he was behind me with a bloody cup of tea, for God's sake?'

'My fault? I couldn't get a word in. You were going on and on about an imaginary Greek Adonis. Besides, I did try to tell you, but you ignored me.' Tara gathered up her notebook and pens. 'I was sitting here minding my own business.'

'I wish that at some point in my life I could stop being an idiot. But I can't seem to help myself. It's like I'm on some kind of sabotage mission, and every time, without fail, I succeed in making a complete arsehole of myself. I need to find the land of arses and hang out there.'

Tara grinned. 'If you think it'd help. Seriously, though, why do you say things like that?'

'It wasn't that bad, was it? I mean, Jack could tell I was joking.'

'Of course he could. That's why he left so quickly.'

I slumped further back into my chair. 'I'm really sorry about the break-in the other day. It was stupid of me not to tell you and Sophie about what had happened in Athens.'

'It's okay.'

'I only wish the guy on the scooter had run me down. At least then I'd be in hospital, or worse. Either way, I wouldn't have slept with Jack last night and made a complete fool of myself this morning.' My stomach was in knots. I couldn't believe I'd acted like such a juvenile.

'Tell me about Marcus,' Tara said, interrupting my thoughts.

I looked up at her, unsure of what to say.

'What were you thinking? Sleeping with your boss, for God's sake?'

'It just happened. It wasn't planned—'

Tara snorted.

'I hate it when you snort. It's like you don't believe me.'

'I don't.'

'I swear to you, Tara, it wasn't planned. But he was so understanding about the mess with George, especially after the bank got involved—'

'Great. So you say thanks and buy him a bunch of flowers or a chocolate muffin. You don't sleep with the guy and say, by the way, would you like a blow job with that?'

It wasn't like that, at least that's not the way I saw it.

'And Jack?'

'He's great, but I don't want to get involved with anyone right now.' I didn't want to be let down again, to find out down the track that Jack was a liar or thief. I couldn't face being betrayed again. So I'd forced the end of our friendship before it could develop any further. 'Perhaps it's for the best,' I heard myself say.

I'd always hated that expression. It was what people said when they couldn't think of anything better to say in a bad situation, designed to make fools like me feel better about themselves. But in my experience, it never worked. Nine times out of ten, it wasn't for the best at all. However, in this instance, maybe it really *was*. Because let's face it, I was off to live in the land of arses and was only ever going to be happy with other arseholes like myself. To date, Jack had failed the arsehole test.

'So?' Tara was still glaring at me.

'So, nothing. I don't want to get involved with anyone so soon after Marcus.'

'But what if Jack's *the one*?'

Was she kidding? I shook my head. 'I don't think so.'

Jack was definitely not *the one*. That is, I hoped he wasn't, because I wasn't ready for *the one* to pop into my life. I needed to work on myself, sort out the mess with Marcus, throw myself into a new job that I loved... I had too much to do to be distracted by *the one*.

'Claudia, you're thirty-nine—'

'Don't remind me.'

'*The one*,' she continued, mimicking quotation marks with her fingers, 'had better present himself soon or you're going to be old and withered before you know it.'

'You can talk.'

'Don't worry about me. I'm doing fine.'

'And I'm really excited for you,' I said, rubbing my cheek. 'You've been awake all night and you're still at it. How are you feeling?'

'I know you're changing the topic, but since you ask, I'm feeling inspired. I don't want to jinx it, Clauds, but I really feel that I might have a story to tell – a long one, this time. I've been planning, drafting characters and scenes. I think it could work.'

'I haven't seen you this animated since... since I can't remember. Where do you think it's coming from?'

'From being here and meeting some great people.' She stretched her arms out wide to take in the island and the volcano.

Hmm. That would be the same inspirational volcano that failed to erupt and engulf me in flames fifteen minutes ago.

'I'm finally starting to understand that I need to make things happen for myself and take responsibility for my writing. I need to look beyond my own fears and doubts and start writing about how I feel.' She paused for a moment. 'It's been a long time coming. I needed to step out of my comfort zone. And now I've done that, it's like a whole new world has opened up to me.'

Was Tara blushing? The wakefulness, the feverish writing – was there more to the story that she wasn't telling me?

'Is there anything else?'

'What do you mean?'

'You're so bright and bouncy.'

'Claudia, I'm finally writing! Writing words that have meaning and potential. Do you know how long it's been? I'm relieved. I'm excited. But most of all, I'm happy.'

'Glad to hear it.' Sophie grinned as she walked down the stairs and onto the patio. 'Hey, Claud, I saw Jack up the road. And he definitely didn't look happy.'

'Ah well. There's no pleasing some people.' The last thing I needed was another lecture, this time from Sophie.

'But,' she continued pleasantly, 'he was kind enough to take Levi off to find some donkeys to pat.'

'Really? So he's coming back?'

'I guess. He has to return Levi.'

'I need to get out of—'

'What? I thought he stayed over. I'm pretty sure I heard giggling followed by eager romping up the stairs in the middle of the night.'

'You did. You did,' Tara said gleefully. 'But sadly, it's all gone pear-shaped because our Ms Claudia wants a fling with a Greek Adonis, not some handsome Jack from the outback.'

'I can speak for myself you know, Tara. I'm right here.'

Sophie sat at the end of the lounger. 'So speak.'

'There's nothing much to say. Yes, Jack stayed the night. Yes, we did the wild thing. And now Jack's gone and we're both moving on.'

'That's a bit of a turnaround from yesterday, isn't it?'

'Not really. We all knew Jack was only ever going to be a quick fling.'

'Could have fooled me.'

'Yes, well, Soph, you're easy to fool.'

I fidgeted on the deckchair. 'I notice that no one's asked about my foot.' I held up my leg for the pair of them to inspect. 'Or my cheek for that matter.'

Only when it became clear that I wasn't going to talk about the Jack debacle any more did Tara and Sophie finally start talking about themselves.

'I've made a decision,' Sophie began.

'All ears,' I said.

'I'm going to see Bryan when we get back from holidays.'

'Who?'

'My friend, Bryan,' Tara said. 'He texted yesterday, inviting Sophie to his studio for a chat when she gets home.'

'After our discussion at dinner the other night and my argument with Alex yesterday, I had a long think about everything. I love fashion and interior design and I think I could make a real go of it. I'm signing up for the TAFE course as well.'

I clapped my hands. 'Brilliant, Sophie.'

'Best of all,' Tara said, 'Bryan has heaps of contacts, so if Soph doesn't want to work for free, I'm sure she could get a paying job.'

'That's the aim, at least when I've finished the course,' Sophie agreed. 'Meanwhile, I can learn the practical aspects from him, like magazine shoots.'

'God help you,' Tara said.

'Seriously, congratulations, Soph,' I said. 'That's wonderful news.'

'I hope you're right. I feel good about it. I need something in my life other than Alex and Levi, or I'll go mad.'

'Nah, really?' Tara and I said together, huge grins on our faces.

'Have you told Alex yet?'

'Only about the course, not about Bryan, but I will.' With that, Sophie disappeared inside, and Tara and I were left on the patio in the sunshine contemplating our navels.

'But they do poo a lot,' we heard Levi say from the top of the stairs.

I couldn't sit there and wait for the flood of humiliation to wash over me when Jack appeared on the patio. I needed to lock myself in the bathroom until he left.

'Quick, Tara, I've got to run,' I said, struggling to extricate myself from the chair.

I was hell-bent on taking the coward's way out and disappearing inside, but my body wouldn't cooperate. It was stuck. Stuck like a rabbit caught in a car's headlights. Where was that bloody volcano when I needed it? Meanwhile, Tara looked on in quiet bemusement.

'It's true,' Levi continued, as he and Jack descended the stairs. 'Tara fell into the donkey poo and got berry angry.'

It was too late to escape, even if my body allowed me to – Levi and Jack were now on the terrace.

Was that a half-smile on Jack's face? I could barely look at him.

Tara sighed. 'Yes, Levi, it's true.'

'And your clothes got stinky,' Levi said excitedly. 'And you got angry and cried.'

'I don't know if I cried exactly—'

'You dib... she dib,' Levi said, turning to Jack.

'I believe you,' Jack soothed then glanced in my direction. 'If you haven't already guessed, Levi and I have been talking about donkey poo.' Jack checked his Fitbit. 'It's a conversation that can last a good fifteen minutes.'

'Where's Mummy?' Levi asked, bored with the adults on the patio.

'Inside,' said Tara, taking his hand. 'Let's find her.'

Please don't leave me here alone with *him*, my eyes begged her. Fat lot of good it did me. Tara and Levi had vanished within seconds. Meanwhile, I was glued to a deckchair with a citrus-smelling Jack hovering beside me.

CHAPTER 25

'Jack,' I said after I'd managed to prise myself out of the chair, 'I am *really* sorry about this morning. I was being *really* silly and I'm *really* sorry for being so stupid.' All I wanted him to do was to hug me and tell me I was forgiven. Call me a people-pleaser, but even though I might not want a relationship, I didn't want Jack to hate me either.

'Don't worry about it,' he said calmly, wrapping his arms around me. 'You were just showing off in front of Tara. It's okay.'

'Really?' I said, my eyes teary. 'I thought I'd screwed up big-time.'

'You did, but I'm a big boofy bloke and I can handle it.' Jack paused for a moment. 'I have to go now but how about we meet up later? Beach maybe?'

'Sounds great,' I said, immediately recalling the foot debacle from the previous day.

'Promise I'll check for sharp objects before I let you in the water. Let's meet at that café you were lurking at the other day? Say one-ish?'

'Sure.'

Jack was clearly not one to stew on trivial arguments. That

boded well for me because I was always putting my foot in my mouth. He was also a take-charge guy. I didn't want a Greek Adonis after all. Jack from Yackandandah would do me just fine.

When he kissed me, I knew we were back on track. It was a great kiss. A passionate kiss. Even my toes danced. Everything was right with the world and I was damn glad the volcano hadn't swallowed me up. Still, I told myself Jack was only a holiday fling. No point beating myself up about a future with him back in Brisbane when I knew it was only going to last until we left the island.

❦

'Thank goodness he's gone,' Tara said, dragging Levi behind her onto the terrace a few moments later. 'Sophie's on the phone to Alex and it's getting quite h-e-a-t-e-d,' she said, spelling out the letters and pointing to Levi.

'Exactly... heated...' I was miles away, kissing Jack on a huge yacht in the middle of the Mediterranean.

'It's getting quite hot in there,' Tara hissed, pointing inside.

'Hot?'

'Bloody hell, Claud. They're arguing on the phone, for fuck's sake, and I don't want Levi to hear.'

'So instead, you brought him out here to listen to you swear?'

'If you could spell, I wouldn't have to.'

I ignored her. 'So, what did you do with Jack this morning?' I asked Levi, pulling him onto my good knee.

'Looked at poo.'

'What else?'

'Patted donkeys. Jack let me sit on one.'

'Jack's nice, isn't he?' Looking for positive reinforcement from a three-year-old. Pitiful.

'Yeah. Not as nice as my daddy.' Levi started crying. 'I want Daddy.'

Before long, Levi was sobbing. Thankfully, Sophie heard the commotion and came rushing out.

'Here, Leev,' she said and handed him her phone. 'It's your turn to talk to Daddy.' Levi took the phone and jumped off me, but only after he'd wiped his nose on my shoulder.

A couple of minutes later, he waved the phone in Sophie's face. 'He's gone now, but he's gonna play ball with me when we get home and take me to the beach.' Levi was beside himself with happiness. Sophie looked exhausted.

'You okay?' I asked her.

She nodded.

'What did Alex say about Bryan?'

'He said I should do whatever makes me happy.'

'That's a bad thing?'

Sophie glared at me, before stomping back into the apartment.

I checked my messages. A text from Marcus, apologising for being abrupt on the phone the other day and adding, *Twenty grand has been deposited into your bank account. What you do with it is up to you.*

Yippee! I texted back. *Twenty thousand thank-yous! Promise I'll track Con down, even if it takes me another month!*

It was close to one by the time I walked into Fira. I had a spring in my step at the thought of meeting Jack for lunch. The fact that I was officially almost debt-free didn't hurt either. But just to be sure, I stopped at an automatic teller, not quite believing Marcus had actually paid me. I punched in my four numbers, asked for the account balance and the machine spat out a slip of paper. I read it and almost keeled over. I had twenty thousand, three hundred and forty-two dollars in my account. This was officially the best day of my life!

Not only was I rich (okay, I had to pay all the money to my bank and American Express, but today I was rich!) now that I'd put things right with Jack, I was happy too.

I loved this place: the cobbled pathways; the donkeys vying for road space with scooters, cars and pedestrians; the funky boutiques and fabulous cafés and bars. But it was the spectacular views that got me every time. Like nothing I'd ever seen before.

As usual, there were crowds of tourists taking pictures, shouting in a jumble of foreign accents, but the town still had a casual unhurried vibe about it. I bought a great straw bag and a couple of postcards. I even stopped by Nikos's to praise him on the craftsmanship of my stunning turquoise necklace.

'You like?'

'Yes, very beautiful,' I told him.

'Now, you buy matching earrings? Come.' Nikos led me inside the shop, thrust a glass of red wine in my hand and proceeded to show me several sets of exquisite earrings.

'Best price for you, Clow-di-ah.'

Several minutes later, I waltzed out of the shop with an enormous smile on my face, feeling rather virtuous at having walked away from Nikos's shop empty-handed. No sparkling turquoise jewels would be dangling from my ears for the foreseeable future.

I was making my way to the café when I spotted Con hurry out of a shop and disappear around the corner. I raced after him, but he'd vanished. I thought about searching for him – after all, I'd promised Marcus, and he had paid me all that money – but the narrow alleyways were a maze and chances were I'd only succeed in getting myself lost.

Con, I texted. Think I just saw you in Fira? Can we meet?

Reading the word *delivered* under my text, I waited a few minutes. When the magic three dancing dots failed to appear, I dropped the phone back into my straw bag. Con's loss. I didn't have the envelope with me anyway.

Jack was drinking a short black when I spotted him. My heart fluttered, he was actually at the café, waiting for me. I tried to remain outwardly calm and cool. Difficult given the blazing heat.

'Well, hello there.' Jack beamed as I sat down. 'You know, I'm glad I looked over your shoulder that morning at the airport.'

'So am I. Who knew we'd end up here?'

Jack's eyes were bright and playful. 'Santorini's special, isn't it?'

Now was my opportunity. I still hadn't asked Jack whether he had a significant other and the time had come to make a few inquiries. Despite me musing whether he had a wife or girlfriend at home, I assumed he didn't. Normally, people volunteer that information straight up. 'You should meet my wife...' Or, 'You'd get on well with my partner, Jenny...'

'Jack,' I began slowly, speaking before I'd fully constructed the question in my mind, 'I should have asked this days ago, but do you have a girlfriend or—' I gulped, 'a wife back home?'

Jack shook his head. 'No. Do you? A husband or boyfriend, I mean.'

'No.'

'And I don't live with my mother if that's your next question.'

Just then, I saw Con again, this time, walking out of a small convenience store barely twenty metres down the road.

'Back in a minute.' Before Jack could say a word, I was off, doing a feeble half-run, half-skip up the uneven road, dodging mopeds, dawdlers and donkeys.

'Hey, Con! *Na stamatísei.* Stop! Con!' I yelled up the road as he disappeared further into the crowd.

Con was gone. At least the Con I wanted was gone. Two other Cons stopped and turned my way.

In the process, I hurt my foot again. Miserable, I hobbled back to Jack, gasping for breath. I was definitely joining a gym when my real life began the next week.

'That's it. That's it,' I cursed under my breath when I'd resumed my seat.

'What's up?' Jack looked puzzled.

'Nothing. Just a business transaction I'm supposed to complete.' I took a huge gulp of water. 'Only I haven't been able to do it yet.' A few droplets fell on my shirt.

'I didn't know you spoke Greek.'

'I don't. Well, I speak enough to get by.' I wiped the water from my chest.

All I wanted to do was relax under the sun in Santorini, the jewel of the Greek Isles, with Jack Harper. Not spend endless, thankless, hours chasing Marcus's mate. And now I couldn't give up. There was no way in hell I was handing the money back.

I sat and fumed while Jack stared at me, bewildered. 'I thought you were here on holidays.'

'I am. My boss asked me to do a bit of work as well... It's no big deal.' There was no point telling Jack about Marcus and Con; that can of worms was best left unopened.

'Really, it doesn't matter.' I smiled awkwardly. 'Now, where were we?'

But Jack had his head in his iPhone.

'Jack?'

He looked up, clearly agitated. 'Something's come up. I need to go.'

'What? Now? But we've—'

'Claudia, I said I need to go.'

All right. I heard you the first time. 'Okay,' I said quietly. 'Will I see you later?'

'Not sure what I'm up to this afternoon.'

Where was the sweet guy from a few minutes ago who said he'd been glad he looked over my shoulder at the airport? He'd morphed into a cocky, *not sure I can catch up later*, guy.

Sad, confused, and with a heartache looming, I stared through him into the crowd. I know I'd dashed off unexpectedly for a few minutes, but why would he suddenly change his tune? Maybe he'd decided that last night had been a mistake. Or perhaps he was paying me back for my stupid Adonis comments this morning.

He must have sensed my hurt because he said, 'Dinner tomorrow night? How about I pick you up at seven?'

'Sure,' I said, surprised at the knots multiplying in my stomach and my growing pang of longing.

Tomorrow night? That left all of three and a half days before I would *never* see Jack again. Shouldn't we be making the most of our time together, even if it was only a holiday romance? Weren't we supposed to be strolling through the quaint cobblestone pathways of Fira, nibbling each other's ears? And when all the nibbling became too much, shouldn't we run full speed back to the apartment for mind-blowing sex? Wasn't that the way it was supposed to be? Obviously not. Those romance books had it wrong. Jack didn't even try to kiss me, let alone race me off to bed.

I spent the rest of the afternoon wandering the streets. Whichever direction I glanced I saw smitten couples kissing.

Eventually, it was too much to bear, and I headed back to the apartment. I wasn't hungry but given that I was arriving home just before dinner, I thought of Tara and Sophie and stopped to buy some essentials – feta, olives, tomatoes and eggplant. All right, so I bought a couple of pizzas too. I ordered the Santorini

Special and the Seafood Surprise, which was a surprise, given that the prawns were the size of pinheads. Levi would appreciate it, I reasoned, even if the others didn't. I showed no restraint when it came to buying chocolate – white, milk, dark, fruit and nut, and liqueur chocolate. That should do it. Along with wine, of course. Wine and chocolate. Comfort food at its best.

By the time I made it back to Marcella's, laden with goodies, the sun was setting. I was quite looking forward to dinner with the girls. In fact, I'd forgotten about Jack. Jack who? I didn't care.

So what that he seemed to be running hot and cold: one minute playful and intimate; the next minute cool and standoffish. I had girlfriends who loved me. What did it matter that Jack wasn't as fond of me as I'd hoped? It was a fling, after all, and Tara and Sophie were more important than a hot heaving date with Jack the lad.

Unlocking the front door, I let myself in and hit the light switch. No one was home.

I dumped the goodies on the kitchen bench, scrounged around for a bottle opener, opened the wine, poured myself a large glass and grabbed a slice of the Santorini Surprise. Back out on the patio, I watched the sunset. Pure magic. The Santorini sky was mesmerising.

And here was I, watching it by myself. Less than a kilometre away, people sipped exotic cocktails at the Sunset Bar. All around me couples in other apartments nuzzled each other's ears, necks and breasts, toasting their good fortune. But I was home alone. Not even Marcella's cat, Ari, was around.

As time ticked by, I kept an eye on the stairs, hoping to see my friends. I'd texted both of them a couple of times but either they hadn't seen my messages or were ignoring me. Just like Con.

My third piece of pizza, third glass of wine. Still no one. The sunset faded. It grew dark and decidedly chilly. I checked my messages again. None. (There *was* one from Marcus, but he didn't count.) At least they could have texted me.

I retired to my room at 8.30pm, but not before I'd scrawled a note to Tara and Sophie telling them about the leftover pizza and wine in the fridge, *not that you deserve any for leaving me alone!*

I waited until a quarter to nine before completely closing my bedroom door. What if something sinister had happened to Sophie and Tara? I shook the thoughts away, determined not to get spooked. But still, I was worried. As I drifted to sleep, I heard nothing. No wind. No meowing. No voices. Nothing but silence. An eerie creepy silence. Only the loud voices in my head.

CHAPTER 26

The next morning, I woke up crying, which was a little unexpected. The more I tried to stop the tears, the more I cried and the more the room crowded in on me. I was a shivering mess. The fiasco with Marcus, meeting Jack, the odd almost-lunch with him the previous day, the Con business. I seemed to be digging ever deeper holes for myself.

I always lived in the present, assuming tomorrow would take care of itself. And it was precisely because of this attitude that I'd ended up where I was. I wanted to turn the clock back. Five years earlier, I was happily working for Riesling Renaissance and living contentedly in my funky flat in Toowong. I was single, in a good place both emotionally and financially, and was loving life. My life specifically. I still remembered the disbelief and shock; the physical heart pain and sadness at being retrenched from Riesling Renaissance. That same week, Marcus mentioned that his office manager had left. The job landed in my lap and being one to believe in the universe having her own plan for each of us, I assumed this was her plan for me. Little did I know Ms Universe has a perverse sense of humour.

My phone beeped. A text message from Con asking me for

my address in Santorini and saying that he would come to the apartment to collect the envelope. He didn't tell me when. A minute later, a message from Marcus asking if I'd received a text from Con. Lord, get it together, guys!

The messages distracted me enough to stop the tears and kick-start my thinking. I needed to square things with Marcus – formally resign and make a real effort to find a job I could enjoy and stick with. I was hopeful I could go back into events management. It might mean starting at the bottom and working my way up, but I wasn't totally out of the loop; at least I could contact people I still knew in the industry.

As for accommodation, I hadn't spoken to Tara, but I hoped she'd still allow me to live in her house, provided I continued paying rent at the market rate. I didn't want to move out on my own just yet.

I reached for *Things To Do Now That You're... 40*. It bugged me that I was reading it, especially as it wasn't aimed at my age group (I was only thirty-nine!), but then again, neither was *Cosmo* and I always managed to get past that.

Opening the book randomly, I found such gems as, 'Learn to play "Stairway to Heaven" on a guitar.' Like that would ever happen! 'Practise juggling three balls in the air and become proficient at it.' So, I assumed, once people reached forty, they had nothing better to do than learn a musical instrument and master magic tricks. As I read through all the things I'd need to do once I eventually reached that milestone, my eyelids grew heavy.

Seconds later, I fell back to sleep.

It was almost midday when I finally made my way downstairs.

'Well, well,' I said when I saw Sophie and Levi playing on the patio. 'Nice of you to finally come home.'

'Sorry, love. Got your note. Thanks.'

'I went to all that trouble to buy pizza and no one came home.'

'Tara and I assumed you'd be out with Jack.'

'Jack Spack. I was here – alone.'

'Was it really as bad as all that?'

'Yes. No. Not really. I went to bed early. What did you get up to?' I asked as I inspected my cut foot. I'd taken off the bandage the previous night to let the skin breathe.

'After the beach, we met up with Angie and Harry. The boys played together, and we ate dinner at Kamari overlooking the sunset.'

'Nice.'

'Sorry, Claud, had we known you were at a loose end, I'd have phoned.'

I rolled my eyes. 'I texted.'

'Don't be like that. Leev wants to go on a boat, so I thought I'd take him to Folegandros for the afternoon. It's an hour away. Want to come?'

'Sure, sounds good.' It'd stop me aimlessly hanging around waiting for Jack to turn up that night. 'I'll just knock on Tara's door and see if she wants to come.'

'Let her sleep. She was having a raucous time when I left to bring Levi home last night. Who knows what time she staggered in?'

'I'll come,' Tara said huskily as she peered out from behind the bathroom door.

🝱

Within the hour, the four of us were on our way to Folegandros. The name meant rocky – good call because the island was tiny, stark and very rocky. Traditionally a place of exile, I could understand why; the island was wrapped in huge cliffs, making escape almost impossible.

Nervously, we peered out the windows of the bus taking us to the town centre as it veered precariously close to sheer cliffs. To take my mind off the treacherous road, I focused on the endless series of dry walls that had been erected over the centuries to create terraces on the island slopes. It didn't help my anxiety, but I appreciated the effort that had gone into their construction.

Happy to have made it into town alive and in one piece, we strolled through the market square, which overflowed with pink bougainvillea and red hibiscus. Every now and again, we stopped to take a picture and wait for Levi to catch up.

He was a wanderer, that child. The slightest distraction and he was off.

We meandered along a maze of crazy paved alleys that were home to masses of vibrantly coloured geraniums and houses with brightly painted wooden balconies.

The three of us could have explored the tiny hamlet for hours, peeking into the locals' homes, checking out their décor, sampling their cuisine, but Levi quickly tired of sightseeing. After grabbing lunch from a tiny taverna offering an extraordinary range – including over twenty types of ice cream, seventy different kinds of beers, as well as traditional Mediterranean dishes such as stuffed peppers, moussaka and smoked aubergine – we sat under a row of magnificent lime trees and watched the locals go about their business. Then, at Levi's insistence, we caught another bus to a nearby beach.

'Have you spoken to Alex again?' I asked Sophie while Levi and Tara amused themselves throwing pebbles into the ocean.

'Not since I blew up at him yesterday.' She paused. 'You know, when you asked me the other day if everything was okay... well, it is. Don't get me wrong. But every now and then when these feelings bubble up inside me, I feel like I'm going to explode.' She took a breath. 'And it scares the hell out of me. I've got to deal with it before it takes over again. I don't want to be a sick or weak person. I want to be in control of my life.'

I nodded. 'You're one of the strongest women I know, Sophie. I can help too, if you let me. We're in this together.'

'I feel so guilty when I look back at that time when Levi was a baby,' she said as we watched him skip along the water's edge. 'Guilty and selfish. It's not what a good mother does.'

'Bollocks. You have to forgive yourself. For goodness' sake, you had postnatal depression.' I hugged her. 'Levi's doing fine.'

'But what if I feel like leaving again, or worse? I have to take charge of my life, take responsibility for my actions.'

'Maybe, but be kind to yourself, and talk to me if the feeling resurfaces.' I understood what Sophie was saying. I needed to do it as well – take responsibility for the way I was living my life. It scared the hell out of me.

Tara walked over and draped her arm around Sophie's shoulder.

'Sometimes I feel like I've been living a lie since Levi was born, like I'm some sort of fraud,' Sophie said. 'Maybe I've been drifting for years.'

I put my hand up. 'Me too. But when you're struggling to keep your head above water, you tend to float with the current.'

'It's not always the most sensible option, though.' Tara looked at me pointedly.

'I know, and I am going to make changes as soon as I get home,' I said. 'No matter how difficult they are, or how much I want to avoid them.'

I knew I'd been coasting, not wanting to make hard

decisions or, in fact, any decisions about the way I'd been living. I'd lost count of the times Tara had warned me that my laissez-faire attitude would get me into trouble because I didn't consider the consequences. As much as I loved Einstein's philosophy, I had to start planning for tomorrow and taking responsibility.

'You're not alone,' Tara said, softening. 'I've done my share of avoidance. I can only imagine what my parents will say when I tell them I'm taking time out to write a novel.' Tara pretended to pull out her hair. 'Ahhh! I have to live the way I want to, even if it means disappointing people. Besides, in the past when I've tried to avoid upsetting others, I've only ended up hurting myself.'

'I'm so glad this holiday has been good for your writing.'

'Good? It's been amazing. Forced me to explore my creativity, to really challenge and push myself. I feel like a new person. I know that sounds dramatic, but this holiday has turned into so much more than I ever could have imagined. I can honestly say I am excited about the future, the possibilities. It's fantastic.'

'The future,' I said, letting the words hang.

'The future,' Sophie repeated. 'The future has new challenges for each of us. And with the three of us exploring new opportunities, we can support each other—'

'Like they do in Weight Watchers or AA,' I said.

Sophie frowned. 'I guess. I know I have to take control for Levi's sake.'

The three of us sat quietly staring out to sea.

'Speaking of which,' Sophie said. 'Where *is* Levi?'

We stood and looked around.

'He was here a moment ago,' Tara said. 'I was throwing pebbles into the water with him.'

The colour drained from Sophie's face. 'Levi!'

'He can't have gone far,' I said. 'He's probably skimming stones down the beach a bit further.'

The trouble was that all along the winding beach were

multiple hiding places for young adventurers. There were also scores of sun worshippers and umbrellas dotting the landscape, so it was impossible to get an uninterrupted view.

'I can't see him.' Sophie twirled around. 'My God. He's not here.' She ran along the beach, shouting Levi's name.

'Tara, I'll go this way.' I pointed in the opposite direction to where Sophie had run. 'You head up there.' There was a pathway directly above us. Tara took off and I jogged along the water's edge, looking for Levi and a lifeguard.

Along the way I asked people whether they'd seen a small boy. 'He's lost,' I explained in Greek.

'*Óchi!* No!' person after person replied.

I peered behind thyme bushes and through caper flowers in the hope that he was hiding. I searched as far as I could go, calling out for him. But after ten minutes, I hit the bottom of a precipice. A sheer drop. Definitely not a hill that Levi could climb. Looking back along the beach, I figured there was no way Levi could have wandered this far in such a short time. He'd been out of our sight five minutes, seven, maximum. It would have been virtually impossible for him to get here so quickly unless he'd been carried.

Staring back the way I'd come, I hoped that by the time I returned to the others, Levi would be found. I strained my eyes as far as I could see, hoping to spot Levi's little pixie face. In the distance, I saw Tara. Sophie held Levi's red cap, but Levi wasn't with them. I ran the last forty metres.

When Sophie saw me alone, she burst into tears. 'I'll never forgive myself if anything's happened to him.' She hunched over and wept.

At her side, Tara was describing events to an official-looking Greek man.

'Claud, can you help?' she asked, stepping back so I was

standing next to him. He wore a navy uniform and clearly wasn't on surf patrol.

I explained that we'd lost sight of Levi fifteen minutes earlier when he'd been throwing pebbles into the water. I wasn't sure how accurate my Greek was, but the officer had a good grasp of English, so between us, we managed. I gave Levi's height, age and description, and the officer jotted down notes on blue paper.

'He was wearing a green T-shirt,' I said.

'It was blue,' Sophie said. 'Blue with dolphins on the front. Bare feet, navy board shorts.'

'*Perímene!*' he instructed us.

'*Efcharistó,*' I replied.

He turned to walk back up towards the path, shouting in Greek on a two-way radio.

'What did he say?' Sophie said, her eyes flickering nervously.

'He's asked us to wait here.'

'Wait here? For how long? What did you say to him?'

'Thank you.'

'Thank you?' Sophie screamed. 'For what? I can't wait here. I have to find my baby. He's lost somewhere in this.' She pointed at the beach activity around us. 'I can't stand here doing nothing. We've got to look for him. He's a little boy. He doesn't know where he is, and he can't swim to save himself.'

'Leev's a great little swimmer,' Tara said in a low calm voice. 'But I don't think he's in the water. I asked him barely twenty minutes ago if he wanted to go for a swim and he put his toes in the water and yanked them straight out again, saying it was too cold.'

Relieved, Sophie inhaled deeply.

'Tara's right,' I said, 'he's just wandered off to where we can't see him.'

'Really, Claudia,' Sophie said, her voice suddenly sharp and hard. 'And you'd be happy about that, wouldn't you? Levi's been pissing you off all holiday.'

'Pardon?'

'Levi's been getting in your way, making it difficult for you to lead your self-centred party lifestyle.'

'Sophie, that's not fair.'

'Anyway, what if he hasn't wandered off?' Sophie yelled. 'What if your friends have kidnapped him? Or worse?'

'He hasn't been kidnapped, for God's sake.' I was trying to remain composed. 'It's not my fault he walked away.'

'No, it's never your fault, is it?' Sophie hissed. 'You, who only ever thinks about herself. How could it possibly be your fault? You just always seem to be around when bad things happen. You're self-destructive, a magnet for the dangerous.'

'Hang on, if we're talking self-destruction—'

Tara stepped in between us. 'Time out. This isn't helping Levi.'

'She was the one who wasn't paying attention to Levi,' I said to Tara. 'He's your responsibility, Soph, not mine.' It was a truly horrible thing to say and I regretted it the instant the words left my mouth.

Sophie turned to Tara. 'You were playing with him. You said you were looking after him.'

'Why was it my job all of a sudden?'

'Come on. It's no one's fault,' I said. 'Let's focus on finding him. We can rip each other apart later.'

It was after four in the afternoon and Levi had been missing twenty-five minutes. The sky was blue. The sun was still hot, but a cool breeze swept over the beach. Thyme fragrance hung in the air. Thankfully, the crowd had thinned, so it was easier to do a broad sweep of the beach.

Sophie wiped her eyes, gathered up Levi's dinosaurs, picked up her bag and once again paced the beach calling his name. I couldn't stand watching her any longer – her pain and distress broke my heart.

I retraced my steps, asking for help. No one had seen Levi. At least, no one had noticed him enough to remember seeing him. Tara walked back up to the path calling to Levi as she hiked through the bush.

&

Ten minutes later, I found Sophie and we walked arm in arm to find Tara, who was covered in scratches and cuts from low-lying shrubs.

'We'll find him,' I said, sick with dread.

'My life's over,' Sophie said. 'Nothing matters if I don't have Levi. I don't have anything.'

'Shhh, don't talk like that,' Tara said, hugging her. 'We'll find him.'

'When? He's gone. My baby's gone and I don't know what to do. He's my life.'

There was nothing I could say. I squeezed Sophie's hand hard, praying we'd find Levi safe and well.

Tara stood back and surveyed the beach. 'I've been thinking, who knew we were coming here?'

'What do you mean?' I asked.

'Who knew we'd be here today? How much do you really know about Jack, Claudia? His scooter looks remarkably like the one that tried to run you over the other day.'

'I thought that at first but look around. Ninety-nine percent of the scooters here look the same.'

'He could easily have followed us.'

'Why do you say that? Besides, I didn't even know we were coming here until this morning.'

'Still,' Tara said, raising her voice, 'I reckon you're involved in some serious shit and you've dragged Sophie, Levi and me into your mess.'

'That's not true,' I said, hoping Sophie might say something in my defence.

She didn't. It was doubtful she'd even heard us talking.

'How could you say something like that? It's not true,' I repeated. If we could just find Levi, then everything would be all right again. The way it should be.

'Really? What about Con?' Sophie said, springing to life. 'What do you know about him?'

I bowed my head.

'You don't ever think, do you? You just go blindly along for the ride, never stopping to consider the consequences.'

Tara nodded.

I couldn't think straight. 'What about Angie?'

'What about Angie?' Tara repeated.

'She's been hanging around as well.'

'Yeah, you're right. I can see the headlines now: *Single mum from London kidnaps three-year-old Australian boy to add to her brood.* What do you reckon?'

'Marcella?'

'Don't be ludicrous!'

'I don't know!' I burst into tears. My head was pounding. Tara and Sophie held me responsible for Levi's disappearance and I didn't blame them. They were right. It probably was my fault. I should have thought twice about getting involved in Marcus's deal, but it was only supposed to involve the signing of some papers! Surely it couldn't be the cause of a child's kidnapping?

'Mummy,' Levi cried as he wrestled his way out of the official's arms.

'Levi, Levi,' Sophie shouted, swooping down to pick him up. 'Mummy missed you, beautiful boy. Where have you been?'

'Looking for sand,' he replied, showing no signs of distress. 'And I found some, way ober dare.' Levi pointed to a speck in the distance.

Sophie hugged him fiercely, tears spilling down her cheeks. Tara and I watched with a mixture of relief, gratitude and wonder. Whether Sophie liked it or not, and no matter how much she might want to escape from time to time, she'd always love, worry and agonise over her child. That's what mothers did, and she was a good mother.

'Come to sand, Mummy,' Levi said, struggling to break free of Sophie's grip, blissfully unaware of the anguish he'd caused.

I looked at Tara. We both shook our heads.

'Thank God,' I whispered.

CHAPTER 27

*B*ack at the apartment, we were all still shaken by Levi's disappearance, and I was worn out from arguing with Tara and Sophie. It had been one hell of an afternoon. The three of us had fought before. We'd had some doozies over the years. Our spats were never irreparable, but sometimes the barbs stung. This afternoon's drama went to show how quickly accusations and recriminations could be hurled about.

The three of us had been careless with our friendship recently. Though we were tight, it was strikingly clear we hadn't spent enough time with each other, and the cracks showed.

Sophie's furious words rang in my head. *Levi's been pissing you off... getting in your way... self-centred party lifestyle... self-destructive, a magnet for the dangerous.*

I'd said hurtful things too.

Still, if you couldn't be honest with your best friends... but there was honesty and there was honesty. We walked a fine line, and sometimes our jibes came awfully close to crossing that invisible 'no-go' zone.

It seemed frivolous to be heading to dinner with Jack; I didn't feel like it at all.

'Go out tonight,' Tara encouraged when I told her I wasn't up to it.

'I should be here with you three,' I argued.

'Levi and I are playing dinosaurs,' Sophie said. 'Go have some fun. Please!'

'At least one of us should be hitting the town tonight,' Tara added.

'Want to come?'

'I don't think so.' Tara looked at the notebook in front of her. 'I've got some serious writing to do.'

'What if Jack really is a gangster,' I said, only half-joking.

'Sorry about that, Claud,' Tara said. 'I was catastrophising.'

I nodded. As if Jack could be a gangster. He was far too handsome... and an Aussie. I mean, he hailed from Yackandandah. 'I'm sorry about everything too.'

'It's over now,' Sophie said, hugging a squirming Levi. 'I'm sorry for what I said, Claud. You're great with Levi and I know you love him. It isn't easy being on holidays with a toddler. I'm the one who should've been watching him.'

'We all should have been.' As difficult as our friendship was at times, I wouldn't swap my best friends for the world. There was something incredible about being able to weather difficult times together.

'Go on, get dressed. Jack'll be here soon.'

I checked my watch. Sophie was right. Jack would be here in less than an hour and I looked like death and felt worse.

❧

In the shower, I washed and scrubbed my body until every pore was squeaky clean. Afterwards, I buffed, waxed, and creamed myself, then plucked every stray hair I could find, including my eyebrows. I had to be careful though; I tended to over-pluck when nervous. Some people chewed their fingernails. I plucked eyebrows. Critically, I examined them in the mirror. Raising one, then the other, then the pair of them together. They were uneven and would never be a match for Jack's beauties. I hoped our children would be blessed with Jack's brows. It would save them a lifetime of torment.

'Yes, Jack darling, I always look this good when I tumble out of bed first thing in the morning!' I said to myself after an hour of primping.

'Go, girl,' Sophie whooped when I walked outside.

Tara wolf whistled.

I couldn't wait to see Jack. Tonight, I was determined to be a dream date. I wouldn't say anything silly, use any offensive language or act inappropriately. I'd be perfect. The perfect date. The perfect girlfriend. The perfect wife. Okay, that was going too far.

I sat down next to Sophie. 'How you doing?'

'Fine,' she answered as she shuffled Angel cards. 'Shaky, but happy. Glad to have Levi with me. Happy with the world. Thankful.' Sophie paused. 'And incredibly sad that I've taken Levi for granted all this time.'

'What happened today could've happened to anyone. We weren't paying attention and Levi scarpered.'

'Yes, but I was wrong when I said my life would be better if I didn't have Levi. I can't believe I ever thought that. I've spent the last three and a half years running away from him, when he means everything to me.'

We glanced over to Tara who was busily scribbling at the other end of the terrace.

'You'd better not be writing any of this down,' Sophie said.

Tara turned to us, raised her pencil and continued writing.

I fidgeted, twitched and looked at my watch again. Jack was half an hour late.

'Do you want to read my Angels while you're waiting?' Sophie held up the cards.

'I don't know.' Tara stopped mid-sentence. 'Do you really want to mess with that stuff anymore?'

'My, how the worm has turned,' I said. 'A week ago, you didn't believe a word of it.'

'I still don't, but I don't want to wish ill fortune upon myself.' Tara chewed on her pencil. 'Or others.'

'Ill fortune?' Sophie said.

'What Tara means is,' I said, 'we shouldn't be relying on destiny, but instead making our own future, and creating our own destiny.' Relying on the Angel cards was a bit like letting someone else take charge of our lives.

'Come on.' Sophie shuffled the deck.

'Okay, but maybe this is the last time.' Perhaps the Angel Oracles should retire... at least while luck was on my side.

The cards always came down to one thing anyway – belief in one's self. And I got that kind of advice from my mother all the time.

'Ready.' Sophie pulled three cards from the pack and laid them on the table.

I stared at the Angels and read from the guidebook. '"Congratulate yourself on a recent decision to change your inner channel."' As in TV channel? '"Don't back down. You won't ever regret breaking with tradition."'

'Are you sure it says that?' Sophie asked.

'Everything is open to interpretation, but yes, that's what it says.'

'Well, we'll leave it at that,' Sophie said, unconvinced. 'Sounds good though.'

'Tara? You up for it?' I waved the cards in front of her.

'I guess, as long as this really is the last time. And I don't want you telling me anything bad.'

'Shuffle!' I handed Tara the cards. She shuffled them reluctantly while I peeked at my watch and ran my fingers through my hair. Tara picked out three Angels and laid them on the table.

'Easy-peasy,' I said. 'It says here in my trusty book that you have to "sort out your priorities and stick to them."'

'Is that it?'

'Why does everyone keep asking me that? Yes, that's it.' I looked around, ignoring Tara's obvious disappointment. 'Where the hell's Jack? He's late.'

'Forget about Jack. What does my reading mean?' Tara asked.

'It means,' Sophie enthused, 'you have to make a list of everything important in your life and work out how to make the most of what you've got and the people you love. Figure out what's vital and follow through with the commitment.'

'I wanted to hear that I'd live happily ever after with the love of my life.'

'What love? What life?' I asked. 'I thought the only love you cared about was your writing.'

'I was joking. Keep your shirt on.'

I shrugged. Tara had a point. I was becoming increasingly agitated. Jack was nowhere to be seen and I was beginning to think he wouldn't show, that he really was too good to be true.

'Here, let me read yours, Claud,' Sophie offered. 'I'm sure the Angels will provide you with the answers you're looking for.'

I shuffled the cards without much enthusiasm. My heart just wasn't in it. Something told me I wouldn't want to hear what the Angels had to say. I chose three cards and Sophie searched for words of encouragement while I disappeared to the bathroom for the eighth time, checking my hair, lipstick and cleavage, in the hope that Jack would materialise by the time I returned.

'Ready?' Sophie said after I'd taken a seat next to her.

'Hit me.'

'Okay. Basically, it says here that you've messed up in the past.'

'What a surprise!' I raised my sore, uneven eyebrows.

Sophie twitched in her seat. 'It says that "although you've been fooled at times and have fooled yourself as well, there is still time to build for the future. The mistakes you've made will add up and ultimately make sense."'

'Jeez, I'm glad we cleared that up,' I said impatiently and looked at my watch. Again. 'That makes me feel *so* much better.' As if I needed reminding that I'd made mistakes. Many of them.

'Why don't you call him?' Tara suggested.

'I've texted and phoned. His mobile's diverted to messagebank.'

❧

After Levi had gone to bed, the three of us had shared leftover pizza, souvlakia and salad. I tried to recall exactly what Jack had said to me the previous afternoon.

'Are you sure you didn't get the time or the night mixed up?' Sophie asked.

'We saw each other at lunchtime yesterday and he said he'd take me out to dinner tonight. Unless...'

'Unless what?'

'Unless that comment about the Greek Adonis really did piss him off. He was quite agitated yesterday.' I stared across the caldera and back at the homes and hotels built into the cliffs, their lights twinkling in the moonlight. 'He's probably looking at me from one of those apartments right now, laughing because he's got his revenge.'

'The way your mind works, Claud!' Tara said.

'What? A couple of hours ago you were convinced he'd kidnapped Levi.'

'And I apologised. I was distraught. On the brink.'

'Jack's okay,' Sophie said.

'How would I know? I only met him a few days ago. He could be an axe murderer.'

I said goodnight and walked into the bathroom to scrub off my make-up. A masterpiece that had taken an hour to create took all of two minutes to destroy.

Patting my wrinkly face, I counted and named several new lines and two new moles (they could have been warts), then unhappily climbed the stairs to bed.

CHAPTER 28

'Claudia, are you awake?'

'I am now,' I answered sleepily, trying to think of a good reason why Sophie would bang on my door at such an ungodly hour. (Whatever that hour was.)

'You've to get up,' she bellowed through the walls. 'Now!'

'Why?' I rolled over and opened my eyes.

Sophie pushed open the door and peered in. 'There's a Greek guy downstairs. Con.'

Oh shit. 'What time is it?'

'10am.'

Damn. Not as unreasonable a time as I'd first thought. Still, I'd been asleep and dreaming about Chris Hemsworth. 'I'll be out in a sec.'

'Could you hurry? He's creeping me out.'

I practically fell out of bed and put on the black dress I'd thrown off in a huff the night before. After brushing my hair and wiping the sleep from my eyes, a half-arsed effort, I glanced at my reflection in the mirror. Good God! I really needed to wash my face and brush my teeth, but first things first. Hand over the envelope and flash drive, get the papers signed and get rid of Con forever. Then I'd shower and clean my teeth. Good plan.

I reached under the bed, fumbled for my daypack, dragged it out and unzipped one of the side pockets. The yellow envelope was exactly where I'd put it the other day. A bit crumpled and covered in chocolate, but all contents in place. Clutching it with both hands, I walked downstairs.

He stood out on the patio. It was Con all right.

Sophie met me in the doorway. 'Here she is,' she sang in an artificially light voice.

'Yes. Here I am. *Kaliméra*, Con. Nice to see you again.'

'*Kaliméra*, you have the papers, *naí*?'

'Right here.' I gave the envelope a pat. I wouldn't miss it at all. 'Better late than never, hey?'

I smiled out across the ocean. The dawning of a new day and my duty was all but done. Sweet relief!

Con didn't acknowledge me as he snatched the envelope out of my hands, his eyes veering off in all directions.

Ingrate.

I was waiting for a tiny word of thanks, when, out of nowhere, Jack ran down the stairs and stopped in the middle of the patio.

Before I'd had time to say, *Nice of you to show up – fourteen hours late*, Jack called out, '*Stamatíste!*'

He was, I noticed even in my confusion, wearing a short-sleeved T-shirt that magnificently showed off his biceps... or was it triceps? Anyway, one of those muscle groups. I was under pressure, couldn't think straight. Whatever those beefy things were above Jack's elbows, they looked amazing. Jack was one hell of a strong guy. But enough of that. Something bizarre was going on in front of me. This wasn't the Jack I knew and had fantasised about. Who was this guy? And could someone tell me why he was twisting Con's arm in some kind of bear hug?

I waited for the laugh. This was a joke, right?

'Jack! What the hell—'

Two men in uniform ran onto our patio.

Jack nodded to the men, then bent down to retrieve the envelope that had fallen out of Con's hand onto the floor. The taller one tilted his head to the side, executed a snazzy body manoeuvre and cuffed Con. The second one grabbed my arms and cuffed my wrists. It was over before I could open my mouth to ask what was happening.

'What's going on?' Sophie and Tara asked from the relative security of the front doorway.

Jack ignored their question. 'I'll need your passport, Claudia.'

I couldn't speak. Why was Jack, the engineer from Yackandandah, allowing these apes to cuff me?

'Your passport?' His manner was detached, almost cold.

'Upstairs,' I mumbled. 'What's going on?'

Con held up his cuffed hands to Jack and the other men, who I gathered were police, showing all ten fingers and shouting in Greek, '*Gamísou!*' which basically meant, 'Fuck you!'

'Hang on,' Tara said when she appeared again with my passport. 'Jack?'

Jack took the passport. 'Let's go,' he said to the men and Con and I were marched up the stairs.

Sophie and Tara ran up behind us.

'Stop a minute, Jack.' Sophie pulled at his shoulder. 'Where are you taking her?'

'Holding room at the airport. She'll be detained there until we get clearance to transfer her to Athens for formal prosecution.'

'Pardon?' I asked. Whatever this misunderstanding was, it was escalating out of control. 'I haven't done anything.'

'Yeah, what's she done?' Tara asked.

'Securities fraud, money laundering, stock manipulation,' Jack said, seemingly unfazed by the growing crowd of observers at the top of the stairs. 'There's an extensive list.'

'I thought you were an engineer,' I said.

'Not quite.'

'This is a mistake. I haven't done anything wrong.'

'We've been watching you for almost two weeks,' Jack said, his voice calm and even. 'The game's over, honey.'

Honey? Honey?

'You've been caught on tape handing this envelope to Constantine Kafentsis here.' Jack pushed Con forward and held up the tattered yellow envelope as evidence. He glanced at the brown smudge.

'Chocolate,' I offered.

He raised his eyebrows. 'Can you deny that?'

'No. But it'll come off. It's only chocolate.'

'We have to go,' Jack said coldly.

Shock stole my words. I kept expecting a goon from Greek *Candid Camera* to jump out at me and yell 'Gotcha', at which point we'd all fall about on the floor laughing. But no, between the stony looks on the faces of the police, Con's pissed-off expression, the horror on Tara's face, and Jack's indifference, I knew this wasn't a stunt.

'Can I at least go to the bathroom and get a few things together?'

Jack shook his head. 'Your friends can bring them to the airport once we've questioned you further.'

'Further?' I shrieked in disbelief. This had to be one helluva mix-up. Why had Jack done this? Had he been following me the whole time? Who was he? And what about Con? And Marcus?

'Jack, this is a mistake.'

Con and I were bundled into a tiny sweaty Greek police car, in full view of the whole street. Dozens of locals and tourists had turned up to see what the commotion was about. Marcella held Levi's tiny hand. Hadn't we caused her enough trouble?

As the police cars inched forward, the crowds stepped back and cleared a path. I watched them through the rear window as we drove away. It was humiliating. And surreal. The cuffing, being crammed into the back seat of a police car and driven to the airport. I couldn't take it all in.

I tried catching Con's eye by coughing and sighing loudly. No such luck. He wouldn't look at me. Even when I asked him if he knew what was going on, he remained silent, pretending not to understand what I was saying. He sweated profusely and stared out the window.

Turning my attention to the police in the front seat, I tried pleading my case. 'Excuse me? There's been a terrible mistake.' They ignored me too. I needed to talk to Marcus. He'd sort this mess out quick smart.

And Jack? What the hell was his story? He'd climbed into the other car. It seemed he'd engineered the whole thing. Jack the engineer! I'd known he couldn't be trusted from the first time I saw him wearing that absurd hat at Brisbane airport.

I was delirious with worry. What if I was locked up for years and no one knew where I'd been taken? What if Greece was one of those countries where nobody received a fair trial? I'd never met anyone who'd been arrested in Greece before. What if no one listened to me and I was thrown in jail with murderers and rapists? What if I was carted away and none of my family or friends ever heard from me again, because I'd been sold into the slave trade or prostitution?

My scrambled brain and vivid imagination invented worst-case scenarios much quicker than I could process them. Nausea crept up my throat.

The car finally stopped in a space reserved for emergency and police vehicles outside Santorini airport. Jack jumped out of the car next to me and spoke with several ground staff. They tilted their heads towards me. Jack motioned to the police in the front seat of the car I was sitting in. They opened their doors, got out and opened the two back doors. One held me, the other guarded Con. It was mortifying.

Moments later, I was frogmarched towards automatic sliding doors by a short rotund police officer carrying a gun in his holster.

Inside the airport, Con was led in one direction and I was escorted the opposite way, along several dark crowded passages. Other tourists, locals and airport workers stared at my cuffs, then at me. No one smiled. People turned away as soon as I attempted eye contact. My throat constricted. I wanted to yell, *I'm innocent.*

'Drugs,' I overheard one say.

'Yeah, drugs,' another agreed.

They were tourists like me. Like I used to be before this nightmare began.

I walked with my head bowed, staring at the floor, barely managing one foot in front of the other.

Finally, we stopped in front of a nondescript grey door. The officer fumbled with his massive keyring until he found the right key and unlocked the door. He motioned for me to enter. Once inside, he closed the door behind me. I heard the click of a lock and listened until his footsteps faded.

Where was Jack? Why had he left me? When was he going to come and sort this mess out? I'd be almost willing to overlook the whole fracas if, when he arrived, he admitted it was a misunderstanding. A big mistake. Sure, I'd be shitty. After all, being handcuffed and driven away by police on your vacation was no picnic. However, after some serious grovelling, I could forgive him.

I waited... and waited.

But Jack didn't come.

No one did.

There was a minuscule window to the outside world, but it was opaque and I couldn't see through it. And the window had bars. Vertical and horizontal.

I tapped the door and called out, '*Kaliméra?* Hello? Is anybody there?' Timidly at first. Much louder by the fourth time. By the sixth attempt, I was screaming.

No response.

I stopped shouting. My cell fell quiet. Quiet, and very hot.

CHAPTER 29

I was alone. And handcuffed. Locked in a room no bigger than Tara's bathroom back home. Speaking of which, I really needed to use the toilet, but this room didn't appear to have an en suite. There was a small table upon which sat a chipped tumbler and a pottery jug of what I assumed was water. The room was a drab grey – the walls, concrete floor, ancient melamine table and two steel chairs, all grey.

The only other item was an earthenware pot. It reminded me of the wee pot my old nanna placed on the floor by her bed at night. Surely, they didn't expect me to use that?

Hands clammy, hair wet, I freaked out. Panicked, I sat on one of the chairs, put my cuffed hands on the table and rested my head in them. I was in a foreign country, about to be charged with God knows what. I sat silently for a long while, in a kind of trance, focusing my attention on a black scuff mark on the grey wall.

Finally, I heard movement on the other side of the door. A key turned in the lock. Jack and a female guard walked in. At least, I assumed the round butterball with big black hair was a guard. Unsurprisingly, she wore a dull grey uniform consisting of ill-fitting pants and a plain long-sleeved shirt.

'Jack, I'm so glad you're finally here,' I said, approaching him, relieved that he'd come for me at last. It didn't matter that he'd brought a Greek mama with him. What mattered was that this whole ugly mess would finally be sorted. 'I've been waiting for you.'

Jack motioned towards the woman. 'This is Nina. She's with the Greek police.'

'*Kaliméra*,' Nina said in a flat voice, her features pinched.

'Claudia, please take a seat,' Jack said, staring through me.

Okay, not quite the response I'd been hoping for, but maybe Jack was being formal because we weren't by ourselves. Protocol and all. I was surprised at how reasonable I was being, given I'd been forcibly removed from my holiday apartment and thrown in a tiny drab holding cell without explanation.

When he motioned for me to sit, I hesitated. 'What's all this about, Jack? It's a mistake. You know that, don't you?'

Jack had a tape recorder in his hand, which he laid on the table. Positioning himself in the chair opposite me, he said, 'Please take a seat. Even though Nina is the police officer in charge,' he gestured towards Nina, 'I'll be conducting the official interview with you.' He ran his hand through his hair. 'Because of our common language.'

'What interview? You're scaring me.'

'I'll be asking questions and taping your answers.'

I stared at the ancient tape recorder. You'd think he'd use something a little more sophisticated. I shook my head. I needed to phone the Australian Consulate. They were always helping troubled travellers out of tight spots in foreign countries.

'Aren't I supposed to have a lawyer present?' I'd watched enough cop shows to know that much. And Jack, I'd concluded, was definitely a copper. Although he wasn't wearing a uniform and hadn't shown me any official identification.

'You can. Do you want one?'

I wanted to slap him. Instead, I quietly answered, 'Yes, thank you.' But where the hell was I going to find a lawyer in Santorini... one who understood English and could get me out of this ridiculous mess? 'And I'll need to see some official identification from you as well,' I said wearily.

Jack nodded to Nina and she walked outside. At last, Jack and I were alone. The perfect opportunity to confront him and make him explain to me what was going on. But I couldn't face him. I just stared at the miserable manacles gripping my chafed red wrists.

'We can get those off for you if you like,' Jack offered.

'I presume you mean the cuffs?'

Jack rolled his eyes in a *for fuck's sake* way and walked around the table to me. From the wad of keys in his pocket, he picked out a small silver one. I held my hands out towards him.

'There you go.' The unfastened cuffs slid from my hands. Turning away from him, I massaged my wrists.

Nina returned with Angie.

'Angie!' I rushed to hug her. I'd totally forgotten she was a lawyer. I selfishly hoped she was a good one. No. A great one. There was no point having an average lawyer defending me when I was being held prisoner in a foreign country. *A prisoner.* I'd been in a few tangles in my time, but I'd never been arrested. 'Thank God you're here.'

'You okay?' Angie asked.

I nodded and turned to Jack. 'If I hadn't asked for a lawyer, you'd have just left Angie standing outside?'

Angie smiled. 'Tara called me as soon as you left the apartment. I'd have found you, sweetie.' Angie was an angel, an angel who, if I was not mistaken, sounded rather regal and kind, not dissimilar to the Kylie Minogue's lovely adopted English accent. How could I ever have imagined she sounded like Hyacinth Bucket? I had every confidence Angie would get me out of this mess. She sat down beside me on a fourth grey chair Nina had wheeled in. It was getting crowded in here.

'Enough pleasantries,' Jack said. 'Let's get on with it. Ready?' Jack's tone wasn't pleasant. It wasn't unpleasant. It was official.

He pushed the record button on the tape recorder.

'Interview with Claudia Taylor. Time,' he paused to check his Fitbit, '12.52pm.' Jack looked across at me. 'Please state your name for the record.'

'But you just said it!' I glared at him. His eyes were cold, his manner hard and remote.

'Just say it, Claudia,' Angie coaxed.

I blinked. 'Claudia Marie Taylor.'

'Is this you?' Jack opened my passport and pointed at the hideous headshot on the inside front cover.

'Yes.'

Jack placed the passport back in his folder and withdrew another photograph. 'Are you acquainted with Marcus Cassoli of Cassoli Imports, Brunswick Street, Fortitude Valley, Brisbane?' Jack held up a picture of Marcus climbing out of his Porsche.

'Yes.'

'Could you speak up, please?' Jack pushed his tape recorder further to my side of the table and laid the photo of Marcus beside it.

'Yes,' I repeated.

'And you are employed by his company as the office manager?'

'That's right.'

'And you're in his employment now?'

'Yes, Jack. I've already told you that.' I could tell he didn't like my tone, but too bad.

'Let's stick with the question-answer format, shall we?' Jack said with an intimidating stare.

I slipped to the verge of tears again.

Angie looked at him and then at me. 'It'll be okay, Claudia. We'll sort this out.'

'How long have you known Con Kafentsis?' Jack showed me another photo, this time of Con.

'I met him for the first time five days ago, I think.'

'You think?'

'No, um, one day before my birthday so... six days ago.'

'But you've spoken to him a number of times over the phone?'

'Maybe once or twice.'

'Well?'

'Well what?'

'What was it?' Jack demanded. 'Once or twice?'

I was shaking. My face flooded with heat. I had no idea how often I'd spoken to Con. My mind was blank. 'I can't remember.'

I figured my arrest had something to do with Con and what I'd seen in Athens. Poor Marcus. He'd be distraught. But what did Jack have to do with it? Where did he fit into all of this? Overtaken by a storm of tears, I cried and cried. I couldn't remember a thing.

'Interview suspended at,' Jack looked at his Fitbit, '1.03pm.' He pressed pause on the tape recorder.

Angie held my hand and let me weep on her shoulder while she patted my back. She handed me a red bandanna so I could wipe my eyes. 'Can you at least tell us what Claudia's being charged with?' she said to Jack.

'Nothing... yet. Right now, I'm trying to place her movements and establish her relationship with Mr Kafentsis.'

'I told you,' I said, sobbing, 'I don't have a relationship with Con Kafentsis!'

I dabbed my face with the bandanna. I was tired, hungry, had furry teeth, dirty knotty hair, and desperately needed to use the bathroom. In short, I was a mess. 'I need to use the bathroom.'

'Okay, we'll have a five-minute break.' Jack motioned to Nina.

'You don't—' I teared up again. 'You don't expect me to use that, do you?' I pointed to the earthenware pot on the floor.

Jack almost smiled. 'That's for cigarette butts. Nina will take you to the bathroom down the hall.'

I felt like a complete idiot. Although in the scheme of things, mistaking an ashtray for a wee pot was nothing compared to being jailed for the term of my natural life for crimes I hadn't committed. As I was led out the door by Nina, Angie handed me a small cosmetics bag, for which I was eternally grateful. At least I could brush my teeth and comb my hair.

Thankful for being allowed inside the toilet cubicle by myself, I sat on the seat and tried to clear my head. It didn't feel real. As much as I struggled to make sense of the last couple of hours, my mind kept wandering to obscure things like rats, wee pots, and mouldy sandwiches. This place made my skin crawl. Scratching myself, I began imagining what it would be like to have cockroaches crawl all over me, into my ears, up my nose...

'*Syngnómi?* Excuse me? You finish?' came Nina's voice from above the stall door. 'We go now.'

I flushed the toilet, walked out and glanced in the mirror. I really should have spent the time fixing myself instead of hunched on a toilet seat, contemplating my fate at the hands of marauding insects. I washed my face, cleaned my teeth and ran a comb through my hair. I examined my eyes. No amount of eye make-up was going to help. There was no disguising the puffy and bloodshot reality.

'Feeling better?' Angie asked when I returned to the tiny grey room.

'Wretched.'

Jack hadn't moved. He sat opposite my chair, his tape recorder at the ready. I hated him. What had I ever done to him? Why did he want to single-handedly destroy my life? I loathed him. I wanted him to die a slow and painful death. And I wanted to watch.

But before my wish could be granted, I needed to work my way out of this hideous situation. So I had to concentrate. There'd be no more tears. No more shouting. I'd do my best to answer Jack's dreary little questions and then get the hell out of here.

CHAPTER 30

The Jackass – yes, I'd resorted to name calling – released the pause button on his silly little tape recorder.

'Interview resumed at 1.15pm. Claudia, how long have you known Con Kafentsis?'

I was ready. I was composed. 'I met him briefly for the first time six days ago. I spoke to him over the phone once, the day before that.' Forthright and in control.

'That's it?'

'Yes.'

'There were no other times you spoke to Mr Kafentsis or saw him?'

I thought for a moment. 'Today, obviously. And then a couple of days ago, I thought I saw him in the crowd. I also texted him a couple of times.'

Jack let out a deep sigh. 'Take me through it from the beginning, Claudia. Why were you so desperate to meet with Mr Kafentsis?'

'I wasn't desperate. Marcus was.'

'As in Marcus Cassoli, your boss?'

'Yes. He wanted me to give an envelope to Con, which contained a flash drive and papers for him to sign.'

Jack tilted his head to the side. 'Why?'

'Because he's a new investor in Marcus's company. Apparently, his company makes the best oils and organic wine in Greece.'

He corrected his head. 'Why were you the go-between?'

'Because I was here in Greece on holidays, I guess.'

'You guess?' Again, with the questioning whine and annoying tilt of his swollen head. 'That's very convenient, isn't it?'

'Not really. Marcus paid me to come over here as part of my job.'

'And exactly how big was the bonus Marcus paid you?'

'Nothing, I mean—'

'Cut the lying, Claudia. How much money was Marcus paying you to hand over the flash drive?'

I shook my head. 'Nothing.' The words caught in my throat as I remembered the money Marcus had deposited into my savings account.

Jack rocked back on his chair, apparently considering my words.

My hands turned clammy. Perspiration trickled down my cleavage. I had an uneasy feeling about the money.

'Isn't it true, Claudia, that you accepted this little jaunt because you wanted a new challenge to make up for your boring average life?'

'I beg your pardon?' I said, willing his chair to topple over. 'Where did you get that stupid idea?'

'Your boring childhood? You told me yourself – you wanted more excitement, more thrill in your life.'

'I never said *thrill*.' The Jackass was making me angry. 'And, if you recall, I was referring to a time when I was a teenager. I also liked *Ace Ventura* and dreamt about becoming Mrs Jim Carrey. I've grown up somewhat since then,' I said through clenched teeth.

'Come on, Claudia, do you really expect me to believe you came all this way to give some papers to a stranger? As a favour to your boss?' Jack glared at me, no doubt hoping to make me cry again.

He referred to his notebook, cleared his throat and read from the pages in front of him. 'Did you or did you not say that your life was, quote, "incredibly normal. Sometimes I find myself asking, 'Is this it?' and I feel like doing something crazy to inject a bit of excitement into my life." Well?'

'My God! You were recording our lunch conversation? When we were drinking wine, getting to know each other?'

'Claudia,' he said, dismissing my outrage, 'we know about your dire financial state. You need the money to pay off a twenty-five-thousand-dollar bank debt. Isn't that correct? And didn't twenty thousand dollars appear in your bank account two days ago, courtesy of Mr Cassoli?'

Angie gasped. 'I don't think—'

Jack put his hand up to silence her. 'I overheard a conversation between you and Mr Cassoli where you specifically—'

'Okay, yes,' I said. 'Marcus agreed to help pay off my bank debts if I passed the flash drive on to Con.'

'No!' Angie shouted as she reached across the table and put her hand out to stop me from saying anything more.

I looked at her, stunned. 'Angie, you've got it all wrong. There wasn't anything untoward going on, I promise. Con is a huge olive oil man. He also makes balsamic vinegars. Marcus is really excited—'

Angie glared at me. 'I think you've said enough, Claudia.'

'But I haven't done anything.'

'Can't you see your boss was bribing you?' Angie said.

'No, you don't understand. Marcus would never do anything like that.'

'Let's backtrack,' Jack said. 'You say that Marcus is innocent, and that the money wasn't a bribe. How can you be so sure?'

'It was a gift.'

Jack laughed. 'Come on. Bribe, gift, bonus... no boss gives his employee money like that unless—'

Anticipating what Jack was about to say, I jumped in and admitted my nasty little secret. 'Marcus and I were having an affair.'

Angie was speechless.

'Half the women in the office were sleeping with him. I didn't figure you—' Jack stopped and pretended to read through his notes.

'I don't believe that,' I said, tears welling in my eyes. Marcus flirted with other women, but there's no way he'd be sleeping with any of them. Would he? I suddenly felt naive and silly. I didn't want to hear that I was just another notch on Marcus's bedpost.

Angie made a strangled noise, then, 'He's married, isn't he?'

'Separated,' I said quietly.

Jack rocked back in his chair. 'Exactly why do you think Marcus sent you to Greece?'

'Other than to meet Con and have him sign a bunch of legal papers?'

Jack nodded.

'I'm not sure,' I said, wiping away tears. 'Marcus wanted me out of the office because we'd ended our affair.'

'So, he offered you this holiday?'

'He said I needed a break. He asked if I'd ever been to Greece and suggested I might like to take a holiday for a couple of weeks, the only stipulation being that en route to Santorini, I get some papers signed in Athens.'

'Go on.'

I took a breath. 'Marcus offered me the holiday of a lifetime. He knew my financial situation. The whole world knew I was in debt up to my ears. There was no way I could get to Europe on my own anytime in the foreseeable future. He booked my airline ticket, organised a great apartment in Santorini, all for meeting Con for ten minutes while he signed some papers.' Breathing deeply, I blinked away a few rogue tears. 'Okay, in hindsight it does seem a bit too good to be true.'

Jack looked at me for a moment. 'What about the money?'

'I truly believed that was my kiss-off. He said as much. I certainly didn't ask for it. I was shocked he even offered. Next thing I knew, he texted telling me he'd transferred it to my bank account.'

As it finally dawned that Marcus had used me, the combination of fear, anger, hurt and betrayal overwhelmed me. My leg trembled, my stomach churned. I thought I might be sick. I felt lost, abandoned and very, very scared.

With a click of the pause button, Jackass suspended the interview. 'Claudia, do you need to take a break, some water perhaps?' He poured Angie and me the remainder of the liquid from the pale grey pottery jug.

Angie sipped from her glass. 'I had no idea about any of this.'

'You must hate me,' I said.

'Everyone has their reasons,' she replied, by no means a ringing endorsement.

'You right to start again?' Jack asked and clicked off the pause button. 'Marcus Cassoli gives you an all-expenses-paid holiday to Greece...'

'When we landed in Athens, I immediately went to the

address Marcus had given me and searched for Con but...'
I hesitated.

'Go on.'

'I don't know if it was the right location. I saw some guy get beaten up and it freaked me out. The place was derelict, surrounded by used syringes and broken glass.'

'You were definitely at the right address.'

'But it was abandoned – Wait! You saw me there?' I couldn't believe what I was hearing... he'd seen me and hadn't tried to help.

'No, not me,' Jack said. 'Go on.'

I hated him saying that. As if I had a choice other than to *go on*. 'I called Marcus and said that Con wasn't there.'

'And how did Marcus react?'

'He told me to fly to Santorini as planned and that Con would call me when it suited him.'

'Go on.'

I wanted to shove Jack's *go ons* down his throat. 'I got on with having a holiday.'

Jack shifted uncomfortably in his chair.

'Celebrated my birthday and did some sightseeing, as you do on holiday.'

'Okay,' Jack said. 'When did you finally make contact with Con Kafentsis?'

'He phoned me a week ago and we arranged to meet at the café opposite the bus terminal at eleven the next day.'

'How did you feel about that?'

'Relieved.' I took a deep breath as I remembered. 'Because I could finally hand over the envelope and get on with my holiday. But I was also worried because he sounded creepy. Again, Marcus told me I was being paranoid.'

'Anything else?'

'I thought Con was a little abrupt over the phone, but I put that down to the language differences.'

'Then what happened?'

'I turned up the next day at the agreed time and Con showed up half an hour late.'

'He was probably watching you. Making sure you weren't with anyone else,' Angie piped up.

'Maybe. Anyway, I didn't recognise him from Athens, which was a good thing, but before I could discuss the contents of the envelope, Con's phone rang and he took off.'

Jack stopped drawing cubes on a blank sheet of paper and looked up. 'Didn't you think his behaviour was a bit odd?'

'Of course, but I don't know many Greek people. I didn't want to make assumptions about a person I didn't know.'

Jack nodded. 'What happened next?'

'I spoke to Marcus and told him I wasn't going to hang around for this bloke anymore. But then he said he'd pay off a significant chunk of my debt—'

'Go on.'

'Jack,' I resisted the urge to call him by his full name, Mr Ass. 'Would you please stop telling me to *go on*? I'm going on as fast as I can.'

'Sorry. Force of habit.'

'Let me see... I was nearly run over by a scooter—'

'Coincidence.'

'And the apartment was trashed—'

'Kids. Though you do seem to be a magnet for trouble, Claudia.'

I raised my eyebrows. 'You were watching me the whole time?' Jack looked away. 'And then Levi disappeared.'

Angie shook her head. 'When you put it all together, a lot has happened to you in the past few days. It does look rather suspicious.'

'Then you turn up in full CSI mode,' I said to Jack.

Jack checked his notes again. 'You said you saw Con in the crowd the other day?'

'I thought I saw him. I started to chase him. I even called out his name, but he didn't stop. So I texted him.'

I took a breath. 'Then I realised there was no point meeting up with him, I didn't have the envelope with me. You were there, Jack. You saw me trying to catch Con's attention a second time. If I'd been privy to a fiendish plan, do you really think I'd have tried to hook up with him while you were with me?'

'Maybe. It's not as if you knew who I really was.'

'No, you're right. I still don't.'

'Let's continue, shall we? What happened with Marcus?'

'By this stage, Marcus was snappy. He told me that Con was a busy man overseeing an enormous enterprise and that he'd come to the apartment when it suited him.'

'Then you met up with him this morning?'

I tried looking out the window.

'He came to your apartment this morning, Claudia,' Jack continued. 'I have the photographs to prove it. Are you saying you didn't invite him?'

'Hardly. I was still asleep when he turned up, hence the reason I'm looking so glamorous now.'

'You didn't prearrange the meeting this morning?' Jack raised one eyebrow. He might have been an arse, but his eyebrows were still fetching.

'I think Claudia's answered the question,' Angie said. 'She had no idea Con would show up at the apartment this morning.'

Jack nodded. 'Before we finish, is there anything else you'd like to add?'

I shook my head.

'Interview one completed at 1.54pm.' Jack pushed the stop button.

'Interview one? How many more interviews are there going to be? I've told you everything I know.'

'What happens now?' I asked Angie after Nina and Jack, armed with his crappy tape recorder, left the room.

'Not sure.'

Not the answer I was hoping for.

'I'll look around and see if I can find out anything more. It might take a while. You okay with that?' Angie squeezed my hand and walked out of the room.

I was left alone to think about the mess I'd gotten myself into – or rather, the mess Marcus had dropped me into, head first. Although all the evidence indicated that he was up to no good, I had trouble believing it. Marcus had always been so easy-going. He never seemed concerned about company finances; in fact he was a generous employer, sparing no expense at the end-of-year celebrations and always rewarding staff with overflowing festive hampers.

Okay, so he hadn't seemed so easy-going since I'd been over here, what with all the carry-on about the envelope. And now I knew why. Still, I couldn't believe he'd really treat me like this, allow me to get caught up in criminal activity. Because if I believed that, then I'd have no choice but to believe that Marcus had been using me the whole time. A humiliating thought.

Much later, Nina delivered some souvlakia, tzatziki, olive bread and a Diet Coke. I'd lost my appetite but forced myself to eat in case this was the last food I saw for a while.

Being in this godforsaken place was a mild form of torture. Perhaps they'd hidden a two-way mirror and Jackass was spying on me to see if I'd crack? I looked around, scrutinising each wall. There didn't seem to be a secret mirror anywhere. But then again, logic told me that if it were concealed, I wouldn't see it. What about a hidden camera? I searched the walls and concluded that it was highly unlikely I was being watched. But I decided against scratching my nose, just in case.

Where was Angie? She and Jack had hit it off right from the word go. Maybe they were getting to know each other better over an intimate airport lunch. Were they both laughing about me right now? Giggling about what a pathetic loser I was?

Just then, Angie appeared in the doorway with Jack.

'I'll leave you to it,' Jack said to Angie and closed the door behind him.

'Angie!' I snapped. 'Is it over? Can we leave now?'

'Not quite.' Angie dragged two chairs together and motioned for me to sit.

'What do you mean, *not quite*? I haven't bloody well done anything wrong.'

'The good news is I think Jack and the police believe you.' She hesitated. 'Or at least,' Angie qualified, 'they want to believe you... It's a start.'

'Who is Jack anyway? An undercover cop?'

'Private investigator.'

I shook my head. 'What's the bad news?'

'Although they've taken Marcus Cassoli into custody in Brisbane—'

I gulped.

'—the police over there haven't finished interviewing him. Jack has to wait to hear what Marcus says. Also, because the Greek authorities are involved, Jack doesn't have the power to release you. That's up to Nina, and she needs permission from their Australian counterparts.'

'Bloody hell.'

'It'll be okay.' Angie stroked my shoulder. 'It's obvious you were caught in the crossfire.'

I wasn't feeling confident. 'What about Con? What's he said?'

'Not a lot. The police over here have had their eye on him for ages. He's a known drug dealer, hacker, into money laundering—'

'Slowly,' I said. 'My head's still fuzzy.'

'Apparently the flash drive has a series of numbers embedded in it – a secret code, if you like – that has the information Con needs to transfer millions of dollars from several Australian bank accounts into Swiss ones. And using the Swiss bank-secrecy laws, Con could've simply turned himself into the invisible man. He already had mechanisms in place – shell corporations, numbered accounts, forged documents.'

'The perfect plan.'

'Theoretically. The irony is that Marcus trusted this swindler, but as it turns out, Con was trying to con Marcus. Marcus thought of Con as his money courier, with you as the go-between, but Con had much bigger plans. Marcus assumed that Con would remain honest and split the money. He had no idea who he was getting involved with.'

'But why did he trust Con in the first place?' I wondered out loud. 'It doesn't make sense.'

'Desperation. Marcus's business isn't as rock solid as it appears.'

'And me?' I asked Angie, dreading the answer.

'I'm afraid Marcus was going to pin it on you if things went wrong.'

I dropped my face into my hands and rubbed my eyes and cheeks. 'How the hell did I get caught up in this nightmare?' But I knew the answer. I'd been taken in by Marcus. I'd believed him when he said he cared about me and wanted to help. He'd been so easy to trust. It never occurred to me that Marcus's business dealings were anything but above board.

'Whenever the office accounts didn't add up, I assumed it was because of my atrocious maths skills.'

'That's what Marcus wanted you to think.'

I shook my head. 'He let me off the hook and told me his accountants would deal with it. I'm a naive idiot, aren't I? And a lousy judge of character.'

'Perhaps you're an optimist who sees the best in people.'

That was one way of looking at it.

'It's going to be fine.' Angie's tone was how I imagined a psychiatrist might sound trying to coax a deranged person off a twenty-metre window ledge. 'We'll all be laughing about this in a few hours' time. Jack knows it's a mistake.'

'It's more than a mistake. I really thought Jack was becoming a friend. To find out he was using me all along…'

'I don't think—'

I held up my hand. 'It's the sorry story of my life. All the men I've known have used me in one way or another. Thanks for being here today, Angie. It's funny, the first time I met you, I thought you liked Jack.'

'As in wanted to shag him?'

'Something like that.'

'Whatever gave you that idea? I don't, by the way.'

'No, I know. Just me being suspicious. I thought Jack was too good to be true. Turns out, he is.'

Angie pulled me into a hug.

'None of this is your fault, Claudia,' she said when she let me go. 'How were you to know what Marcus and Con were up to?'

I shook my head. 'I can explain about Marc—'

'You don't have to. It's none of my business. I'm sure you had your reasons.'

Did I? Did I have a reason for sleeping with Marcus, or did I just do it because it felt good when he paid attention to me? Because I felt special when Marcus paused for an extra couple of minutes in my office every morning when he did his rounds?

'So the memory stick held a code?' I asked.

'Yeah, and once accessed, vast sums of money could have

been drained from the company's bank accounts, including overdraft facilities which ran into the millions.'

'And I was the one who almost made it all possible?'

'Unfortunately, that's exactly what Jack thought.'

Moments later, the doorknob turned, and in he walked. 'Claudia,' Jack said, putting his hand on my shoulder, 'you're free to go.'

Thank goodness. I couldn't believe it. I shrugged off his hand. 'You mean it's over?'

'Not quite.'

He had to rain on my parade.

'We'll print out a transcript of your interview and I'll need you to sign it tomorrow. We'll also need you present at Marcus Cassoli's hearing in Brisbane later this year.'

'Sure.' Whatever. I wanted to get out of there, go back to the apartment and have a shower. 'Just one thing, Jack – they won't be coming after me because I dobbed, will they?'

'Who?'

'Con and his mates.'

'Doubt it. Con's on his way to Athens. He's going to be busy for the next seven to ten years. You don't have to worry about him.'

'And Marcus?'

'Marcus will also be busy.'

I nodded and walked towards the door with my head held high and Angie beside me.

'Claudia,' Jack called out. 'You'll need to repay the twenty thousand dollars as soon as you land in Australia.'

Excellent. Financial Armageddon.

Part of me wanted to ask why Jack had lied to me, why he hadn't simply asked me about all this before it got out of hand. But I couldn't face him a moment longer.

I was over it.

And over him.

I walked out the door, still feeling wretched. Of course the holiday had been too good to be true. Even though I'd had an affair with Marcus, a free European holiday was an extravagant pay-off. Not to mention the money. He'd never cared for me at all, he'd just been using me. The same with Jack bloody Harper. What was it with men and me?

CHAPTER 31

*I*t was close to five by the time we arrived back at the apartment. I vacillated between tears and blind rage; there were so many things I was upset about I didn't know where to begin.

Firstly, I was furious with myself for allowing Marcus to use me for his sinister ends. None of this would have happened had I not slept with him. And then to find out there were other women as well! Still, I couldn't help feeling shocked that Marcus would do something like this. He might have been a faithless jerk, but I wouldn't have picked him as a criminal with international connections. Would Marcus really have let me take the rap for this? Apparently so.

'Claudia, it happens a lot more than you'd think, sweetheart,' Angie said as we sat on the terrace with Sophie and Tara some time later.

'That makes me feel *so* much better.' Obviously, there were a hell of a lot of idiots like me in the world. Not a comforting thought.

'You couldn't have known,' Tara said.

'Yes I could. You told me I was getting into serious shit, but I didn't listen.'

'There's one thing I don't get,' Sophie said, twirling her ringlets in contemplation. 'Angie said that you'll have to pay back the thousands of dollars Marcus gave you. Why'd he give you so much money in the first place?'

Tara and Angie looked at me and then uncomfortably at each other but said nothing.

'I'll see what the boys are up to,' Angie said finally.

'I'll join you,' Tara said, and they disappeared inside.

'Sophie—'

'What is it?' Sophie squeezed my hand.

I couldn't believe I was about to destroy her faith in me again.

'I slept with Marcus.'

'No,' she started.

'I did.'

'What? You're kidding? He's married, for God's sake.' She practically spat out the words.

'Separated.'

'Do you love him? Did you intend becoming his second wife?'

'No. I don't know. I was confused.'

My answer seemed to infuriate her further. 'If you weren't in love with him, why the hell would you do it? Why would you play with people's lives that way? His wife? Their children?'

'It wasn't like that, I promise. I had no intention of going to bed with him, but he was so kind and sympathetic about all the stuff with George...'

Sophie rolled her eyes.

'Okay.' I put my hands up. 'It was inexcusable.' I slept with a married man. End of story. No matter how much I tried to reason why, I couldn't. My morals were in the gutter. Marcus didn't force me. He didn't declare his undying love for me. Neither of us did.

Sophie was seething. 'It was just something you did to pass the time?'

'It wasn't that either. I like – liked – Marcus, a lot.'

'The fact that this man had a wife and children didn't matter?'

I didn't answer. How many times could I tell her Marcus was separated? Besides, it was beginning to sound lame even to me.

'How can I compete when there are women like you, waiting to pounce on every married man who comes along? Women like you, who are funny and charming and don't have to worry about doing the laundry or grocery shopping?'

'This isn't about you, Sophie.'

'Of course it's about me. It's about every married woman who's cheated on by their husbands with single women who don't give a damn about anyone but themselves. They think they're so goddamn special.'

'I'm not special.'

'You got that right,' Sophie fumed. 'You're a walking cliché!'

I shook my head. An affair was only a cliché until you were smack bang in the middle of it, living the lie every day.

Sophie wasn't finished. 'You're a disgrace, Claudia.'

'I'm so sorry,' was all I could manage.

'It's not me you should be apologising to.' With that, Sophie turned and walked inside.

I thought about following her, but I couldn't face another scene. Maybe after she'd had time to think, she'd calm down. And as angry as she was with me, I was even angrier with myself. I knew what I'd done with Marcus was wrong.

'That went well,' Tara said when she and Angie walked back outside.

'Where is she?'

'In her bedroom.'

'What am I going to do?'

'She's in shock. Give her time,' Angie suggested.

Tara wrapped her arms around me. 'God, you get yourself into some situations.'

'I know. I'm sorry for dragging you into this mess. I keep going over everything again and again. My brain won't let it rest. I know that sleeping with Marcus was selfish and I have no one to blame but myself. And I know he used me to get to Con—'

'I doubt Marcus knew how far Con's criminal tentacles stretched,' Angie said. 'Jack thinks Marcus was duped into believing Con was the answer to all his financial worries.'

'And he had me to pin it on if things went wrong.' I closed my eyes and shook my head. 'I can't forgive myself for putting you guys in danger.'

'We were never in danger,' Tara said. 'It was our overactive imaginations.'

Just then, Sophie walked outside. I got up out of my chair and walked over to her. 'I'm so sorry, Soph.'

'So am I.' Sophie sighed. 'You thought he was separated. It happens.'

'Thanks, but I had no business sleeping with him.'

'It takes two. Anyway, how are you feeling? About Jack?'

I burst into tears. Jack! I couldn't get over the fact that he'd used me as well. He'd been following me since Brisbane airport, maybe even before.

'Jack never liked me,' I said coldly. 'He never fancied me.'

Sophie shook her head. 'I really do think he liked you.'

'Whenever the two of you were together, he did seem attentive,' Tara observed.

'He was fucking attentive, all right,' I yelled, finding my fury and pushing away the almond cake Angie had given me. 'He was pumping me for information. That's all he cared about. It wasn't a coincidence we met in Brisbane, or in Athens, or again in Santorini. How dumb am I? Why couldn't I see he was following me? I was vital to his investigation. Prick. Pratt. Pig face.'

The three of them sat there, mouths open, staring at me.

'Feeling better?' Tara said finally.

'Yes, actually.' I blew my nose and wiped away my tears. 'I swear, as God is my witness,' I crossed my heart, 'I will never have another boyfriend! I'm going to become a nun.'

'Now, now,' Sophie said.

'Why not? My life's fucked anyway.'

Sophie knew better than to try to reason with me.

'He fooled us as well,' Tara said. 'Men, hey?'

'All this time he was just stringing me along. Doing his job.' I was so furious, spittle flew out my mouth. 'I was part of his investigation.' I stopped as the memory of Jack's legs entwined with mine hit me full force, then screamed, 'Which makes the fact that he slept with me an absolute disgrace!'

I was exhausted and ashamed. I wanted to go home to Tara's cosy little terrace on the other side of the world and hide from everyone for a month, a year – longer if I could. Who cared that I was destined to end up wearing Sophie's knitting, surrounded by cats? I'd had enough. I was defeated. I never ever wanted to think about Jack Harper again.

'Have you done a poo today, Mummy?' Levi asked Sophie when she and I walked back inside to check on the boys. Sophie pretended she didn't hear him. He followed us into the kitchen where we retrieved two enormous chocolate blocks from the fridge.

'Poo? Did you do a poo, Mum?'

'Levi, I really don't want to talk about this right now.'

'Mine was huge. The biggest poo I've eber done. Bigger than

a dragon's. I watched it swirl down the toilet. Now Harry's doing one and I'm watching him. We neeb toilet paper.'

Sophie retrieved a roll from the kitchen cupboard. 'I really don't want to know.'

As we walked out of the kitchen, Levi ran ahead to the bathroom, presumably to check on the state of Harry's bowels. Then I noticed Sophie's wide-open jaw. 'You okay?'

'There,' Sophie said quietly, pointing out to the terrace. I looked. Tara and Angie were locked in a passionate embrace. It was a sweet, intimate moment and I felt as though we were intruding.

I turned a very rigid Sophie around and marched her back towards the kitchen.

'What was that about?' she exploded, moments later.

'Well, they evidently like each other.' I paused. 'A lot.'

'But how? When? Where? When did all this happen?'

'A few nights ago,' came a voice from around the corner. Tara helped herself to a piece of chocolate, then wrapped her arms around us. 'Isn't it great? I think I'm falling in love.'

As she twirled back out to the patio, Sophie and I peeked outside. Angie wasn't there but there were voices coming from the bathroom. Angie was on toilet duty. Sophie and I saw our chance and ran out onto the terrace with our chocolate.

'This is where your inspiration sprang from?' I squealed to Tara, hugging her. 'Angie!'

'I'm stunned.' Sophie dropped the chocolate onto the table and flopped into a deckchair.

I lunged at Angie when she rejoined us. 'I can't believe you kept this from us. Spill!'

'We wanted to tell you,' Tara said, holding Angie's hand, 'But what with Levi disappearing yesterday and your arrest today, Claud—'

'Apparently I wasn't arrested,' I corrected. 'I was detained.' I'd momentarily forgotten about the whole humiliating debacle. 'Anyway, enough about me, tell us about you two.'

'I knew Angie was special as soon as we met,' Tara admitted.

Angie smiled. 'Same.'

'Those first few days when we all hung out together with Harry and Levi, we just clicked.'

'Obviously.'

'Then that night after the beach, after you left, Soph, we kissed.'

'I had no idea,' I said.

'I thought you might have guessed something was up when I didn't come home,' Tara said.

Sophie and I looked at each other and I slapped Tara's arm. 'We had no idea you didn't come home.'

'You didn't come home?' Sophie said. 'At all?' Sophie's jaw was still lying rigid on the floor.

'Nope. After we put Harry to bed, we stayed up all night talking, kissing...'

'Making plans,' Angie continued.

'Plans?' I repeated, raising my eyebrows.

'Well, we have to do something,' Tara said excitedly. 'Angie lives in London, I'm in Brisbane. We have to sort it out, and pretty damn quickly.' Tara seemed so together, so relaxed. 'Kissing Angie's the best thing I've ever done. You know when we kissed, the earth really did move.'

Angie swooned. 'My heart was laid bare.'

Tara wrapped her arms around Angie and together they danced on the patio.

They were happy and I was happy for them, truly. But a part of me couldn't believe Tara had fallen for a woman who lived on the other side of the world. Now I knew how parents felt when their child waltzed into the family home one day and, seduced by fantasies of bright lights, fame and fortune, announced that they were leaving boring Brisbane and moving overseas.

Tara couldn't leave me. We'd been a team for too long. She was my *plus one*.

CHAPTER 32

For a split second when I woke up the next morning, I was happy. Thrilled for Tara and Angie. Thrilled to be on holidays in beautiful Santorini. Thrilled to have met Jack.

Jack. Suddenly I remembered everything, and my happiness evaporated. I couldn't believe a holiday that had started out so well could end so sadly. All I wanted was to go home. I couldn't enjoy it here anymore. I didn't even want to try.

Why had I thought Jack liked me? Hadn't I learnt anything from George and Marcus and the rest of them? Men were not to be trusted! Ever!

'Fucking prick. I hate you!' I shouted.

'Claud,' Sophie gasped, flinging open my bedroom door. 'Are you okay?'

'No, I'm not. I'm a loser. I used to joke about people like me. Now the joke's on me. T-shirts across the globe will be printed with my face – Claudia Marie Taylor, ultimate loser.'

Sophie sat down beside me on the bed. 'You'll get through this.'

'Unlikely. I can't ever show my face in public again. I'm an imbecile, nitwit, moron, dimwit, jerk, fool, simpleton, dunce, dolt.'

'You forgot idiot.'

'Thank you. Idiot.'

'Okay, I get the picture, but don't you think we've all felt like that before?'

'Once, maybe, but with me it's every couple of days.'

'So you were caught handing over illegal papers. It's not the end of the world. I know your heart's broken, and I'm truly sorry about that, but whatever's happened, it doesn't make you any less the great person you were yesterday or the day before.' Sophie kissed me on the cheek. 'We'll get through this together. You, me and Tara, if you let us. Except, of course, when you're in the loo, or the shower. With all that's happened with Tara, I want you to know that this is purely a best friend thing.'

And I thought I was paranoid.

'Oh, Sophie, and here I was thinking you were wanting to share my firstborn!'

Sophie grinned. 'Are you sure you're okay?'

'Yeah, I just need to be by myself for a while, but before that, I want to say how truly sorry I am about sleeping with Marcus—'

'It's none of my business. You're both adults. I had no right to react the way I did or to tell you how you should live your life.'

Sophie left and I stayed in bed until I heard them leave the apartment. When all was quiet, I slipped out of the bedroom. It felt good to have some time alone and pad about the place in my pyjamas. Eating a bowl of yogurt, I walked outside and squinted out across the Mediterranean. It was a sunny, wind-free, very pleasant twenty-seven degrees. Maybe my life wasn't too shabby. I had two amazing best friends and a very cute, if poo-obsessed, godson. I could survive without Jack Harper and I bloody well would.

But just then Jack walked down the stairs and onto the patio. 'Hope I'm not interrupting?'

I couldn't believe it.

'Jack,' I said coolly. When would this nightmare end? And when would he realise that it was impolite to walk in on a lady who was not yet dressed for the day? Jack Harper had no holiday etiquette. 'I can't talk to you now. Please leave.'

'I will, but I need you to sign the transcripts from yesterday.' He gave me the once-over as he handed me several pieces of paper. 'Nice pyjamas.'

'You disgust me. Do you have to wait? Can't I send these to you?'

'No, I need them today.'

I ignored him and began reading. As I did, Jack tried explaining his inexcusable actions.

'I'm sorry,' he started.

'You had a job to do, Jack.' Arsehole.

'Thanks for understanding.'

'That's where you're wrong.' I got up and poked him in the chest. 'I don't understand at all.' However, it was hard to be superior whilst dressed in pink satin. I backed away and headed inside to change, hoping he'd do the decent thing and leave.

Ten minutes later he was still on the terrace.

'So, you're a private investigator, not an engineer?'

'Did you have your heart set on an engineer?'

'Excuse me?'

Jack managed a weak smile. 'Marcus's wife, Trish, hired me initially. She knew about some of his affairs, and that the business wasn't going as well as he made out. With a divorce looming, she wanted to get the financial side of things squared off. There were dodgy transactions going on. And most of them were heading to bank accounts in Switzerland. But the USB flash drive was the real biggie.'

I glared at him, wishing he'd leave but also keen to hear the full story.

'The papers in the envelope were actually a furphy. The flash drive was what Con needed. The deal was he'd hack into the nominated Australian accounts and transfer vast sums of money out of Australia into several Swiss bank accounts. Of course, once Con had the code, he was going to snatch everything for himself. I don't know why Marcus couldn't see that, but then his business was going down the tube. He was desperate. I guess he thought he had no choice other than to trust a criminal. Desperate and stupid.' Jack took a deep breath. 'Had the transaction gone through, Trish would've been left with nothing.'

I felt ill.

'Claudia, can't you see why we thought you were involved in the scam? There were a few nights there when you and Marcus were the only ones who stayed back after everyone else had gone home.'

'You were watching me in Brisbane?'

'No. What I mean is my company had the building under surveillance. We'd been monitoring Marcus for five months. According to our notes, you were usually out the door at five, sometimes earlier.'

That *was* true. 'Yes, but—' But what? Those nights I worked back late I was bonking Marcus? I knew it. Jack knew it.

'Think about how it looked from our point of view. Next thing we know, you're booked on a flight to Athens. We suspected you were carrying something. We had to notify the Australian police, who in turn related the information to their Greek counterparts.'

'Why didn't you just tell me who you were and ask me for the envelope? I'd have given it to you.'

Jack put his hand underneath my chin and raised my head, so I was forced to look into his attractive brown eyes. 'I thought about it. When we went up to Oia that day, I was going to ask, but then you hurt your foot and the moment passed. Then, while you were chasing Con a couple of days later when we were at lunch, I got word that twenty thousand dollars had been transferred into your bank account.'

'I can see how that might look a little—'

'Suspicious?'

I nodded.

'I wanted to tell you who I was and what I was doing. When I first saw you at the airport, I thought you were cool. But I couldn't jeopardise the operation.'

What dickhead says *cool* anymore? It was so twentieth century.

'Besides, I had to stick to the facts. You were a suspect.'

'A suspect you slept with?'

'That was before I knew about the money—'

'Very unprofessional.'

'Yes, I'll admit I got too close to you. It was definitely the wrong thing to do.'

He was the jackass after all. There was nothing personal about this. Anymore. 'Do you sleep with all your suspects?'

'Of course not! Do you sleep with all your bosses?'

I glared at him.

'Claudia, as I got to know you, I realised you couldn't possibly be involved, and by then I'd started to fall for you – really fall for you. When I found out about the money transfer, I didn't know what to think. It seemed like I'd totally misjudged you.'

'How did you know about the money?'

'Australian police were monitoring Marcus's accounts.'

We sat in silence for a good minute before Jack spoke again. 'Claudia, I'm sorry, but can't you see this wasn't about you? Or about Marcus for that matter, although I am sure Trish will be very pleased. It's about Con Kafentsis.'

I gave Jack one of his *go on* looks.

'Once we notified the Greek police we were looking for Kafentsis, they filled me in. Con's been involved in this sort of thing for years. But the wheels of justice take a bit longer to turn over here. They'd only come on board the day before we caught you handing over the envelope to Con. And now they've finally got the hard evidence needed to put him away.' Jack puffed himself up and continued without my prompting.

'From what I know of Marcus and my conversations with the Queensland police since his arrest, he's a white-collar criminal. He had no idea who he was dealing with. He's a complete amateur. He'll crumble quickly and cooperate to save his own skin. Most importantly, he'll give the cops the information they need to put Con away for a very long time.'

'So Con doesn't make the best olive oils and organic wines in Greece?'

'Afraid not. He makes shabby oil as part of an elaborate business front for his illegal operations.'

'Good on you,' I said with all the sarcasm I could muster. 'Your mother must be very proud. Country boy from Yackandandah makes good.'

'That part of it is true, I swear.'

'You also told me you were an engineer.'

'I never said I was an engineer. I told you I *studied* engineering at university.'

'You deliberately lied to me?'

'No. You didn't ask the right questions.'

'Jack, you wouldn't have told me the truth even if I'd asked.'

'I might have.'

'What? Are you here on holidays?'

'Well, no. On that front I'll admit I was being economical with the truth. But I really am an investigator.'

Big deal. 'I'm sorry we didn't meet under better circumstances,' I said graciously.

I lowered my eyes and read the rest of the transcript. On paper, I sounded like a five-year-old. Talk about stranger danger. I had no idea.

'It's not too late, is it?' Jack asked.

Was he trying to sweet-talk me? Lure me back to the cot for one more romp before departing Santorini's shores? I might not have had a lot of dignity where Jack was concerned, but I was doing my best to salvage some self-respect.

'How dare you! I was a suspect you slept with to get information.'

'I told you, sleeping with you was never part of the investigation. By then I'd fallen for you and wanted to be with you. I—'

'Get out, Jack.'

I threw the signed papers at him and went back inside the apartment, locking the door behind me. I watched from my bedroom window as he walked away. No doubt there were other ladies on the island who'd succumb to his charms. The day was young. If he hurried, he could bed at least a couple before sundown.

I allowed myself another ten minutes to wallow before mentally slapping myself and pulling on sensible walking shoes. (I took Tara's Birkenstocks from her room.)

Then I was out the door and heading towards Oia. I trekked up the narrow path that overlooked the cliffs. At one particularly hairy point along the way, I stared out across the perfect sapphire sky and the turquoise ocean. Moving as close to the edge of the cliff as I could, I looked down and threw pebbles over the precipice, one by one. I watched as they bounced against the cliff face and into the ocean. Maybe if I threw myself off, my death would be quick and painless.

On the other hand, knowing my luck, I'd survive the fall and be left with hideous injuries... scarred for life and feeling even sorrier for myself than I already did.

CHAPTER 33

*A*fter the drama of the last couple of days, Sophie didn't hesitate when Marcella offered to babysit so we could have a child-free dinner in Fira. You'd have thought Marcella would have kicked us out by now, but no, she was a real champ and took my cavorting with a felon in her stride.

'Clow-di-ah,' she said. 'It's very, how do you say, *exciting*? Neighbours are talking.' Marcella was delighted at being the centre of attention and able to regale the neighbours with her on-the-spot account of what had happened. Apparently, my detainment was the most gripping entertainment since a tourist had fallen into the volcano the previous summer. At least our visit to Santorini wouldn't be forgotten in a hurry.

'How many broken bones do you reckon you'd get if you went over the cliff?' I asked Tara and Sophie as we walked into Fira for dinner.

'Depends on whether you took a running leap and flung yourself over, or whether you just sort of fell,' Sophie said.

'I think you'd get more injuries if you ran off,' Tara said.

'Really? I've thought about this at length,' Sophie said, 'and I think you'd have fewer breakages if you took a running leap because there's every chance you'd end up in the water.'

'As opposed to bonking yourself against the cliff numerous times on the way down if you just fell off?' I asked.

'You'd probably break most of your bones,' Tara agreed.

'Probably best not to do it, then,' I said.

The others nodded in agreement. Still, it was comforting to know that my best friends thought about flinging themselves off cliffs during their dark moments. It made me feel less like a freak.

'Who'd have thought it?' Tara said, taking a long sip of her Santorini Sling. 'This holiday has completely changed my life, my outlook, my... everything. Thanks for dragging me along, Claud.'

'You're welcome.' I smiled to hide my pain. 'Not only are your words flowing, but you've fallen in love.'

Tara's life had changed for the better. Mine, on the other hand, was swirling further and further down a filthy stinking toilet bowl. What did I have to go back to? I had to give back the twenty thousand, for a start. That would hurt – a lot. And I'd still have the bank manager breathing down my neck. He'd have a conniption when I became suddenly unemployed. I had no idea what would happen to Cassoli Imports now Marcus had been arrested. Who'd be in charge? And what about my living arrangements... would Angie and Harry emigrate and move into Tara's house? If they did, there'd be no room for me. I guess I could (at a pinch) live with Mum and Dad. Plenty of thirty-somethings did that these days. But I couldn't see myself handling it for long. The more I thought about what a mess my life was, the more depressed I became.

'I never thought of you as being gay,' Sophie said to Tara once we were settled.

'Neither did I,' I said, 'I know there was Jules—'

'But everyone experiments,' Sophie said.

'I've never kissed a girl before,' I said. 'Neither have you, Soph.'

'That's not strictly true,' Sophie said. 'Remember that time when we didn't speak for six months?'

'We were kids,' Tara said dismissively.

I nodded.

'Well, Tara and I kissed. There, I've said it,' Sophie said breathlessly.

'Sophie!' Tara squealed.

'You did not!' I yelled. 'Why have you never told me? What happened?'

'I can't remember,' Tara said.

Sophie shook her head. 'Thanks a lot.'

'Okay, I do remember. I just don't want to make a big deal about it. It was the middle of winter, freezing cold and raining—'

'And we were at your house,' Sophie continued. 'Listening to Madonna, and you said she was so gorgeous you could imagine kissing her—'

'And you said, "I wonder what it would feel like to kiss a girl."'

'Because I'd just broken up with Craig.'

'Then we sort of kissed,' Tara said.

'And I remember thinking how soft your lips felt.'

'Hello! Why wasn't I told?' I shouted over the top of them.

Both Sophie and Tara shrugged.

'And more importantly, why didn't either of you try to pash me? Am I so unattractive?'

Tara laughed. 'Yep. That's the reason.'

'I take it romance didn't blossom between you two?'

'Soph went back to boys.'

Sophie punched her on the arm. 'And you went back to having the hots for the PE teacher.'

'Okay, so let's clear it up once and for all,' I said. 'Sophie was the first girl you kissed?'

Tara nodded.

'And you're falling in love with Angie?'

Again, Tara nodded.

'Really?' I asked.

'Claudia, why is it so hard for you to believe?'

'Because you and I are a team, Tars. We've always had disastrous relationships—'

'Thanks a lot.'

'—and each other to fall back on. Now there'll be just me.'

'I'm sorry, darl, but I do think Angie's the one.'

I sighed. 'And that's why your writing's taken off?'

'Exactly. It's like I've been repressing part of myself. But once I set myself free and allowed Angie in, the words began to flow. I'm so grateful, thankful and—'

'Don't tell us,' Sophie and I said in unison. 'HAPPY!'

'What happens now?' Sophie asked after we'd all calmed down.

Tara thought for a moment. 'Angie and I want to be together, and because she has Harry, it makes more sense for me to move. Eventually, that is... if things work out between us.'

I gasped. 'What? Leave Australia? You've only known her a few days.'

'I know what I want,' Tara said firmly. 'At least I think I do. In fact, after we leave here, I'm going back to the UK with Angie for a couple of weeks. She wants to show me her home.'

'Then what?' I asked, hardly believing what I was hearing. 'What about your job? Your house? Your life?' I was trying not to sound selfish, but Tara was all I had. Plus, I was living with her.

If she moved overseas, she'd want to sell her house or at least rent it out to people who could afford to pay her the going market rate.

'I've called Melinda and resigned over the phone.'

'No!'

'Yes, and she's given me an extra two weeks' holiday "to think things through". So I've taken her up on her offer. But when I go back home, I'll resign permanently. After I tie-up other loose ends, hopefully I'll be back over with Angie and Harry within a couple of months. Then we'll see if we still feel the same way about each other. But I have a good feeling about us. I'm seriously hopeful.'

This was moving way too fast. Surely Tara hadn't fully thought this through. 'But how can you both be so sure about your feelings after such a short time?'

'I can't. There are no guarantees. But I'm willing to give it a shot.'

I didn't like the sound of that. It implied she'd made up her mind.

'I'll also have to tell my parents.'

Okay, she'd definitely made up her mind. 'The good news is you're probably too old for them to try another intervention,' I said.

'It's my life. They'll have to deal with it. And if they can't, too bad. Now I've met Angie, I feel at peace, like it's all coming together for me. I can finally see my way forward.' Tara took a sip of wine. 'Still, what if Angie gets back home and realises it's a mistake... that I was only a holiday diversion?'

'She won't, Tara,' Sophie said. 'Besides, she's probably thinking the same thing about you. Only it's worse for her.'

'How so?'

'Because Angie's got Harry to consider. She's probably wondering why you'd take her on when she comes with a child as well as all the everyday crappy baggage all of us carry around.'

Tara looked out across the Santorini sky. 'Because I think I could really love her, and Harry too.'

'You're so ready for this, aren't you?' I said. 'All the other would-be Angies never worked out because the timing wasn't right.'

Tara reflected for a moment. 'Yeah, I was scared before I met Angie. Scared because I couldn't seem to make a go of it with men and I didn't know why. Aside from the obvious.'

'Which is?' Sophie asked.

'I don't find them remotely attractive,' Tara answered. 'I'm not saying that a few of them aren't appealing, I just don't want to see all their bits. They don't interest me. But some part of me still wanted to believe I was hetero.' Tara shrugged. 'Truth is, women have always made my head turn.'

'Can't say I've ever felt like that,' Sophie chimed in, then smiled at Tara and blew her a kiss.

'Now that I've made peace with myself and accepted that I want to be with Angie, I can actually see the two of us in our old age, sitting on the porch together, holding hands and drinking cups of tea.'

'Who's going to share my verandah?' I wondered out loud.

Tara and Sophie wrapped their arms around me but didn't answer the question. I didn't expect them to. They're not psychics.

We clinked glasses and toasted Tara and Angie and the magnificent Santorini sunset.

'Let's face it,' Tara continued, 'most men are idiots.'

It was a hard fact to argue with, but Sophie gave it a shot. 'There have to be some decent guys in the world. Alex and Levi for starters.'

'True, but I deserved to fall in love with a woman,' Tara said triumphantly. 'I deserved it.'

Who was I to argue with her? I was going to be celibate for the rest of my life. Penises, breasts, butts, eyebrows, none of the physical attributes meant anything to me anymore. I'd embarked on a higher level of life – spiritual freedom.

'Now I'm sorted,' Tara said, 'what are we going to do about you, Claudia?'

Avoiding eye contact, I picked at invisible fluff on my jeans.

'Come on. You're in debt up to your eyeballs and yet you continue to spend money like a Kardashian.'

'Not that we don't love your gorgeous gifts,' Sophie said. 'But you're too generous.'

'When I shop, I feel better about myself. It's my way of telling people I love them,' I confessed.

'We love you too,' Tara said. 'But—'

'I don't need to buy people's affection?'

'Exactly. If you keep going the way you are, you'll be trapped by debt forever.'

'What should I do?'

'Let's work out a realistic budget, one you can stick to,' Sophie said.

'That means only buying essentials, right?'

'Right. No more gift-giving,' Tara said. 'And no more credit cards. And definitely no more internet shopping when you're bored.'

I groaned.

'You have to get rid of your debts, hon,' Sophie said. 'It won't be too bad, you'll see.'

No, I thought, *it won't be bad, it'll be hell. Walking past a shoe shop and not buying a pair, using Olay instead of Clinique, no more Dior lipsticks or impulse buys for friends...* 'What about—' I started.

'No!' They shouted me down before I could finish my question.

Bloody hell! In times of crisis, everyone splashes out on a pair of outrageously high sandals with no real intention of wearing them, don't they? And what about that new miracle body toner, the Power Plate? (Apparently, it involved standing on a vibrating plate and performing exercises while jiggling up and down.) I had my heart set on buying one when I got back home. Okay, so I'd have to rethink a few expenses...

CHAPTER 34

*O*ur second-last day on Santorini. How did I want to spend it? I'd already travelled extensively around the island and had my favourite restaurants and bars. I'd become quite fond of a Greek salad with every meal; I particularly liked the way the feta cheese was served as a slab on top of the lettuce, not cut into a hundred pieces as it was back home.

But I didn't feel like eating at another café. I liked to believe this was because I was now adhering to a very strict budget and not because I was afraid of bumping into Jack.

I wasn't even sure he was still on the island. He was probably in Athens, or en route to Australia preparing for his next big case. Liar that he was. Deceiver, swindler, imposter. Hang on, I was getting him mixed up with Marcus. Marcus was the swindler. Jack was the deceiver and imposter.

I decided only to leave the apartment to venture to the pool. That way there'd be no temptation to spend money. I was more than ready to use my remaining time in Santorini working on a killer tan, swimming laps and reading magazines. But for now, I was happy to lie in bed a bit longer.

I was done with the whole self-analysis thing. I didn't want to think about me anymore. I knew I was going home to a dire situation, especially if Tara decided to swap countries and live with Angie. And I wouldn't be able to shop my way out of missing her as I had no choice but to cut back on all areas of spending to pay back the twenty grand. It wasn't like I desperately needed new accessories and trinkets. Shopping was a habit with me, a comfort when everything else in my life was going wrong. I'd have to find a better way to feel good though, because Tara, Sophie and I had worked out a spending plan for me. I'd be living frugally for a few years. But there was light at the end of the wretched tunnel.

It helped that I wasn't going to be playing the dating game anymore. I'd have no one to dress up or wear make-up for, and eating out was a no-no. You could take your eligible bachelors and your not-so-eligible married, divorced and separated men, and push them into the nearby volcano for all I cared. I wasn't interested. I was going to enjoy a celibate life. In fact, I was looking forward to it. And not because I had to, but because I wanted to.

I was confident my new lifestyle would suit me fine, because, let's face it, the alternative had never been kind. A whole new world was about to open before me, one which involved my touring the globe giving lectures on how to maintain celibacy without losing your mind. *Hello, my name is Claudia Taylor and I am celibate. It's been three years, two months, six days and four hours since my last bonk.* Raucous clapping.

I was lying in bed, in my underwear, congratulating myself on being the worldwide spokesperson for celibacy, when Tara rushed in.

'Ooya!' I jumped. 'Ever heard of knocking?'

'No time for that, missy,' Tara whispered and quickly shut the door behind her before plonking herself down on my bed. 'I went downstairs, and guess who's here?'

'God! Not Jack again?' I said, pulling back the sheets in preparation for getting out of bed.

'Jack?' Tara raised her brows. 'No, it's not Jack.'

'Who then?'

'Alex.'

'Alex? Here? Now? For God's sake, woman, why aren't you perched at the top of the stairs listening to their conversation?'

'Because that, my snoopy friend, would be really rude.'

'Rude, schmood! It's never stopped you before.'

'Has too.'

'Has not.' I put my hand up to stop the conversation from getting puerile. 'Did you speak to him?'

'I sort of spluttered out a big "Alex, lovely to see you" before Sophie shot me her death stare and I scurried up here to you.'

'What were they talking about?'

'I don't know if they were saying much at all. Levi was climbing all over Alex and they were doing that male rumbling, fighting for dominance, sort of thing.'

I raised my eyebrows. 'Playing?'

Tara wrinkled her nose. 'I guess you could call it that.'

'Get down there and listen in to what's going on. After all, you're Sophie's best friend.'

Tara glared at me. 'Me? What about you?'

'In mourning, Tara. I couldn't possibly concentrate. I'd be a waste of space. No, you run off and tape their conversation and I'll listen to it when I'm relaxing by the pool.'

'That's illegal—'

I got up out of bed. 'Snap to it. You're wasting valuable eavesdropping time. You know you want to.' I opened the door and started pushing her out of the room with my foot. 'Call it research.'

'No!' Tara put up more resistance than I'd anticipated.

'Tara! Go and sit on the stairs.' I raised my arm and pointed to the stairs. She didn't move. 'Go on. You've got everything. A great life, a wonderful girlfriend, and you have the ears for the job.' Nothing. 'Come on, do it for Sophie.'

'Do what for Sophie?' Sophie yelled out as she climbed the last stair at the top of the hallway.

'Sophie,' I squealed. 'Tara was telling me the great news.'

'Was she just?'

'What a nice surprise, Alex turning up.'

'Yes. Isn't it?' Sophie said through gritted teeth.

'Where is he now?' I asked.

'With Levi at the pool.'

Drat! There went my peaceful day slothing by the pool. 'Alex has made a huge effort, hasn't he?' I said as the three of us sat on my bed.

'What?' Sophie barked. 'Flying over for the last day? That's so typical of Alex. Impulsive. Doesn't think things through. Anyway, I don't want you two hiding up here all day. It's safe to come downstairs.'

I stayed in bed while Sophie showered. She was in there for what seemed like hours. Goodness knows what she was doing to herself. When she emerged, finally, Tara scuttled into the bathroom and another few 'hours' disappeared.

Once dressed, Sophie came up to say she was off to the pool to see Alex. 'Be brave and strong,' I said, hugging her and sending her on her way.

I wandered downstairs and retrieved the yogurt and honey from the fridge and poured a bit of both into my bowl. As was my holiday ritual, I meandered to the patio and ate my breakfast as I watched a new fleet of cruise ships make their way into the port. Cruise boats sailed in. Cruise boats sailed out. Rhythmic. Calming. Constant.

'Did you save me any, greedy?' Tara asked when she walked

out, one towel wrapped round her torso and another wrapped around her head in a turban.

'Um, a little,' I replied, suddenly feeling very greedy indeed. I made to stand.

'Don't bother. I'll get some later.' Tara sat down and gestured towards the pool. 'Any sign of them?'

'Nope.'

'Any noise? Screaming?'

'No. Very quiet. When are you seeing Angie again?'

'Soon. We're going off to one of the more remote beaches today.'

'Ooh,' I said, licking my spoon. 'To do a spot of nude bathing?'

'Do you mind? Harry will be with us.'

'Still, I'm sure there'll be a bit of time for groping and fondling, won't there?' I winked.

'Seriously, you need to talk to someone.'

'What? You know you want to.'

'Claudia, take a cold shower, girl.'

'I guess I'll have to after the amount of time you and Sophie spent in there this morning.'

CHAPTER 35

*Y*awning, I stepped inside the cubicle. Nothing like a long hot soak to recharge the energy. I turned on the taps, but the water was lukewarm.

I was out within two minutes, ready to unleash my fury on Tara. But she'd already taken off. Must have heard my shrieking and fled. I put on swimmers and covered up with a hand-painted sarong I'd bought at a Fira market stall – before budget constrictions had kicked in.

What to do now? I could stroll the streets of Fira and pick up a few last-minute pressies, but I'd already bought too many and my baggage limit was blown. Besides, I was determined to stick to the plan and get rid of this bloody debt, legally.

Another option was to head down to the pool as I'd originally intended, but that would mean talking to Sophie and Alex and possibly interrupting their heart to heart. I grabbed a handful of dark chocolate from the fridge, made a cup of tea and snatched several magazines from the dining table. Magical option number three. Eat chocolate, drink tea, read magazines, browse Instagram and check out the catfights on Twitter on the patio.

'Excellent,' I said to myself as I settled down for some serious reading. What a good idea! I was more than enough company for myself. Celibacy would be a cinch.

Amazing weight loss! Amazing weight gain! We tell you what the stars don't want you to know. I devoured page after page of photos and quotes from 'friends' spilling the beans on diet secrets of the stars. Kim Kardashian slurps on watercress soup; Ivanka only drinks bancha-twig tea (when she's not guzzling Red Bull and vodka). These people were all insane. How did kids today have a hope in hell of eating normally?

Excuse me. Did I just say *kids*? Yes, I think I did.

I'd crossed the line. I was officially middle-aged. Fancy me, of all people, talking about balanced lifestyles. What had I become? I was a tut-tutter. I was turning into one of those people who rang the police at ten in the evening to complain about the neighbour's music being too loud. I used to be the one with the loud music, the loud parties, the loud life!

I used to be the tut-tuttee!

I'd morphed into my mother, except I was twenty-five years younger and didn't sport a pink rinse. Next, I'd be watching the weather channel and listening to elevator music.

While Sophie was slugging it out with her man and Tara was getting it on with her woman, I was fretting over the way kids today were doomed because of celebrities and their bizarre obsession with looking like lollipops. What had celibacy done to me? Would I ever be able to read another trashy Facebook post? Was I too old for tabloid press? I silently begged the gods, *Please don't take this away from me. It's all I have.*

I was contemplating the hideousness of my shallow life when I clicked on another story and found what I'd really been searching for. *MAKE-UP-FREE CELEBRITIES.* It didn't get much better than this. *Girls, perhaps if you ate a morsel of food every now and then, you wouldn't look so pained and haggard when snapped by a pesky photographer at six in the morning*, I thought while scoffing a Greek Cherry Ripe. Still, it gave me a perverse pleasure to read that beautiful, famous and wealthy women had the same mundane issues to deal with as we ordinary folk.

I closed my eyes and enjoyed the warm sunshine on my skin. Again, I'd forgotten to slather myself with sunscreen. Not that it mattered. I'd given the sunspots and skin cancers a good two weeks to form, and thirty-odd years before that. No amount of cream was going to help now. They partied happily, confident I'd given up the fight, and they were right – there was no way I was getting up again to lather my limbs with lotion. It felt so good lying in the sun, soaking up the rays. That is, it did after I'd pushed silly notions about sunspots and skin cancers to the back of my mind.

'Ahem. Excuse me.'

I vaguely heard someone coughing politely beside me, but I refused to open my eyes. I was sailing with Matthew McConaughey and he was about to pull the string on my bikini top and kiss me.

'Claudia?'

Too late, Matthew was gone. Maybe if I rolled over, he'd float back.

'Claud, am I interrupting you?'

I opened my eyes, squinting. The sun was blinding. I couldn't see anything. Blinking, I strained to see who was talking to me. 'Oh, it's you.' I quickly reached for my sarong.

'I didn't mean to startle you. I just came around to say sorry and to see that you're okay.'

'Of course I'm okay. I'm not about to throw myself off a cliff, if that's what you're thinking.'

'I hadn't actually thought of that.' Jack seemed surprised, which in turn surprised me. I assumed it was well known that one always felt like throwing oneself off a rocky cliff when one was arrested – no, detained – made a thorough fool of and dumped by a private detective masquerading as a handsome sexy tourist. Although technically, I kept reminding myself, we hadn't been going out, so I hadn't been dumped – just used and abused.

'I'm really sorry. I meant what I said yesterday.'

'Which was?' With everything that had been going on, I could barely remember this morning, let alone the previous day.

Jack looked down at the ants trudging along the concrete. 'That I really liked you from the moment I met you. I thought you were fun.'

'From memory, I think you used the word "cool".' I stood and fixed the sarong firmly around my body. 'Thank you for your kind words, Jack. You're free to leave.'

I paced the patio so I wouldn't have to look at him. 'What else do you want me to say? Thank you for apologising? I've said it. Goodbye.'

Jack grabbed me by the arm as I turned to walk inside.

'Let me go!' I tried to yank my arm away.

'No. Not before you look me in the eye and tell me you accept my apology.'

'I already have.' I gave him the briefest of looks. 'Now let me go.'

'At least let me take you out to dinner tonight.'

I hesitated but remained strong. 'Thanks, but I don't want to go out with you tonight. It's my last night here and I really want to be with my friends.'

Jack released me from his grip. 'Lucky friends.'

'I'm lucky I've still got them after what I've put them through.'

'Are *we* friends?'

I laughed. 'I don't think we'll be getting together for tea parties back home.'

'I guess not.' Jack looked disappointed.

Serves you right, boyo, given you deceived me, cuffed me, interrogated me and treated me like trash. 'I have to say, I thought you were a real arse that morning you arrested me.'

'I didn't actually arrest you,' Jack protested.

'Your cronies cuffed me! And you treated me appallingly. Not to mention you slept with me under false pretences.'

'I said I was sorry.'

'Sorry? You lied to me. You arrested me because you suspected me of being a criminal, and to top it off, you were inexcusably rude during the interview process. Sorry's not going to cut it.'

I was strong. I walked inside and didn't look back. So he was sorry. Big deal. His behaviour had confirmed all my worst fears about ever getting serious with another man. What was I thinking, letting myself be taken in by him? I was also well (very well) into my thirties, single and was facing a precarious work situation. Pretty much where I'd been at the start of the holiday, but at least back then I was only thirty-eight and had this holiday to look forward to.

'That went well.' It was Tara.

'I thought you'd already left.'

'I did, but I realised I'd forgotten my wallet when I got to the bus stop, so I came back, right around the time Jack was begging for forgiveness.'

'You heard?'

'A little. And I'm not saying you don't have every right to be pissed off.'

'Super pissed off!'

'Okay, super pissed off. Look, what Jack did was reprehensible.'

'You think?'

'But, Claudia, I can see how much he really likes you. I don't approve of his actions, but everyone makes mistakes.'

'You of all people—'

'Exactly. Me of all people can be objective. Yes, he had a severe lapse in judgement, but don't condemn him for the rest of his life. He seems decent enough.'

'Decent enough's not good enough, Tara. I've been through this shit before. I'll need a guarantee next time.'

'That's not realistic—'

'I don't care. It's how I feel. Besides, I've got bigger problems than Jack. My career's in the toilet, I have nowhere to live, I'm up to my neck in—'

'Whoa! Back up a minute. You live with me.'

'Tara, you're probably leaving. And besides, my living with you was only ever meant to be temporary. Now you can lease your place properly and get the rent you deserve.'

'You can't move out. I can't entrust my beloved terrace to strangers! Once I know when or even if I'm leaving, we'll interview for a new flatmate. You'll be in charge. Sort of like a manager, but you will need to look after my garden and keep the place in good working order.'

'Thanks,' I said, my eyes welling with tears.

'Now, what are we going to do about Mr Harper?'

I shrugged.

'I'm not going to butt in—'

'Any more than you already have.'

'Claudia, love doesn't come along often. I know George was a complete fuck-up—'

'And Marcus, and Ben, and—'

'Okay, you're right. There've been a few. But that doesn't mean you should shut yourself off from living. You fall off the horse, you pick yourself up and get back in the saddle again. That's what we do.'

'Maybe *you* do, but I'm not. It's too damn hard.'

'Yes, but you can't let real opportunities pass you by. I know how you feel – lost, alone and sad – I've been there. But sometimes you have to give in to your other feelings of excitement, nervousness, lust... and take risks.'

I raised my eyebrows.

'Okay, so you've taken more than your fair share of risks. What harm could come from taking one more?'

'Don't you have a bus to catch?'

CHAPTER 36

*A*fter Tara left, I couldn't settle, so I decided to make the most of the glorious sunshine and the Santorini sights. I walked and walked, hiking up steep cliffs, navigating ancient cobblestones and strolling through tiny hamlets, striding straight past shops and market stalls, only stopping to pat donkeys and admire the occasional garden.

I made my way down to the port, then wandered around to the small pebbly beach nearby. I sat down with a bottle of water and contemplated my circumstances.

Perhaps Tara was right. I had to keep living, moving forward. Though I couldn't switch off my feelings for Marcus, I had to stop feeling so guilty. It wasn't my fault he was a bastard. Yes, I had to take responsibility for my part in our affair but not for his criminal actions. I had to be kinder to myself. This was a wake-up call, and I was certainly now wide awake.

I stared at the huge cliff I needed to climb to get back up to Fira. It'd be easy to lie and say I used my two good legs and walked myself up the hill. But I didn't. I didn't take the donkey option either. I caught the cable car. The one time I'd ridden in a cable car – Taronga Park Zoo, Sydney – I'd felt moments away from disaster, terrified the carriage would snap from its support wires and crash to the ground, leaving me at the mercy of marauding orangutans. Despite the absence of apes, my fear today was no less overwhelming. So, instead of enjoying the view, I spent sixteen and a half excruciating minutes gripped to the seat, my eyes firmly fixed on the wires above.

On the walk home, I popped into my favourite stores and picked up essentials for our last night, not that I knew what Sophie or Tara would be doing. Likely, they'd be out on the town with their beaus. That was okay. Perhaps Levi and I could spend the evening together hustling dinosaurs and eating M&Ms. He wasn't such a bad kid. In fact, Levi could be a delight when he wasn't fixated on poo or throwing a tanty.

Rather than buying everything in the shop, as I would have done in the past, I limited myself to one packet of pasta, a small tub of olives, one dip, eight dolmades and one mid-priced bottle of wine. Frugal, thy name is Claudia. When I arrived back at the apartment happily not laden with goodies, I felt quite pleased with myself. I'd finally shown some restraint.

Angie and Tara were on the terrace, reading quietly and giggling like a couple of teenagers in love, arms linked. I stopped and observed as they whispered secrets into each other's ears. I'd never seen Tara like this before, not with Jules, certainly not with Anthony.

Alex was next to them, reclining on a sun lounger, sound asleep and snoring loudly. Nearby, Levi and Harry sat quietly, half-heartedly pushing cars and trucks through dinosaur roadblocks. A couple of empty chip packets and a bowl of half-eaten popcorn sat beside them.

Tara looked up at me. 'You had the same idea, hey?'

'What's that?'

'Gather enough food and drink to feed a small nation.'

'Err, I did buy a few bits and pieces but not as much as I

normally would've. I'm sticking to my budget.' I nodded in Levi and Harry's direction. 'How you guys doing?'

'Tired,' Levi admitted.

'I'm not tired,' Harry said.

'Yes, you are,' Levi replied.

'I'm not going to sleep,' Harry said.

'Me neither,' Levi agreed.

I found Sophie in the kitchen. 'How's it going?' I asked, dumping my grocery bag on the bench. She looked great, dressed in a simple white singlet, a multicoloured patchwork skirt and beaded thongs. If I'd seen that skirt hanging in a shop, my first reaction would have been 'yuk', but it suited her perfectly. Soph could wear a paper bag and still look stunning.

'Okay. Tea?'

'Sure.' I was desperate to ask her about Alex but didn't want to pry. Thankfully, I didn't need to. Sophie was happy to divulge.

'Before you ask, Alex and I haven't had a chance to talk. He's been entertaining Levi most of the day, and when we got back, Tara, Angie and Harry were here, so we spent the afternoon with them. And now Alex is asleep.'

'Yeah, I heard him cutting logs out there. So, what do you think's going on?'

Sophie let out a long slow breath. 'Alex said he missed us.'

'Clearly! He flew halfway around the world to see you!'

Sophie handed me a mug of tea and we walked out into the lounge room and sat down. 'I was furious when he barged in here this morning. Angry that he'd invaded my holiday. I felt like he'd come to spy on me. But now that he's been here a while, I don't think that was his intention. When the three of us were at the pool today, it was relaxing and peaceful.' Sophie drank her tea. 'Levi's beside himself with happiness. It's been nice.'

'You sound surprised.'

'Yeah, I keep thinking Alex's going to tell me he's leaving.'

'Soph, ever since I've known Alex, you've been saying he's going to leave you.'

Sophie shrugged. 'Blame it on the insecurities that come with being a second wife.'

'Unfortunately, you're always going to be Alex's second wife. You need to get over it.'

'You're so full of clichés. *Get over it?*'

'I'm just saying Alex isn't going to leave you.'

'He left Harriet.'

'She was having an affair. And if he hadn't left her, you two would never have met.'

Sophie waved me away with her hand. 'I keep having panic attacks about being alone, and in a couple of years I'll be forty with absolutely no hope—'

'Like me!'

'No, not like you. I have Levi.'

'Thanks. That makes me feel better.' I took a moment. Sophie could be thoughtless at times, but I didn't take her words to heart. Finally, I said, 'You're being silly. He loves you.'

'What's all this about?' Alex asked, ambling through the open door from the patio. 'Who loves my gorgeous wife?'

'You do!' I jumped up to greet him.

'Too right.' Alex smiled at Sophie before embracing me in a tight bear hug. 'How are you, old girl?' he asked, stepping back and taking a good look at me. 'I hear you've had a busy couple of days.'

'Yes, but it's over now,' I said firmly. 'This is a big surprise. Couldn't bear to be parted from Soph another few days, hey?'

Alex sat down next to Sophie and put his arm around her. 'Yeah. I missed Soph and I missed my little guy and I wondered what the hell I was doing stuck in an office in the middle of winter, going home to a cold lonely house when I could be drinking ouzo with you guys and swimming with my son in the Mediterranean. So I packed up and came over.'

'Just like that?'

Alex snapped his fingers. 'Yep.'

'Pity you arrived on our second last day,' Sophie reminded him.

Alex looked down and kissed her head. 'Claud, what do you think of Sophie heading off to do a design course and working with Tara's mate to become an interior designer?'

'Great,' I said, pleased at his enthusiasm.

'Great? It's bloody fantastic,' Alex boomed. 'I've always thought Soph should do something like that. You've got the gift, babe.'

Personally, I'd always hated the word 'babe', but when Alex said it, it sounded incredibly sexy and he only ever used it when talking to Sophie.

Sophie looked at him and shook her head. 'You're getting a little ahead of yourself there. You don't think I'm abandoning Levi, do you?'

'Honey, Leev should be going to preschool more days than he does. He loves being with friends, and if this new venture makes you happy, then we're all going to be happy. That's all I want.' Alex kissed her again, then got up and walked into the bathroom.

'"If this new venture makes you happy…"' Sophie mimicked.

'What's up?' I asked.

'New venture, argh. He makes it sound so easy when he talks about happiness.'

'And?'

'It's not that easy. You can't just snap your fingers and be instantly happy.'

'You can if you try.'

'Really? You try it!' Sophie glared at me and then towards the flushing sound coming from inside the bathroom before looking back at me. 'Anyway, you're not one to give advice on this.'

'I'm not giving advice. I'm talking to you.'

'Yeah, well, you're annoying me.'

'Sophie, what's the matter?'

She glanced towards the bathroom again. 'I don't know.'

'I'll tell you what the matter is, Sophie. Nothing! You like creating dramas for yourself.' I was trying to control myself, but I'd had enough. After all, Sophie had a loyal husband who'd flown halfway across the world to spend time with her, she had a healthy, happy son, plus she was wealthy, gorgeous and about to embark on a new and glamorous career.

'That's rich coming from you,' Sophie shouted. 'You jump from one disaster to the next. You'd think after the wake-up call you got the other day, you'd grow up.'

'I have.'

'How? By sticking your head further into the sand and announcing to the world that you're taking a vow of celibacy. Please!'

'Would you rather I pour salt on my lunch or tip water on my dinner to stop myself from eating?'

'Stop it.' Sophie slapped the dining table. 'You're being a complete bitch.'

It was as if she'd slapped me across the face. Sophie had only ever called me a bitch once before (fucking bitch, actually) – during that fight at high school when I'd found her gobbling chocolates in her bedroom. It wasn't something you called a friend in jest. In no way could it be regarded as a term of endearment, as in, 'You're a silly old *bitch*, let's have coffee', or 'You look great in those shoes, you crazy, wacky *bitch*!'.

Was I a bitch? Was I such a bad friend? Granted, I might have neglected our friendship a little over the past year or two, but I still loved Sophie and had her best interests at heart, which is why I thought I could tell her some uncomfortable truths.

It took me a moment or two to regain my composure, but I did.

'At least I don't blame everyone else for my unhappiness. You're responsible for your own happiness, Sophie. Don't you get that? I've had enough.'

'You've had enough? For years I've put up with you! You're hopeless around men, money and moderation of any kind.'

'Then why are you friends with me?'

'I'm asking myself the same question. You don't even like kids. Why the fuck did I ever let you be Levi's godmother?'

This was getting out of control. 'That's not fair, Sophie. I love Levi—'

'You? You're not capable.'

'Don't you dare say that. I love Leev with all my heart. What about you?'

'I adore Levi. I hated being a mother. Being different to you and Tara. Being married. I hated it.'

'What's going on?' It was Alex. 'What do you mean you hate being married?'

'I did hate it, Alex. I don't anymore.' Sophie burst into tears.

'I don't understand,' Alex said.

'No, you wouldn't. We never talk about it, do we?'

'Sophie, please don't,' Alex pleaded.

'Don't what? Don't talk about the fact that sometimes I find myself so repulsive I put my head underwater until the feeling goes? Or don't talk about the fact that up until Levi was a year old, I wished he'd drown in the bath?'

'Sophie!' Alex cried. 'Stop! You had postnatal depression.'

'And I took drugs to control it.'

Alex winced. 'That's nothing to be ashamed of.'

'I'm not. Are you?'

I turned round. Thank God Levi was outside with Harry and hadn't heard a word.

Sophie was crying. 'I love Levi with all my heart. I really do. I'd never hurt him. He's my life.'

'Then what the hell's going on? You're scaring me. You're supposed to be on holiday having the time of your life and instead you're a mess.'

'Yes, I'm a mess.'

'I didn't mean it like that. What can I do to help you?'

'No one needs me, Alex. No one has ever needed me. I just fit in with everyone else's life. Yours. Levi's.' She took a breath. 'I could die tomorrow, and no one would care. After a couple of days, you'd all get on with your lives because nobody needs me.' Sophie collapsed on the sofa and sobbed as Levi ran in and jumped on her lap.

'Please don't die, Mummy. I lub you.'

I was in tears but didn't dare look around the room. Alex hurried over and wrapped his arms around Sophie and Levi. 'Mummy's not going to die, darling. She's just very sad because she thinks we don't love her and need her.' With his hand, Alex lifted Sophie's chin so that he could look at her. 'But she's wrong. I need you so much, Soph. Why do you think I'm here?'

Levi squirmed between them, not understanding what was going on.

He kissed her forehead lightly. 'Aren't you excited about this interior design course? I am.'

'Really? It's a world away from corporate life.'

'Who says you have to stick with the same career forever? The only reason I haven't suggested you go back to work or do a course is because I didn't want to add to your stress. You seemed to have your hands full.'

'I did, but—'

'But you need more, I get it. I've always admired the fact that you can be with our little guy twenty-four hours, seven days a week.' He dropped his voice slightly. 'It'd drive me insane.'

Sophie said quietly, 'I'm scared I'm heading in that direction. And you're so busy.'

'Maybe my hours have gotten a bit crazy over the past few months.'

'Try two years.'

'Okay, work's been out of control for a while. I'll look at that, but we also need some objective advice.'

'My psychologist?'

He nodded. 'For both of us. I only stopped going with you because I got so busy with work. But I want to start again. Soph, I'm with you for the long haul, forever.'

'I'm sorry—'

'Please don't be sorry.' He pulled her into a bear hug.

'I'm thinking about going on antidepressants again.'

Alex looked alarmed.

'Sometimes it's like I'm in this black hole and I can't claw my way out, no matter how hard I try. I feel like you and I have nothing to talk about except Levi. Meanwhile, Claudia and Tara are living these amazing lives. I get so sad. I want to go to bed and never get up again.'

Clearly, she was talking about a different Claudia, one who wasn't a bitch and who had a great job, money, her own apartment, was slim, perky and owned an amazing designer wardrobe. Oh, and had bouncy shiny hair like the women in the Pantene commercials.

'Sophie—' Alex said.

'I know it sounds irrational but that's how I feel.'

'It's not irrational. We're going to get through this. Most of the time I thought it was about dirty laundry.'

Sophie managed a half-smile – at last. 'There is that as well.'

'Babe, the long hours at work are only for you and Levi. So

that I can give you everything you want.' He kissed her lips. 'The house is empty without you. I can't bear it.' Were those tears in Alex's eyes?

I looked around the room and suddenly realised I was the only onlooker. OMG! Talk about being the rudest, most inconsiderate, person in the world.

Shielding my face from their view, I sprinted outside as quickly as my nimble legs would carry me. I cursed under my breath as I hurtled onto the patio.

'Thanks for joining us,' Tara said.

'Bloody hell. I thought you guys were inside as well.'

'Us? God, no.'

❧

Neither Tara, Angie nor I dared go inside, and Sophie and Alex didn't venture out. The only ones who didn't care where they wandered were Levi and Harry. Within minutes, Levi seemed to have recovered from the episode. He'd probably need therapy in later life, but for now he seemed fine. Personally, I found it all rather traumatic. Holidays were hard work.

When Sophie finally came outside, she sat down and apologised. Tara and Angie quickly excused themselves again.

'I don't know what you're apologising for,' I said. 'I was the one who called you—'

Sophie put her hand up. 'I called you a bitch. I win.'

I hugged her tight. 'Water off a duck's back. I can be a bitch. Thanks for setting me straight.'

She looked like she might burst into tears again.

'Soph, it's okay. Now tell me, do you really feel like you're trying to claw your way out of a dark hole?'

She sniffed. 'Most days, yes.'

'I knew something was up, but I didn't want to pry. I'm sorry I haven't been there for you. I've really been an absent friend.'

'Hey, I haven't been around for you either. If I'd spent more time with you, I'd have sniffed out the situation with Marcus and it never would've come to this.'

'On the flip side, we'd never have had this holiday.'

'True.' Sophie took a breath. 'You know, I'm probably jealous of you, and your freedom. Ever since Levi was born, I've pushed you away. I've resented Alex for so long, pushed him away too. Even at my lowest, I refused his help, wanted to do it all on my own. He thought he was being a nuisance at home. He didn't seem to notice I was drowning.'

'I think we all—' I started to say as Alex walked out to join us.

'I noticed,' Alex said. 'But I didn't know what to do.'

'But, Alex, you didn't notice my hair, my clothes. I once wore the same tracksuit for eight days and went for seven of them without washing my hair. You didn't say a word.'

'So it was a test, Soph?' Alex said, visibly stunned. 'And my pass or fail was based on whether I noticed your hair was dirty?'

Sophie shook her head as the tears started falling again.

'Harry is my best friend eber,' Levi said as he and Harry galloped past us on their way to the bathroom, neighing and pretending to be horses.

'Levi's a great kid,' I said. 'And you've seen how much fun he's had with Harry this holiday. Soph, if Alex or someone else does something different to you when they're looking after Levi, it doesn't mean it's wrong, it's simply different.'

Sophie nodded. 'I know. I'm used to controlling things. I need to learn to let go. Claud, I'm sorry I said you couldn't love Levi. I know you do and I'm glad you're his godmother. Thank you.'

Tara and Angie walked outside, each holding an antipasto

platter. It was time to sit back and admire the Santorini sunset one last time. Alex ambled back inside for wine and glasses and soon we were enjoying the tranquillity of the burnt orange sun as it dipped to the horizon. The scene felt strangely calm and serene. Or maybe we were all just completely and utterly shattered.

CHAPTER 37

With the early evening's drama, I'd forgotten about Jack. But apparently, he hadn't forgotten about me.

'Hope I'm not interrupting,' came an annoying voice from behind a massive bunch of flowers.

Of course he was interrupting. This was a party. A party to which Jack Harper had not been invited.

'Come in, Jack,' Tara said. 'Are those for me? How sweet.' Laughing, she relieved him of his gift without waiting for a reply.

He also handed over a couple of bottles of champagne. Expensive. French.

'Very nice. Thanks, Jack.' Tara skipped away with the champagne and flowers, but not before nudging me and saying, 'Have you thought about what I said earlier?'

I made a face but said nothing.

'Jack, this is my husband, Alex,' Sophie said agreeably. 'Alex, Jack.'

What short memories Tara and Sophie had. This was the

man who'd ruined my holiday. Detained me against my will and destroyed my good name.

The two men shook hands and exchanged pleasantries. I continued sitting silently, sipping my wine and staring towards the sunset. But I couldn't concentrate because there were too many sets of eyes drilling into my head.

'Claudia, could I have a moment?' Jack asked.

'I guess so,' I replied in a bored voice. I stood and put my wine down on the table.

'Inside?' he pointed. Reluctantly, I followed.

Tara came bouncing out as we walked in. 'Drink this,' she said to Jack, handing him a Greek beer.

'Don't you know anyone else on this island you can torment?' I asked him after we'd taken a seat on the sofa in the living room.

'No one I care to torment as much as you, Claudia. I'm sorry.'

'You said that already.'

'But I really am. I mean it.'

'I know, Jack. What do you want from me?'

'I want you... I want us to get to know each other better and to—'

'We're different people. It just won't work.'

'Why?'

'Because it never does,' I answered truthfully. There was no way I was going to pay attention to Tara's advice. I liked Jack and I couldn't deny the physical attraction between us, but I needed to be able to trust the man I was with, and Jack had betrayed my trust. I wasn't prepared to put myself in a vulnerable position again.

'I can learn to love karaoke,' he joked.

'Look, Jack, I think you should leave.'

'No. I haven't had a fair chance at explaining myself. Besides,

Tara's given me a beer. Why don't I stay for one drink, and if after that you still find me repulsive, I'll go?'

'Promise?'

'You have my word.'

Like that was worth anything. 'Fair enough, but don't expect me to talk to you.'

'Wouldn't dream of it, Claud.'

'And don't call me Claud!'

'I am truly sorry for letting things get out of hand with us and for thinking you were involved in Marcus's scam.'

I nodded and walked back outside.

'Jack's staying for one drink,' I announced to the group. 'And then he's leaving.'

We resumed our positions on the patio. Tara opened the champagne that Jack had brought, and we watched the Santorini sky change colours over the sparkling Mediterranean.

'So, Jack, I hear you're a bounty hunter,' Alex said as he poured Jack a glass of champagne after he'd drained his beer in less than four minutes.

'I don't know if bounty hunter is quite right. Most of the time I'm an ordinary private investigator.'

'Must be fascinating,' Tara said. 'Travelling all over the world to exotic places.'

'Honestly, Tara, this is a first,' Jack said, doing his best to charm the crowd. 'Most of the time it's just your run-of-the-mill investigative work. Cheating spouses, insurance fraud and dodgy companies.'

'Beats working in an office, I'll bet,' Sophie said.

'Yeah, it's got that going for it. I love it. There's always something new going on, and some of the cases I've worked on have been fascinating, but Greece has been the best... and the worst.'

I refused to acknowledge him or say another word. When he

caught my eye, he raised his glass and winked. I wrinkled my nose.

Tara and Angie disappeared inside before reappearing a few moments later carrying the main course – moussaka, olive bread, salads and souvlakia. A further invitation for Jack to stay if ever there was one.

'I should leave you guys to it,' Jack said, making a feeble attempt to rise out of the wicker chair he was sitting in.

'No. Stay,' Tara insisted. 'We've more than enough food.'

'I really should be going,' he said again.

That's right. Get up out of your chair, big boy. Say your goodbyes and get the hell out of my life.

'You *must* stay for dinner, Jack,' Tara said. 'Hey, Claud?'

'If he has to go, he has to go,' I said.

Jack smiled. 'I don't have to leave.'

'I am sure you've got other people to see and places to go,' I said firmly.

'Not really.'

'It's settled then. Sit down and eat,' Tara said as she served him a huge helping of everything. 'You were saying, Jack?'

'What were we talking about?' Jack asked, staring straight at me as I seethed into my champagne.

'You were saying that Santorini has been the best place you've worked,' Sophie prompted as she tucked into her moussaka.

Despite my agitation at Jack being here, I was relieved and happy to see Sophie eating again.

'Yeah,' Jack said. 'I got to be part of a big international investigation. Met some great people too.'

Oh please! Did he really think I was buying all this crap? I'd seen more shit this evening than I would at a cow manure convention.

'I'll second that.' Tara sat down next to Angie and the two of them immediately began canoodling on an oversized chair that wasn't built for snogging adults.

Alex looked up from his plate. 'So, Tara, I can clearly see that you and Angie are in love. But I haven't heard how it all came about.'

'It just happened,' Tara said dreamily.

I could almost hear Alex's mind ticking away. 'Really?'

'Yes, Alex. Are you in love with Sophie?' Tara asked.

'Of course. More and more every day.' He looked at Sophie and smiled. 'But it's not really the same, is it? I mean, neither of you have got a...'

'Penis?' Angie obliged.

'So we couldn't possibly be in love?' Tara said.

'Help me out here, Jack,' Alex said.

'Mate, you're on your own. My aunt had five kids in six years. She's a lesbian now.'

'Alex,' Tara began, 'I'm surprised at you. Women can fall in love just as easily with women as they can with men.'

'Yeah, it's all about desire and attraction,' Sophie said, standing up and hugging him. 'You can't fight chemistry.'

'But you can give it a damn good nudge,' I said.

'You can only protest for so long,' Angie said, leaning over to kiss Tara's lips.

Alex and Jack squirmed in their chairs, though they continued to look, unblinking, as Tara and Angie played tonsil hockey. Perhaps they were hoping the girls would rip their gear off, smear each other with whipped cream and start licking and nibbling. I was quietly confident that wasn't about to happen, but in case, I snapped my fingers several times to move it along. Eventually they stopped kissing and the men stopped gawking.

'What's your theory then?' Jack asked Tara.

Was the pervert hoping for another demo?

'We got lucky, I guess,' Angie said.

Alex considered Angie's comment for a moment before turning to Tara. 'I've been meaning to ask, how's your writing going?'

'Brilliantly.' Tara beamed. 'I'm writing a love story.'

'You? A love story?' I blurted. 'Like Elizabeth Bennet and Mr Darcy!'

'Kind of.'

'But, Tara,' Sophie said, 'love stories are the kind of books you hate the most. Appalling, self-indulgent and meaningless fairy tales, I think you've called them.'

'True, Soph, I might have thought that once. But recently I've received some serious inspiration and I just can't help myself. Words keep tumbling out of my brain, and wouldn't you know it, they're all about love.'

'Good for you,' Alex said as he and Jack stood, collected the empty plates and took them into the kitchen.

Sophie walked over and sat beside me. 'Tara's on the right track. Sometimes we need to open our hearts to love... You never know, he might be standing right in front of you.'

'Yeah,' Tara agreed.

'Easy for you both to say,' I sulked. 'Your loves *are* right here in front of you.'

Sophie looked over at Jack, who was strolling back out onto the patio. 'You've got yourself a great guy too.'

'You reckon?'

'I reckon.' Sophie laughed. 'Don't let him go.'

On cue, Jack wandered over, crouched down beside me and reached out to hold my hand. 'I'm sorry for not trusting you.'

I accepted his hand and led him inside to sit on the sofa where we could be alone.

'Jack, I know you're sorry. I'm sorry for this bizarre mess too.'

'It's not your faul—'

I sighed. 'Please let me finish. I don't want to get involved—'

'Is this about Marcus?'

I nodded. 'Sort of. Marcus made me feel good about myself. I'm not saying I was in love with him, but I did have feelings. I knew he was newly separated, and I still did what I did. I have no one to blame but myself.'

'I'm not married, and I don't have a girlfriend.'

'The thing is, I got sucked in by Marcus, by his charm. I believed what he told me.'

Jack was slowly sinking into the sofa, his face crumpled.

'But it's not only about Marcus. I've made a mess of most of my romantic relationships and the time has come to sort myself out – to look after my own wants and needs. I need to get my career and head together before I can think about starting a new relationship.'

Jack continued slumping silently.

I put my hand on his knee. 'Can you understand? I'm not in the market for a boyfriend.' As soon as I said the words, I felt relieved, knowing I'd made the right decision. I had to be free to get my world back on track on my terms, and at my speed.

'How about a friend then?'

'Sure,' I said cautiously. 'Friends are good.'

CHAPTER 38

*T*ara stared at the packed bags lined up at the front door. 'I can't believe it's really time to go.'

I was on the terrace where we'd first stood that breezy afternoon, looking out across the caldera, barely daring to dream that I'd finally arrived. I'd come here a different person – a woman consumed by guilt, doubt and minimal expectations. Somehow, most of my fears, regrets and insecurities had vanished into the sea. I wasn't perfect – far from it – but I wasn't a lost soul either. I had dreams and aspirations just like anyone else and I was looking forward to doing my best to fulfil them. It might take me a year, or ten years, but I was setting my sights high – like I should have done twenty years ago. My life wasn't about to start, I was living it. I breathed in the familiar scent of lemon blossoms wafting through the air and turned back towards my friends.

Marcella had already come to wish us bon voyage, with an open invitation to return. 'All the time it is full excitement with you girls. Now everyone come to Marcella's. I am famous.' Marcella had kissed Levi and smiled. 'You come next year, gorgeous boy.'

'I'll miss you,' I'd said, hugging her.

'We all will,' Tara had agreed.

'What about these?' Sophie held up my Angel cards.

'Leaving them here for the next travellers to enjoy. I need a break from the mighty Oracles.'

'You're actually leaving your Angels in Santorini?' Tara said.

'Yeah, it's time. I need to concentrate on creating my own future for a change.'

Once home, I'd go back to the office and deal with Cassoli's administrators. Jack had already briefed them, but I needed to explain everything in my own words. Through Jack, they'd asked if I'd work with them to sort out the mess Marcus had left behind. A pleasant surprise. I'd have thought they'd turf me out quick smart, but Jack said they were pleased I was coming back. With the company in upheaval, I wasn't about to walk out.

Besides, it would give me time to spruce up my résumé and line up some appointments with people in the industry. I was hopeful I could get back into event planning; if not in the food industry, there were plenty of other businesses that needed help organising seminars, conferences and festivals. I wasn't opposed to doing a course either, to brush up on my skills.

In addition, Tara and I would find a new flatmate for me, if and when it came to that. 'If you're game, so am I,' Sophie said, pulling me back into the conversation.

'This doesn't mean I'm giving up on the mystical world,' I said, strumming my fingers on the table. 'I'll still read my stars every week and attend the odd John Edward extravaganza.'

Tara nodded, then turned to Levi and presented him with a gift. 'I have a very special present for you.'

Levi tore through the wrapping paper and found two copies of the same book. One for him and one to give to Harry. Handwritten by Tara, the book described all the island adventures the boys had shared. The main characters were Levi, Harry and a couple of wayward dinosaurs lost on Santorini. There were photographs of the boys, Angie, Sophie, Tara and me.

Tara hugged Levi. 'Sweetheart, this book is especially for you and Harry, so you'll always remember the magical time we shared here in Santorini.'

'Hey, Tara,' Sophie said after she'd thanked her, 'isn't that a peasant top you're wearing?'

Indeed it was. I'd been so overcome by the book-giving ceremony, I'd failed to notice Tara was wearing a floral chiffon top with a small V-neck, a drawstring hem and sleeves that trumpeted (practically bellowed) at the elbows – gypsy girl meets peasant princess with a hippie and happening edge.

Angie floated in and wrapped her arms around Tara. She was dressed in something similar. 'Doesn't she look divine? We bought them together yesterday.'

'What do you think?' Tara asked shyly.

'I think...' Sophie said carefully, 'you look great. Glowing, in fact.'

Tara's new look did suit her. Who'd have thought love could have this effect on her. The garment floated and draped just enough to reveal her cleavage and toned forearms. She looked fantastic.

'Sophie, I'm sorry for ragging you about the boho look. The clothes in Santorini do grow on you.'

'Hey. No problemo.'

Angie busied herself with Levi and Harry while Sophie and I said our final goodbyes to Tara on the patio.

'When am I going to see you again?' I mumbled through tears.

'For goodness' sake, two weeks.' But Tara's bravado was cracking. 'You'll have two whole weeks to enjoy the house without me.' The three of us stood on the patio, hugging and crying.

'Before I need to find a new flatmate,' I yelped.

'We'll make sure he—'

'She!' I boomed.

'—is a good one!'

Tara took me by the hand and whispered, 'Everything will work out, you'll see. And remember, love is there for you too.' She motioned towards the patio. It seemed Jack had turned up to say his goodbyes. Tara squeezed my hand. 'Simply open your eyes and embrace it. You of all people should be open to messages the universe is sending you.'

What was going on? First, Tara had adopted a contemporary fashion look and now she was talking about messages from the universe!

'Email me as soon as you land,' I said. Tara was heading off to Angie and Harry's place at Kamari for another two days before flying to Heathrow with them.

After she disappeared up the stairs, I turned to farewell my other best friend. 'Hey, you three!' I said, wiping my eyes, 'I guess you're ready to leave as well.'

'Sure am,' Levi said. 'Daddy's taking me sailing.'

The previous night, Alex had asked Sophie and Levi to join him on a private yacht cruising around the Greek Islands for two weeks. Some people!

'Lucky boy.' I reached down and picked him up. 'I'm really going to miss you, sweetie. Promise me you'll ring as you get home, so I can come over to visit and see how much you've grown.'

'We'll only be gone another two weeks,' Sophie pointed out.

'A lot can happen in two weeks,' I said as Alex and Levi walked outside to talk to Jack. 'I'm sorry for all the mean things I said the other day.'

'Claud, we wouldn't be friends if we didn't argue occasionally. If you can't scream at your best friend and expel a few demons from time to time, what's the point? We might as well be friends who meet every couple of months for coffee and compliment each other on how well we're looking. I have enough of those friends. I need you and Tara to be honest with me.'

'I still can't believe you guys kept your kiss hidden all these years,' I whispered.

'I'd truly forgotten until we talked about it. I'm glad Tara and Angie have found each other. I really hope it works out for them...'

'But what?'

Sophie shrugged. 'What do I know? Life's a gamble, but you've got to give it your best shot.' Her tightly wound ringlets had disappeared and in their place were loose blonde curls with a soft centre part. She looked effortlessly glamorous, as well as happy and relaxed. Making love clearly did wonders for the skin and hair.

'Well, guys, enjoy your adventure around the Mediterranean,' I said to Alex when he, Jack and Levi lumbered into the lounge. 'Don't spare a thought for me flying cattle class back to Australia. By myself. You kids just enjoy your champers, private chef and personal maid. I'll be fine,' I said as Sophie and Alex began kissing in front of me.

No response.

'All right!' I said, butting in between them. 'Save it for the boat.'

'Yacht,' Alex corrected.

'Boat, yacht, canoe, whatever. Just save it all for the cabin, okay?'

'I guess that's it,' I said to Jack as we carried out a final check of the apartment. 'The holiday's over.'

'For you it is,' Jack said with a smile. 'Not for others.'

'Thanks for reminding me.'

'Have you decided what you're going to do when you get back home?'

'I'll sort things out at work and stay there until I find another job. I'm hoping to get back into event planning.'

'Sounds good, but I was hoping you might think about becoming a PI.'

'Don't be silly!' I mulled it over while patting my Angels one last time. I guess it would be kind of exciting, working outdoors, getting to nose about in people's private lives... What on earth was I thinking? It was complete madness. 'Besides,' I said, 'I don't know the first thing about investigative work.' That was putting it mildly. I knew less than zero. *Moonlighting* and *Remington Steele* reruns from the eighties were the closest I'd come to investigative work. 'Returning to event planning will be enough excitement for now.'

'No rush. You'll be at Cassoli's for at least the next three months.' Jack took my hand. 'I've just got one more question for you.'

Here comes the clanger, I thought to myself. 'What's that?'

'I seem to have an extra business-class seat to Brisbane. Happen to know anyone who'd like an upgrade?'

THE END

ACKNOWLEDGEMENTS

I am thrilled that *My Big Greek Holiday*, previously published as *Claudia's Big Break*, has been offered a new lease of life. I had a lot of fun revisiting Claudia, Sophie and Tara's lives and editing their stories for a 2021 audience.

Many thanks to Betsy Reavley at Bloodhound for loving Claudia's story as much as I do and for publishing this updated version. To Fred Freeman, my editor Morgen Bailey, editorial manager Tara Lyons, proofreader Shirley Khan, and publicist Maria Slocombe. Thank you. You are a joy to work with.

Thank you to my amazing agent Michael Cybulski, and all at New Authors Collective Literary Agency, especially Ros Harvey and Dennis Fisher who make me feel supported and trusted to get on with what I love most: writing.

A massive thanks to Andrea Barton, my editor at NAC. You are brilliant. I'm so glad our paths crossed. Looking forward to crossed paths for many years to come.

To my friends, you know who you are, thank you for your encouragement, honesty and friendship – and for telling me to 'get on with it' when sometimes I don't feel like it!

Josh, Noah and Mia, I love you... maybe one day you'll read my books!!

Finally, Chris, thank you for your unwavering support and love. I am very blessed.

A NOTE FROM THE PUBLISHER

Thank you for reading this book. If you enjoyed it please do consider leaving a review on Amazon to help others find it too.

We hate typos. All of our books have been rigorously edited and proofread, but sometimes mistakes do slip through. If you have spotted a typo, please do let us know and we can get it amended within hours.

info@bloodhoundbooks.com

Printed in the USA
CPSIA information can be obtained
at www.ICGtesting.com
LVHW041457090124
768261LV00015B/416